SONIC™
THE HEDGEHOG

THE FATE OF DR. EGGMAN

SEGA®

Facebook: **facebook.com/idwpublishing**
Twitter: **@idwpublishing**
YouTube: **youtube.com/idwpublishing**
Tumblr: **tumblr.idwpublishing.com**
Instagram: **instagram.com/idwpublishing**

COVER ART BY
NATHALIE FOURDRAINE

SERIES EDITS BY
JOE HUGHES
DAVID MARIOTTE

COLLECTION EDITS BY
JUSTIN EISINGER
AND ALONZO SIMON

PRODUCTION ASSISTANCE BY
SHAWN LEE

ISBN: 978-1-68405-406-0   25 24 23 22   8 9 10 11

SONIC THE HEDGEHOG, VOLUME 2: THE FATE OF DR. EGGMAN.
JUNE 2022. EIGHTH PRINTING. © SEGA. SEGA, the SEGA logo and
SONIC THE HEDGEHOG are either registered trademarks or
trademarks of SEGA Holdings Co., Ltd. or its affiliates. All rights
reserved. SEGA is registered in the U.S. Patent and Trademark
Office. All other trademarks, logos and copyrights are property of
their respective owners. The IDW logo is registered in the U.S.
Patent and Trademark Office. IDW Publishing, a division of Idea
and Design Works, LLC. Editorial offices: 2765 Truxtun Road, San
Diego, CA 92106. Any similarities to persons living or dead are
purely coincidental. With the exception of artwork used for review
purposes, none of the contents of this publication may be
reprinted without the permission of Idea and Design Works, LLC.
Printed in Canada. IDW Publishing does not read or accept
unsolicited submissions of ideas, stories, or artwork.

Originally published as SONIC THE HEDGEHOG issues #5–8.

Nachie Marsham, Publisher
Blake Kobashigawa, SVP Sales, Marketing & Strategy
Tara McCrillis, VP Publishing Operations
Anna Morrow, VP Marketing & Publicity
Alex Hargett, VP Sales
Mark Doyle, Editorial Director, Originals
Lauren LePera, Managing Editor
Greg Gustin, Sr. Director, Content Strategy
Keith Davidsen, Director, Marketing & PR
Topher Alford, Sr. Digital Marketing Manager
Patrick O'Connell, Sr. Manager, Direct Market Sales
Shauna Monteforte, Sr. Director of Manufacturing Operations
Greg Foreman, Director DTC Sales & Operations
Nathan Widick, Sr. Art Director, Head of Design
Neil Uyetake, Sr. Art Director, Design & Production
Shawn Lee, Art Director, Design & Production
Jack Rivera, Art Director, Marketing

Special thanks to Anoulay Tsai, Mai Kiyotaki, Aaron Webber,
Michael Cisneros, Sandra Jo, and everyone at Sega for their
invaluable assistance.

STORY
IAN FLYNN

ART
TRACY YARDLEY (#5–6)
ADAM BRYCE THOMAS (#7)
EVAN STANLEY (#8)

LETTERS
SHAWN LEE (#6 & 8)
COREY BREEN (#5 & 7)

INKS
JIM AMASH (#5–6)

COLORS
MATT HERMS

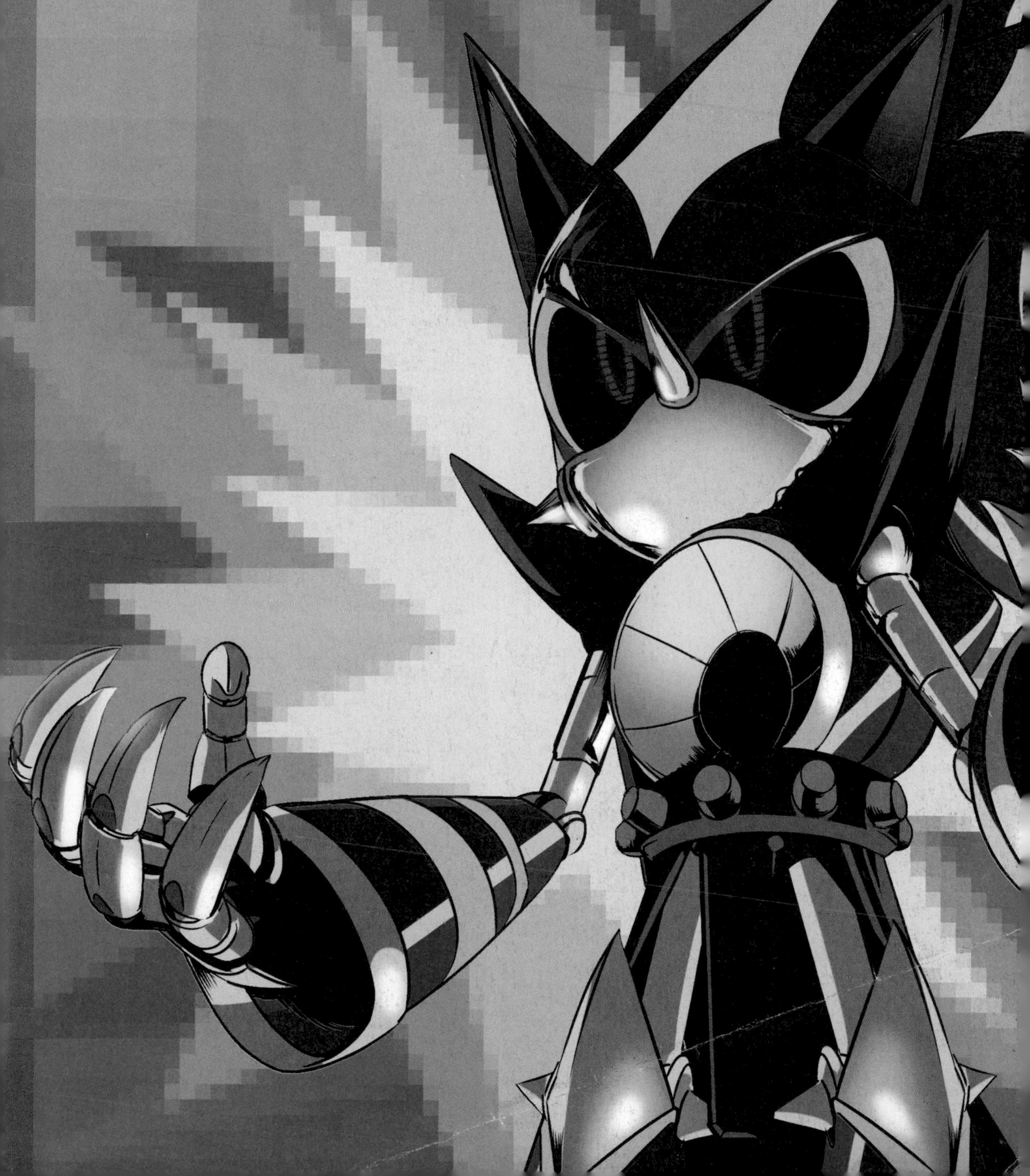

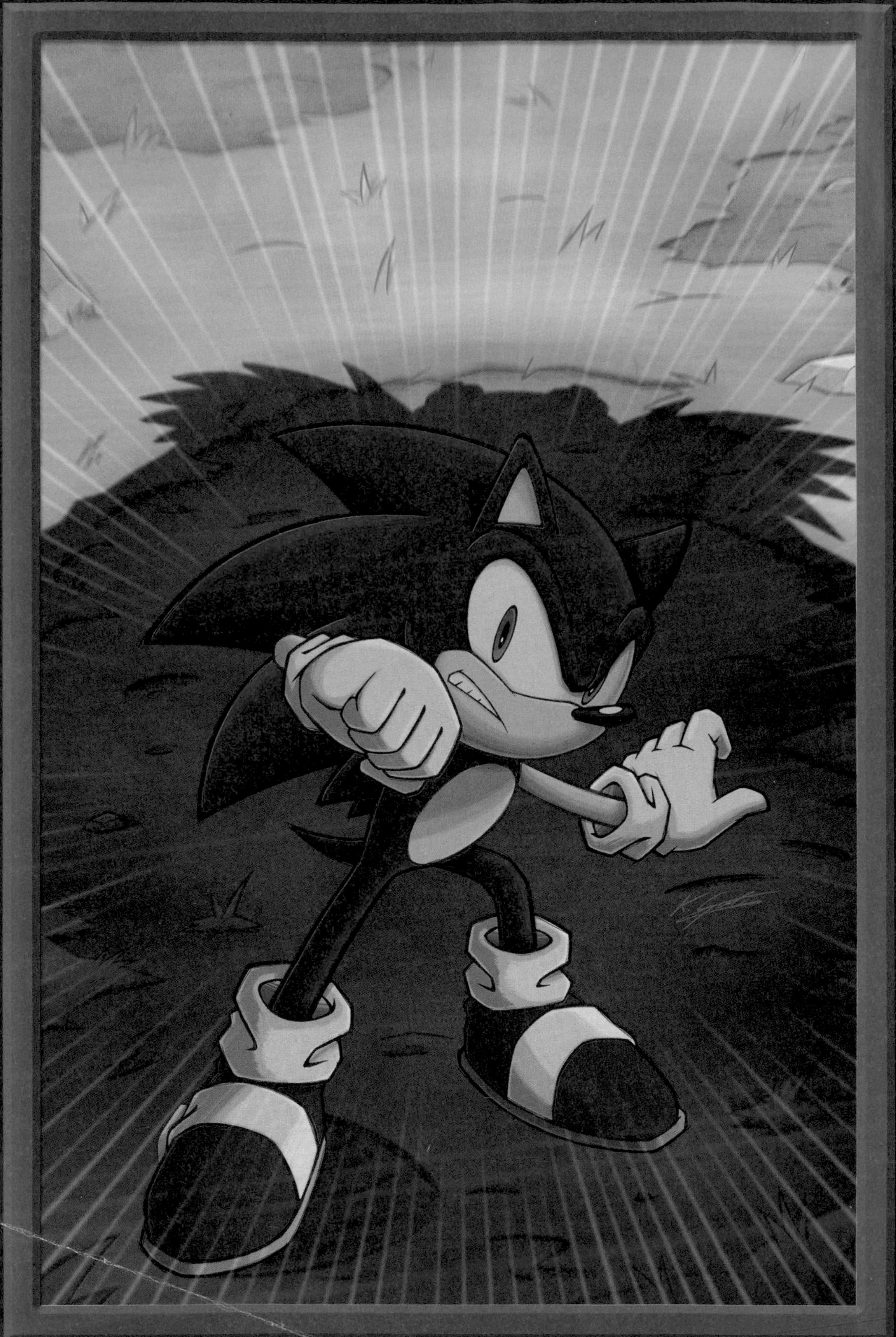

ART BY **KIERAN GATES**

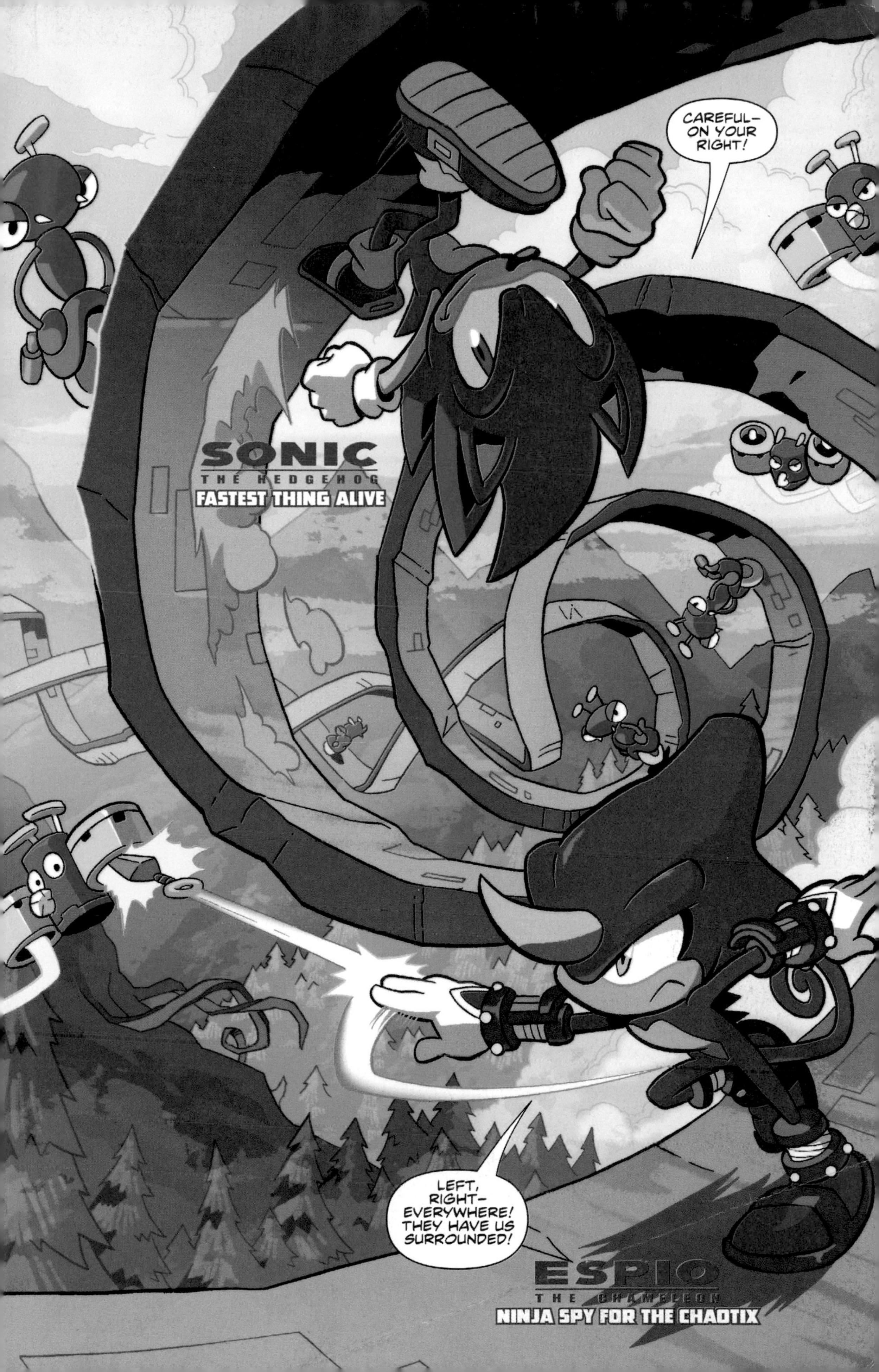
CAREFUL—
ON YOUR
RIGHT!
SONIC
THE HEDGEHOG
FASTEST THING ALIVE
LEFT,
RIGHT—
EVERYWHERE!
THEY HAVE US
SURROUNDED!
ESPIO
THE CHAMELEON
NINJA SPY FOR THE CHAOTIX

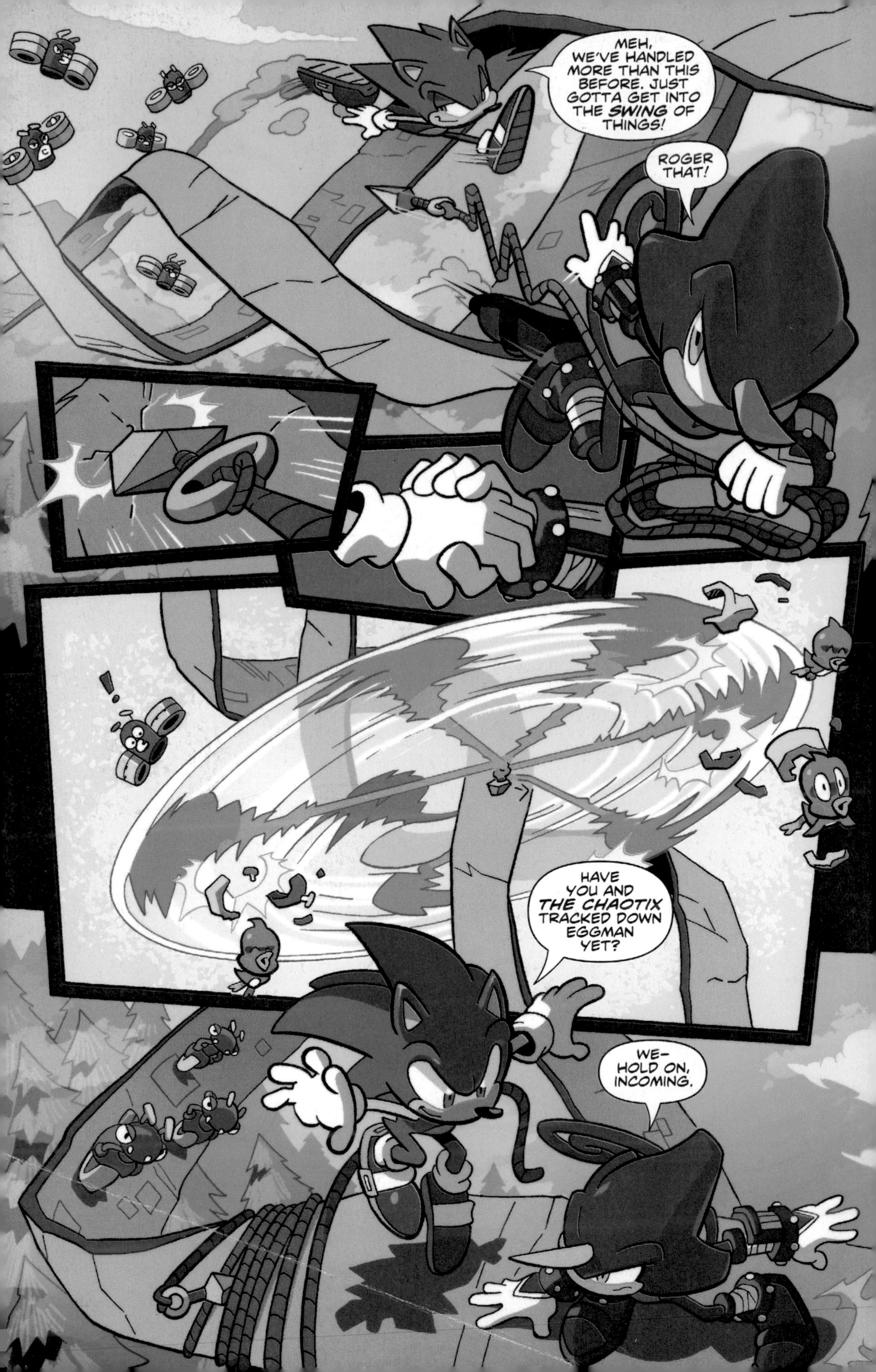
MEH, WE'VE HANDLED MORE THAN THIS BEFORE. JUST GOTTA GET INTO THE *SWING* OF THINGS!
ROGER THAT!
HAVE YOU AND *THE CHAOTIX* TRACKED DOWN EGGMAN YET?
WE— HOLD ON, INCOMING.

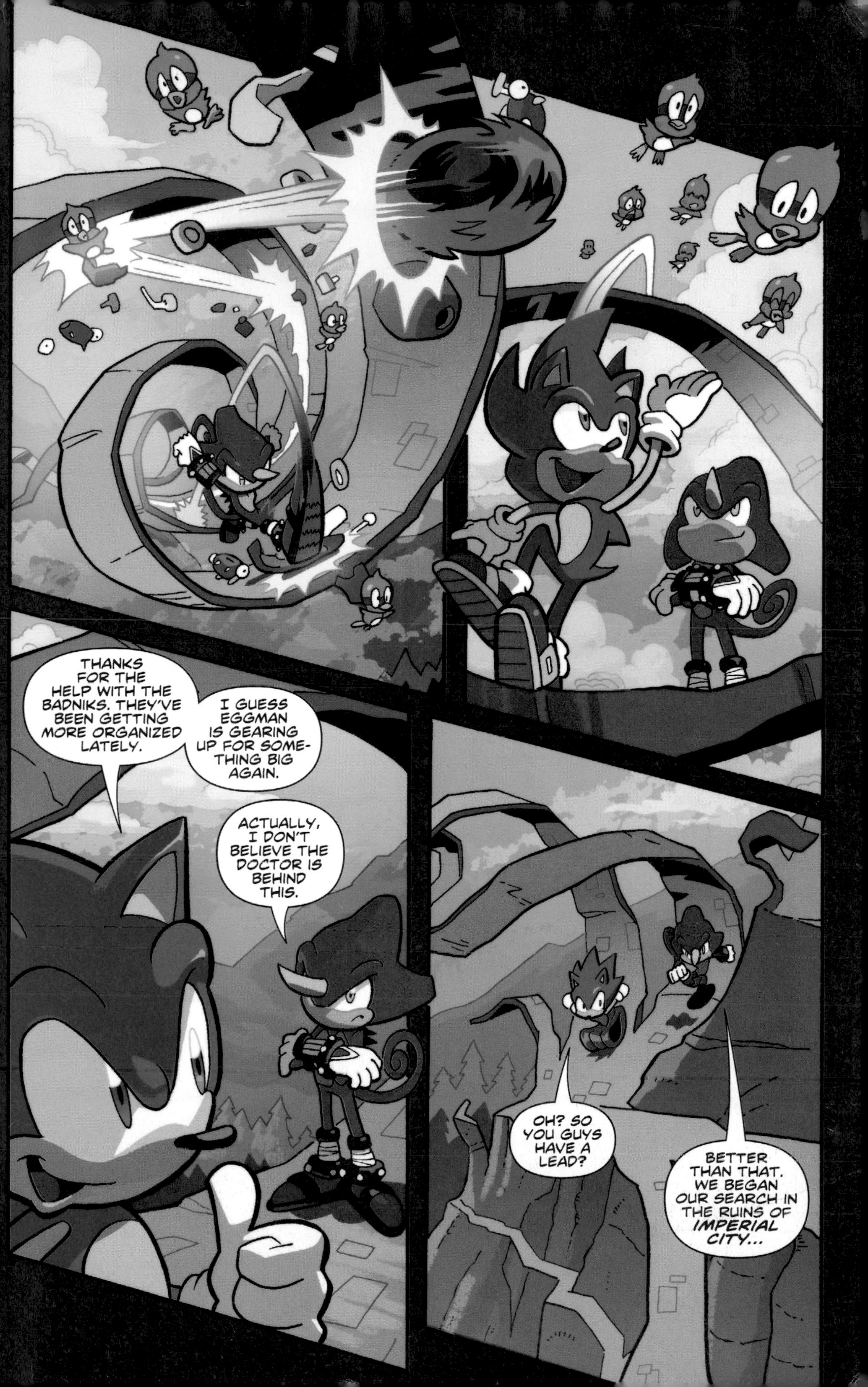
THANKS FOR THE HELP WITH THE BADNIKS. THEY'VE BEEN GETTING MORE ORGANIZED LATELY.
I GUESS EGGMAN IS GEARING UP FOR SOMETHING BIG AGAIN.
ACTUALLY, I DON'T BELIEVE THE DOCTOR IS BEHIND THIS.
OH? SO YOU GUYS HAVE A LEAD?
BETTER THAN THAT. WE BEGAN OUR SEARCH IN THE RUINS OF *IMPERIAL CITY*...

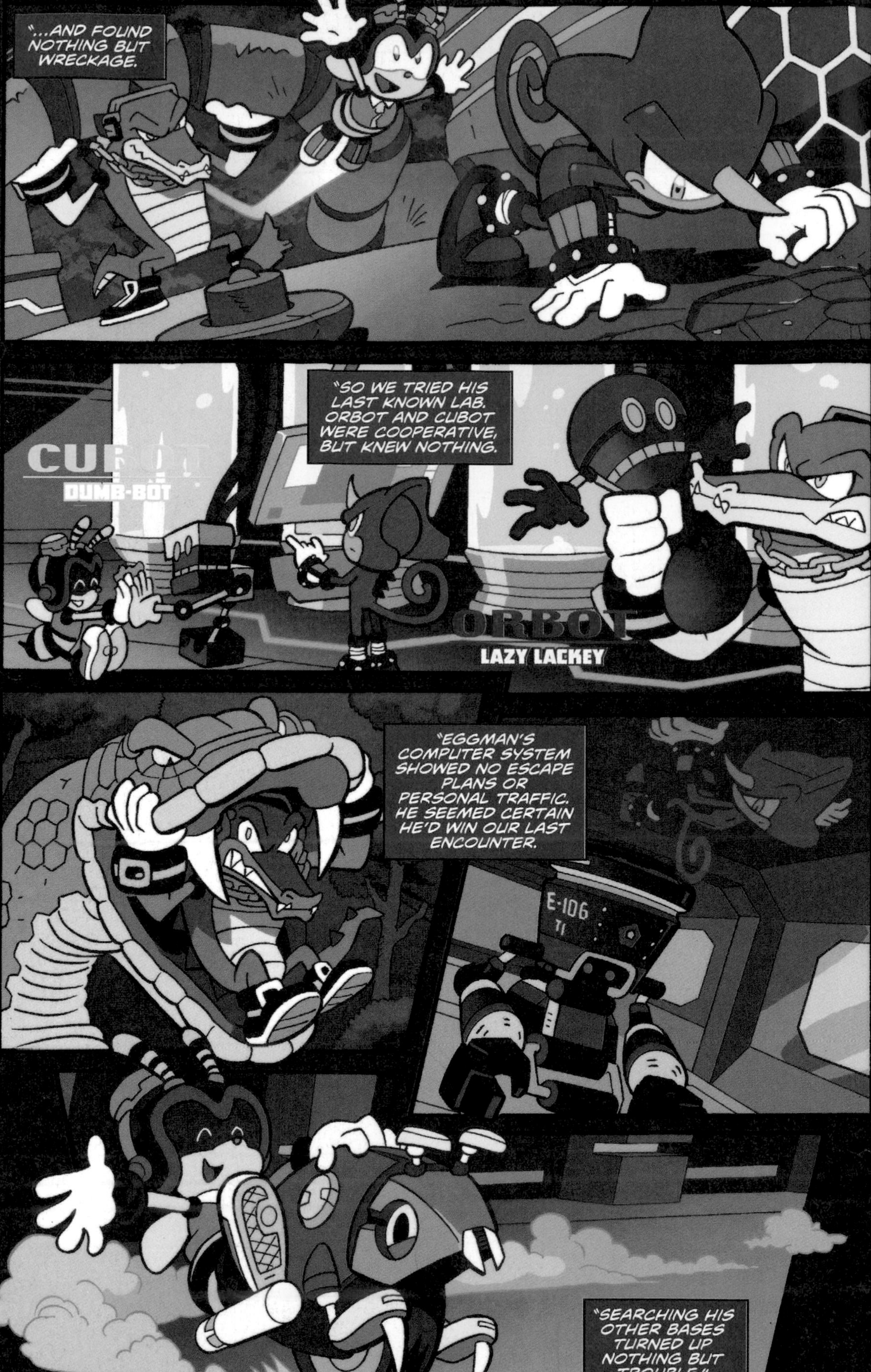
"...AND FOUND NOTHING BUT WRECKAGE.
"SO WE TRIED HIS LAST KNOWN LAB. ORBOT AND CUBOT WERE COOPERATIVE, BUT KNEW NOTHING.
CUBOT
DUMB-BOT
ORBOT
LAZY LACKEY
"EGGMAN'S COMPUTER SYSTEM SHOWED NO ESCAPE PLANS OR PERSONAL TRAFFIC. HE SEEMED CERTAIN HE'D WIN OUR LAST ENCOUNTER.
E-106
"SEARCHING HIS OTHER BASES TURNED UP NOTHING BUT TROUBLE."

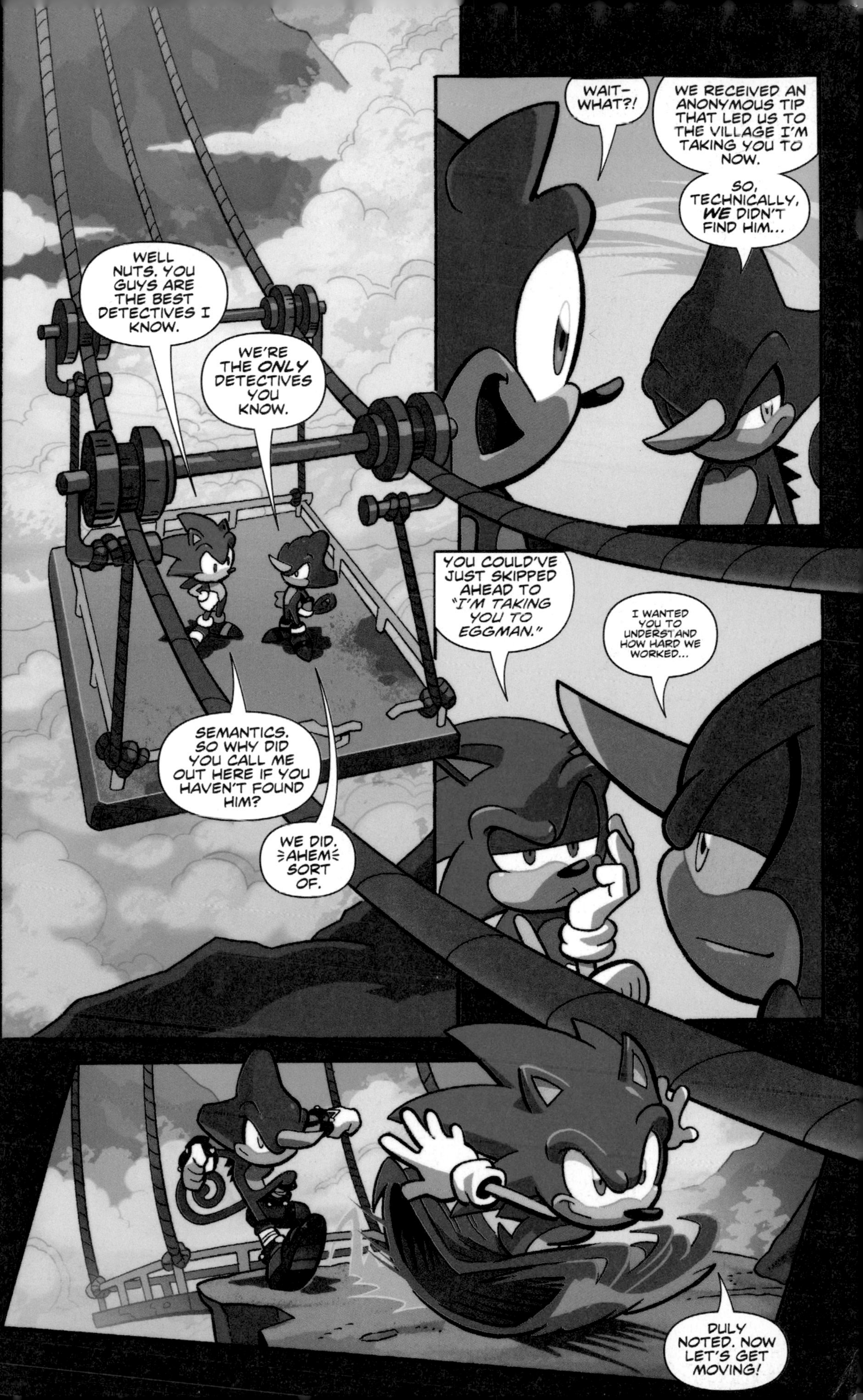
WELL NUTS. YOU GUYS ARE THE BEST DETECTIVES I KNOW.
WE'RE THE ONLY DETECTIVES YOU KNOW.
SEMANTICS. SO WHY DID YOU CALL ME OUT HERE IF YOU HAVEN'T FOUND HIM?
WE DID. AHEM SORT OF.
WAIT- WHAT?!
WE RECEIVED AN ANONYMOUS TIP THAT LED US TO THE VILLAGE I'M TAKING YOU TO NOW.
SO, TECHNICALLY, WE DIDN'T FIND HIM...
YOU COULD'VE JUST SKIPPED AHEAD TO "I'M TAKING YOU TO EGGMAN."
I WANTED YOU TO UNDERSTAND HOW HARD WE WORKED...
DULY NOTED. NOW LET'S GET MOVING!

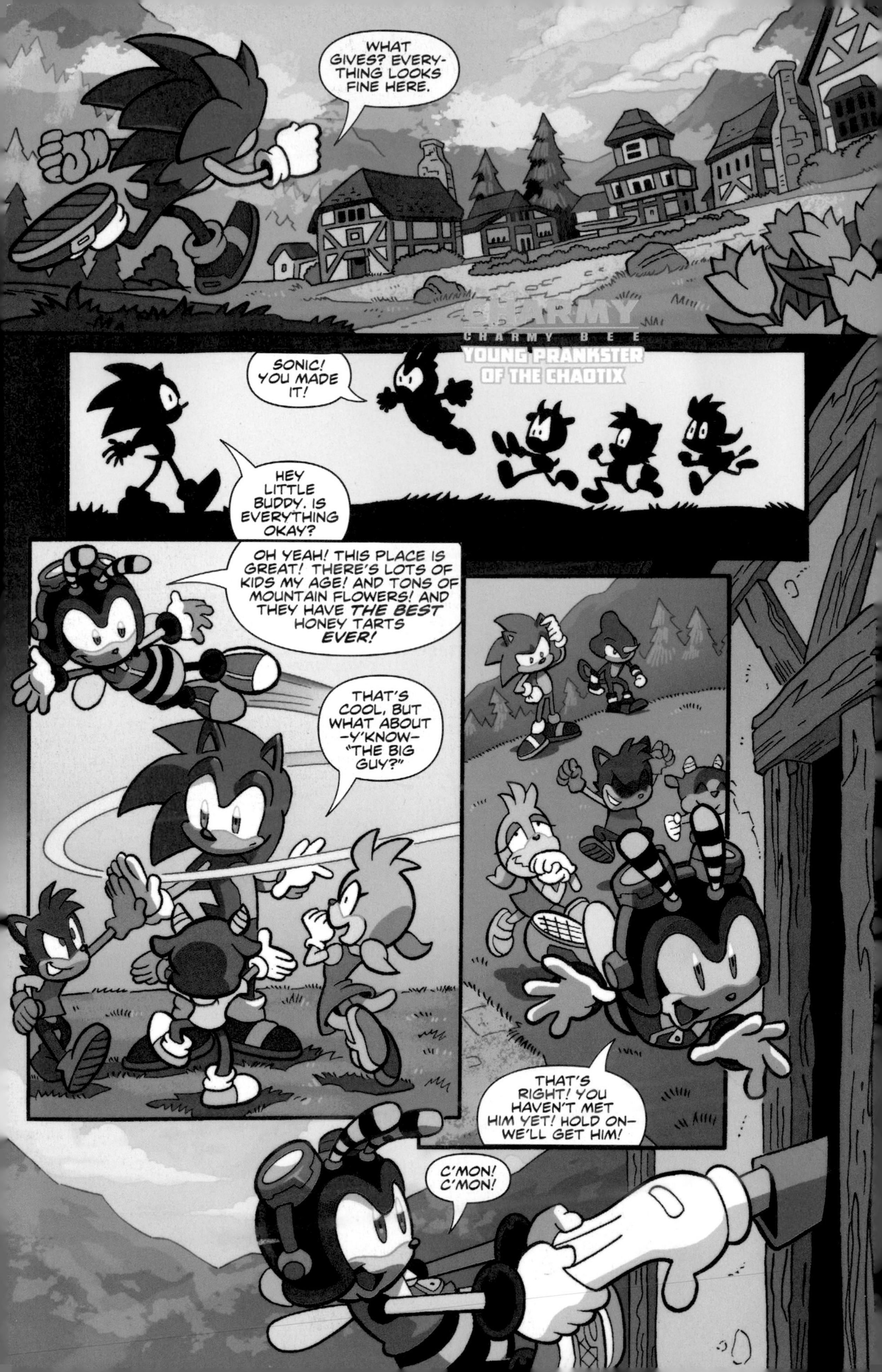
WHAT GIVES? EVERYTHING LOOKS FINE HERE.
CHARMY
CHARMY BEE
YOUNG PRANKSTER OF THE CHAOTIX
SONIC! YOU MADE IT!
HEY LITTLE BUDDY. IS EVERYTHING OKAY?
OH YEAH! THIS PLACE IS GREAT! THERE'S LOTS OF KIDS MY AGE! AND TONS OF MOUNTAIN FLOWERS! AND THEY HAVE THE BEST HONEY TARTS EVER!
THAT'S COOL, BUT WHAT ABOUT —Y'KNOW— "THE BIG GUY?"
THAT'S RIGHT! YOU HAVEN'T MET HIM YET! HOLD ON— WE'LL GET HIM!
C'MON! C'MON!

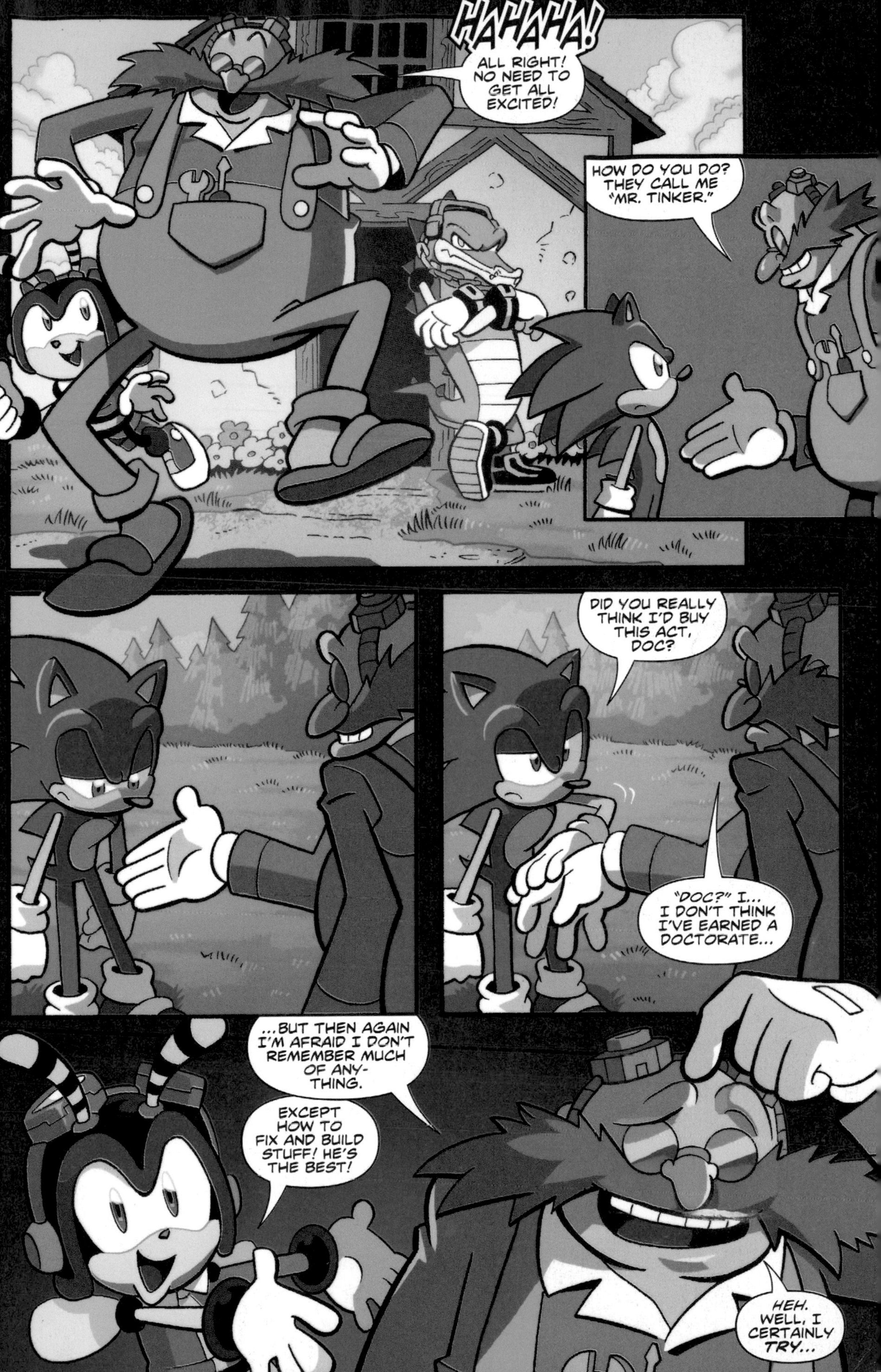
HAHAHA!
ALL RIGHT! NO NEED TO GET ALL EXCITED!
HOW DO YOU DO? THEY CALL ME "MR. TINKER."
DID YOU REALLY THINK I'D BUY THIS ACT, DOC?
"DOC?" I... I DON'T THINK I'VE EARNED A DOCTORATE...
...BUT THEN AGAIN I'M AFRAID I DON'T REMEMBER MUCH OF ANY-THING.
EXCEPT HOW TO FIX AND BUILD STUFF! HE'S THE BEST!
HEH. WELL, I CERTAINLY TRY...

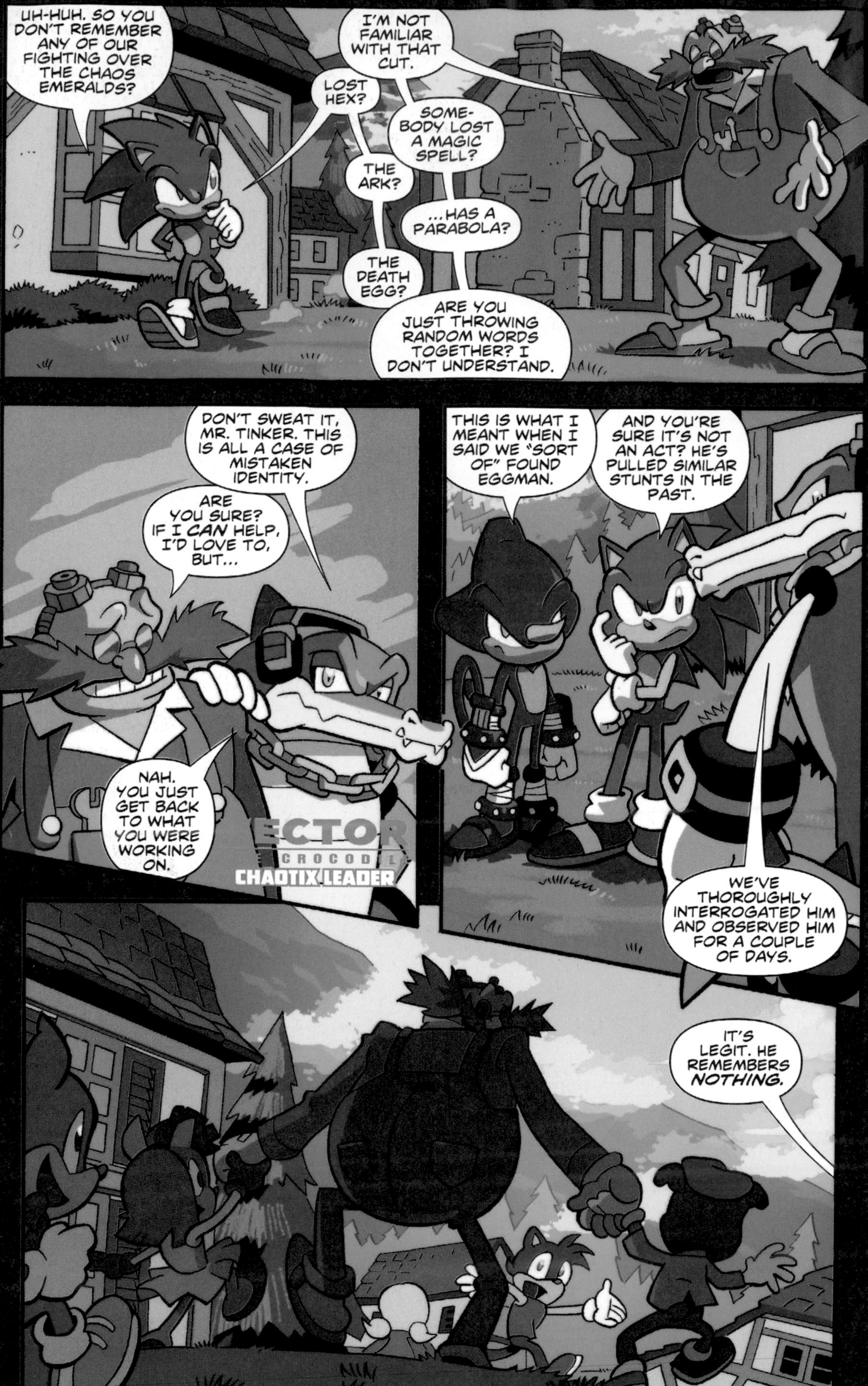
UH-HUH. SO YOU DON'T REMEMBER ANY OF OUR FIGHTING OVER THE CHAOS EMERALDS?
I'M NOT FAMILIAR WITH THAT CUT.
LOST HEX?
SOME-BODY LOST A MAGIC SPELL?
THE ARK?
...HAS A PARABOLA?
THE DEATH EGG?
ARE YOU JUST THROWING RANDOM WORDS TOGETHER? I DON'T UNDERSTAND.
DON'T SWEAT IT, MR. TINKER. THIS IS ALL A CASE OF MISTAKEN IDENTITY.
ARE YOU SURE? IF I CAN HELP, I'D LOVE TO, BUT...
NAH. YOU JUST GET BACK TO WHAT YOU WERE WORKING ON.
CHAOTIX LEADER
THIS IS WHAT I MEANT WHEN I SAID WE "SORT OF" FOUND EGGMAN.
AND YOU'RE SURE IT'S NOT AN ACT? HE'S PULLED SIMILAR STUNTS IN THE PAST.
WE'VE THOROUGHLY INTERROGATED HIM AND OBSERVED HIM FOR A COUPLE OF DAYS.
IT'S LEGIT. HE REMEMBERS NOTHING.

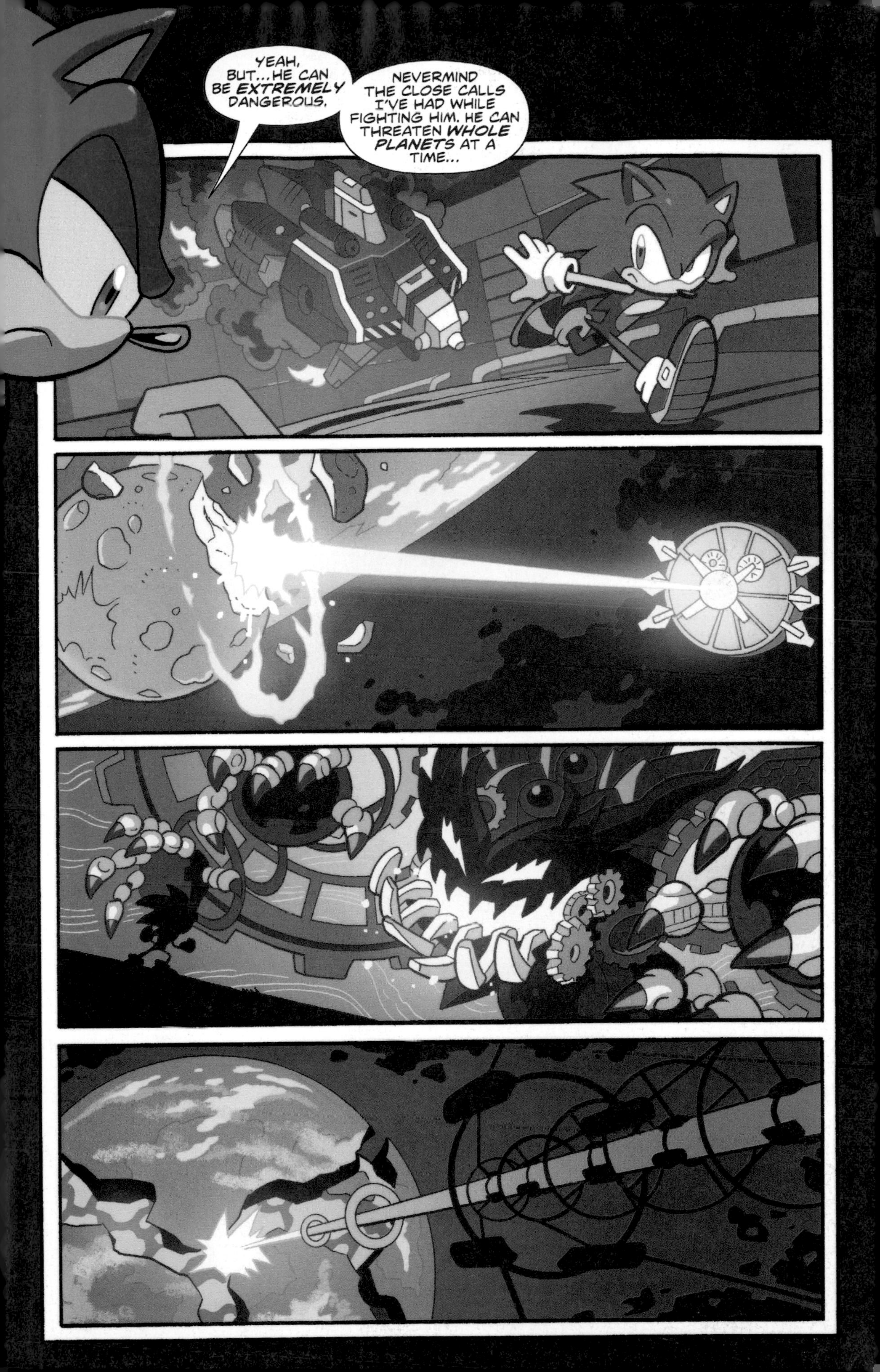
YEAH, BUT... HE CAN BE EXTREMELY DANGEROUS.
NEVERMIND THE CLOSE CALLS I'VE HAD WHILE FIGHTING HIM. HE CAN THREATEN WHOLE PLANETS AT A TIME...

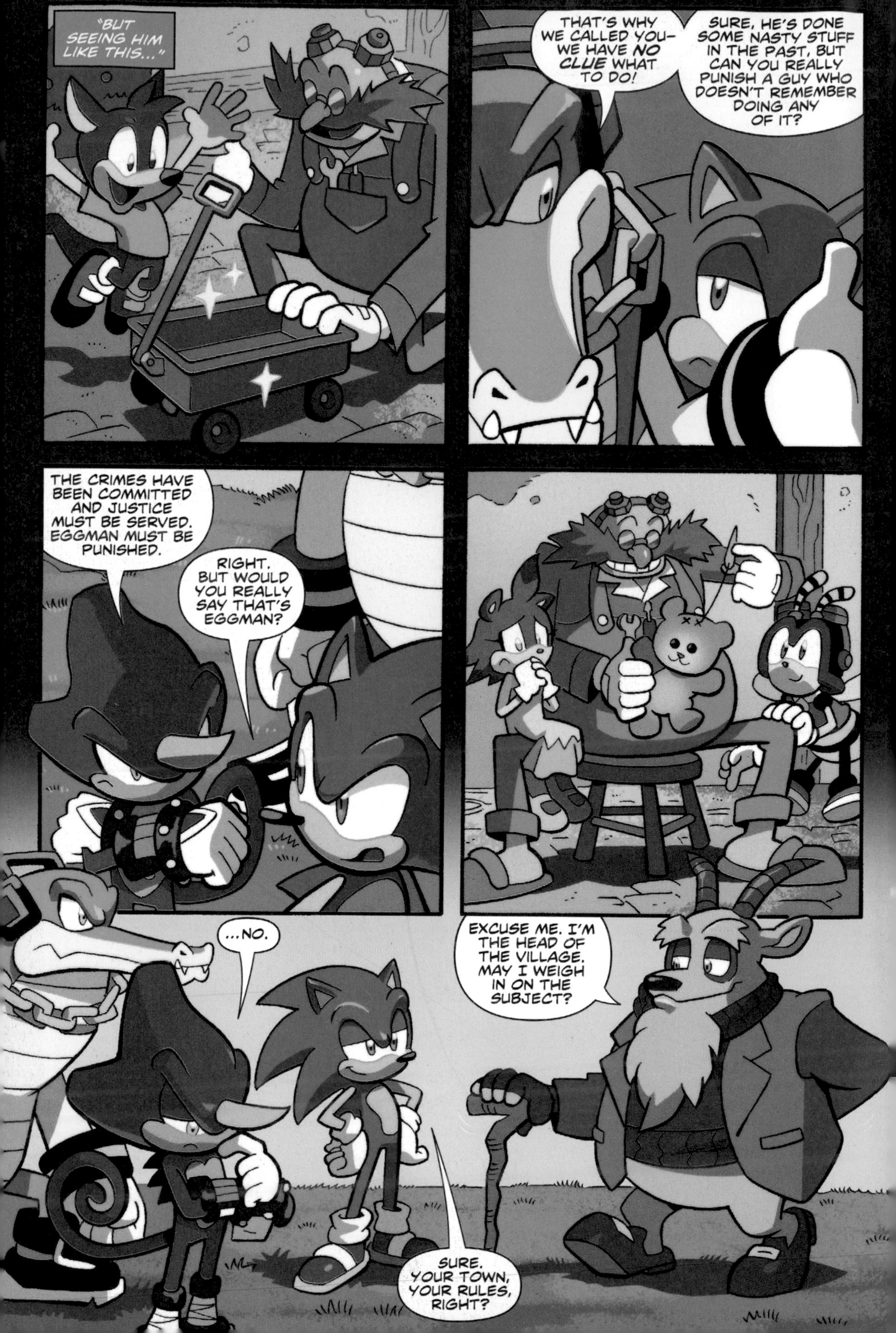
"BUT SEEING HIM LIKE THIS..."
THAT'S WHY WE CALLED YOU- WE HAVE NO CLUE WHAT TO DO!
SURE, HE'S DONE SOME NASTY STUFF IN THE PAST, BUT CAN YOU REALLY PUNISH A GUY WHO DOESN'T REMEMBER DOING ANY OF IT?
THE CRIMES HAVE BEEN COMMITTED AND JUSTICE MUST BE SERVED. EGGMAN MUST BE PUNISHED.
RIGHT. BUT WOULD YOU REALLY SAY THAT'S EGGMAN?
...NO.
EXCUSE ME. I'M THE HEAD OF THE VILLAGE. MAY I WEIGH IN ON THE SUBJECT?
SURE. YOUR TOWN, YOUR RULES, RIGHT?

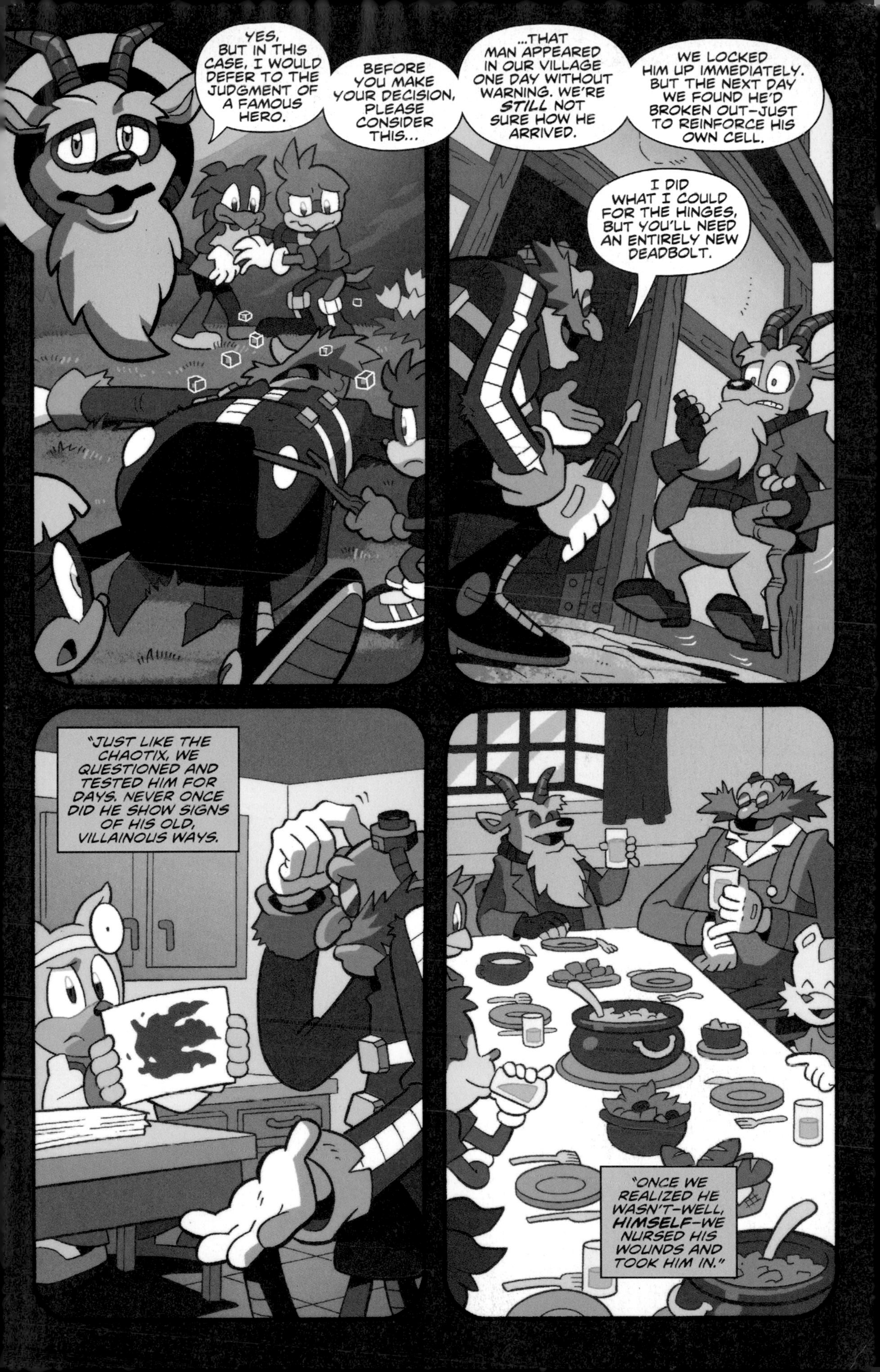
YES, BUT IN THIS CASE, I WOULD DEFER TO THE JUDGMENT OF A FAMOUS HERO.
BEFORE YOU MAKE YOUR DECISION, PLEASE CONSIDER THIS...
...THAT MAN APPEARED IN OUR VILLAGE ONE DAY WITHOUT WARNING. WE'RE STILL NOT SURE HOW HE ARRIVED.
WE LOCKED HIM UP IMMEDIATELY. BUT THE NEXT DAY WE FOUND HE'D BROKEN OUT–JUST TO REINFORCE HIS OWN CELL.
I DID WHAT I COULD FOR THE HINGES, BUT YOU'LL NEED AN ENTIRELY NEW DEADBOLT.
"JUST LIKE THE CHAOTIX, WE QUESTIONED AND TESTED HIM FOR DAYS. NEVER ONCE DID HE SHOW SIGNS OF HIS OLD, VILLAINOUS WAYS.
"ONCE WE REALIZED HE WASN'T–WELL, HIMSELF–WE NURSED HIS WOUNDS AND TOOK HIM IN."

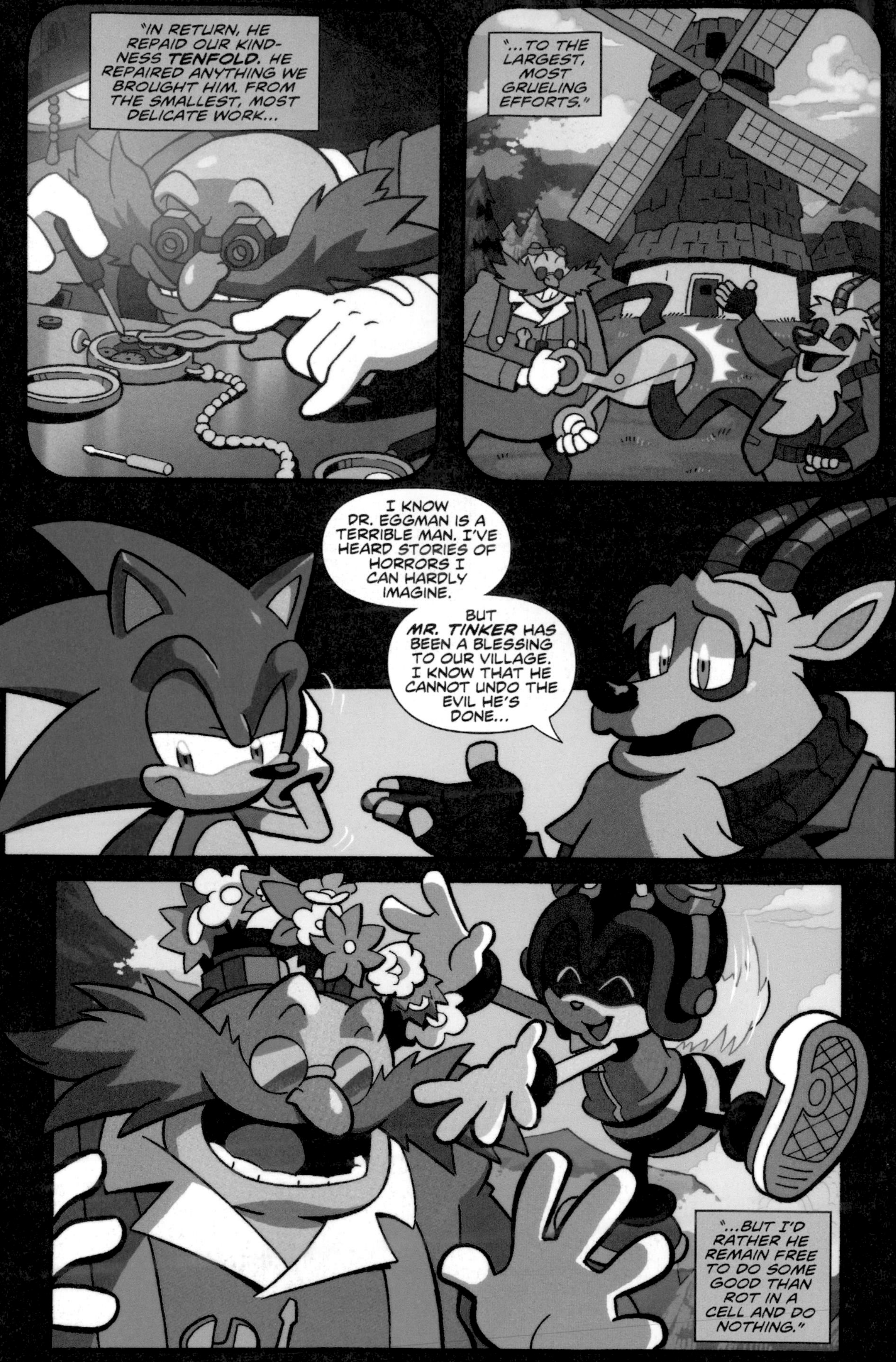
"IN RETURN, HE REPAID OUR KINDNESS TENFOLD. HE REPAIRED ANYTHING WE BROUGHT HIM. FROM THE SMALLEST, MOST DELICATE WORK...
"...TO THE LARGEST, MOST GRUELING EFFORTS."
I KNOW DR. EGGMAN IS A TERRIBLE MAN. I'VE HEARD STORIES OF HORRORS I CAN HARDLY IMAGINE.
BUT MR. TINKER HAS BEEN A BLESSING TO OUR VILLAGE. I KNOW THAT HE CANNOT UNDO THE EVIL HE'S DONE...
"...BUT I'D RATHER HE REMAIN FREE TO DO SOME GOOD THAN ROT IN A CELL AND DO NOTHING."

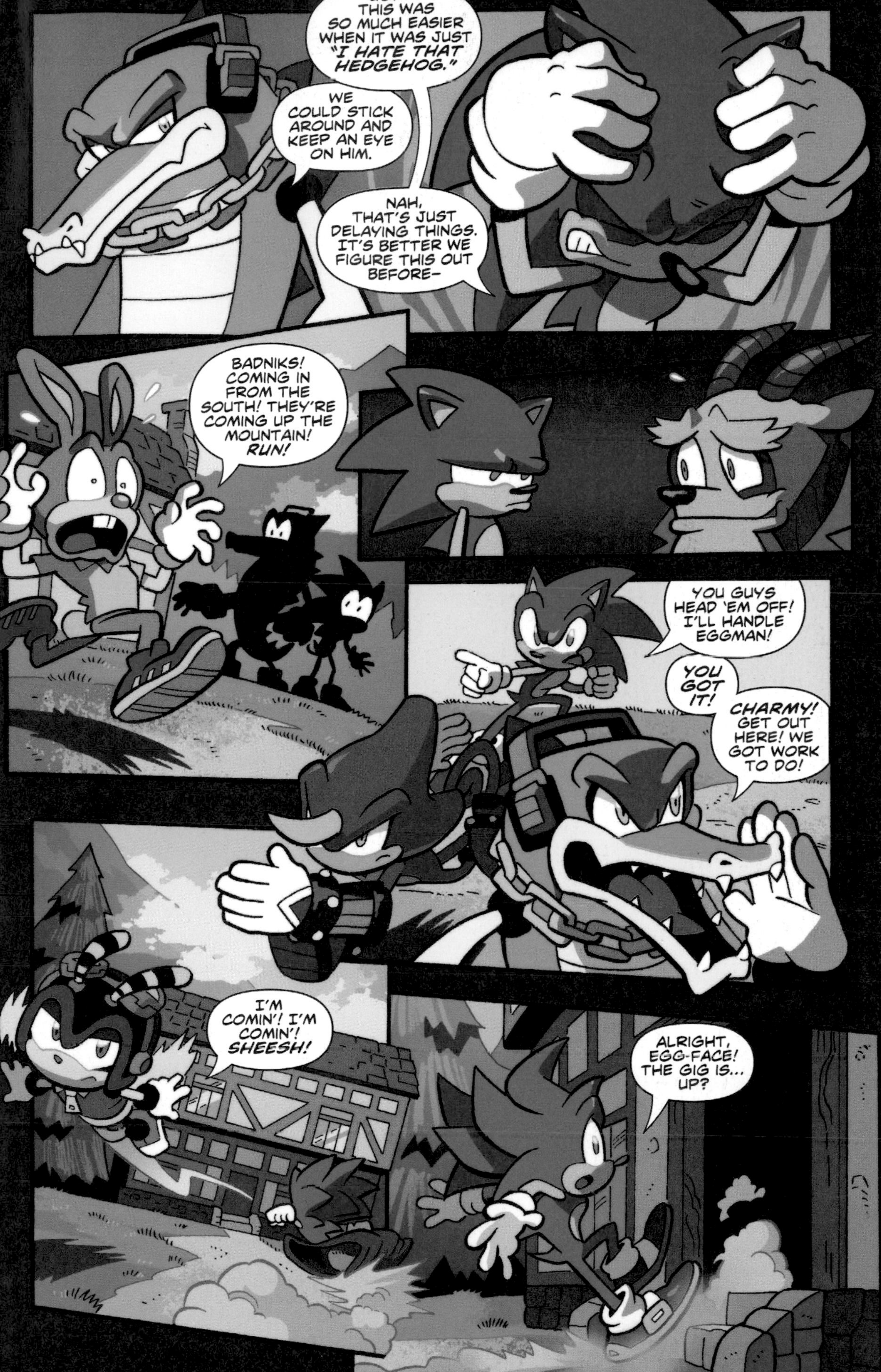
UGH... THIS WAS SO MUCH EASIER WHEN IT WAS JUST "I HATE THAT HEDGEHOG."
WE COULD STICK AROUND AND KEEP AN EYE ON HIM.
NAH, THAT'S JUST DELAYING THINGS. IT'S BETTER WE FIGURE THIS OUT BEFORE–
BADNIKS! COMING IN FROM THE SOUTH! THEY'RE COMING UP THE MOUNTAIN! RUN!
YOU GUYS HEAD 'EM OFF! I'LL HANDLE EGGMAN!
YOU GOT IT!
CHARMY! GET OUT HERE! WE GOT WORK TO DO!
I'M COMIN'! I'M COMIN'! SHEESH!
ALRIGHT, EGG-FACE! THE GIG IS... UP?

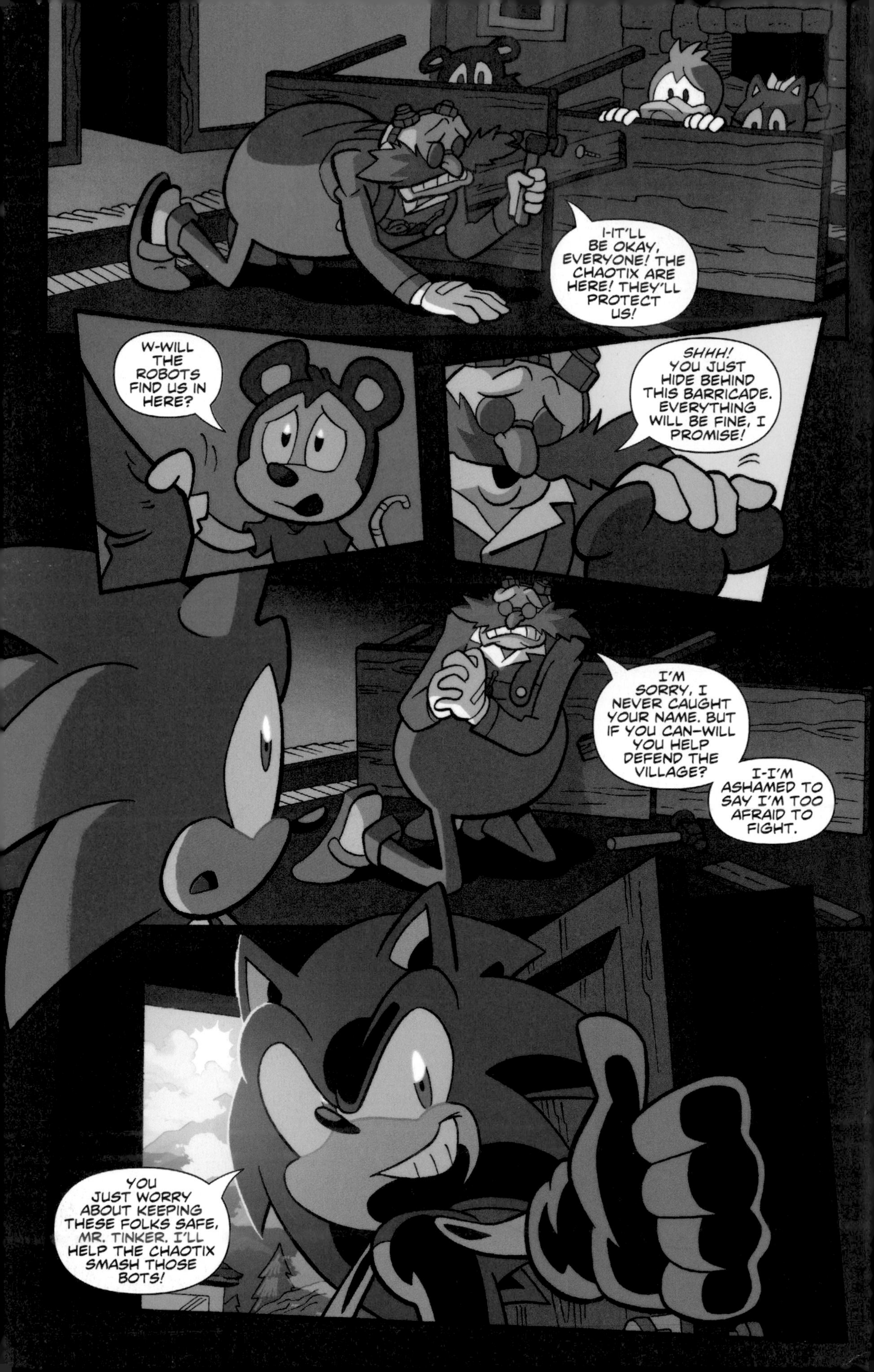
I-IT'LL BE OKAY, EVERYONE! THE CHAOTIX ARE HERE! THEY'LL PROTECT US!
W-WILL THE ROBOTS FIND US IN HERE?
SHHH! YOU JUST HIDE BEHIND THIS BARRICADE. EVERYTHING WILL BE FINE, I PROMISE!
I'M SORRY, I NEVER CAUGHT YOUR NAME. BUT IF YOU CAN—WILL YOU HELP DEFEND THE VILLAGE?
I-I'M ASHAMED TO SAY I'M TOO AFRAID TO FIGHT.
YOU JUST WORRY ABOUT KEEPING THESE FOLKS SAFE, MR. TINKER. I'LL HELP THE CHAOTIX SMASH THOSE BOTS!

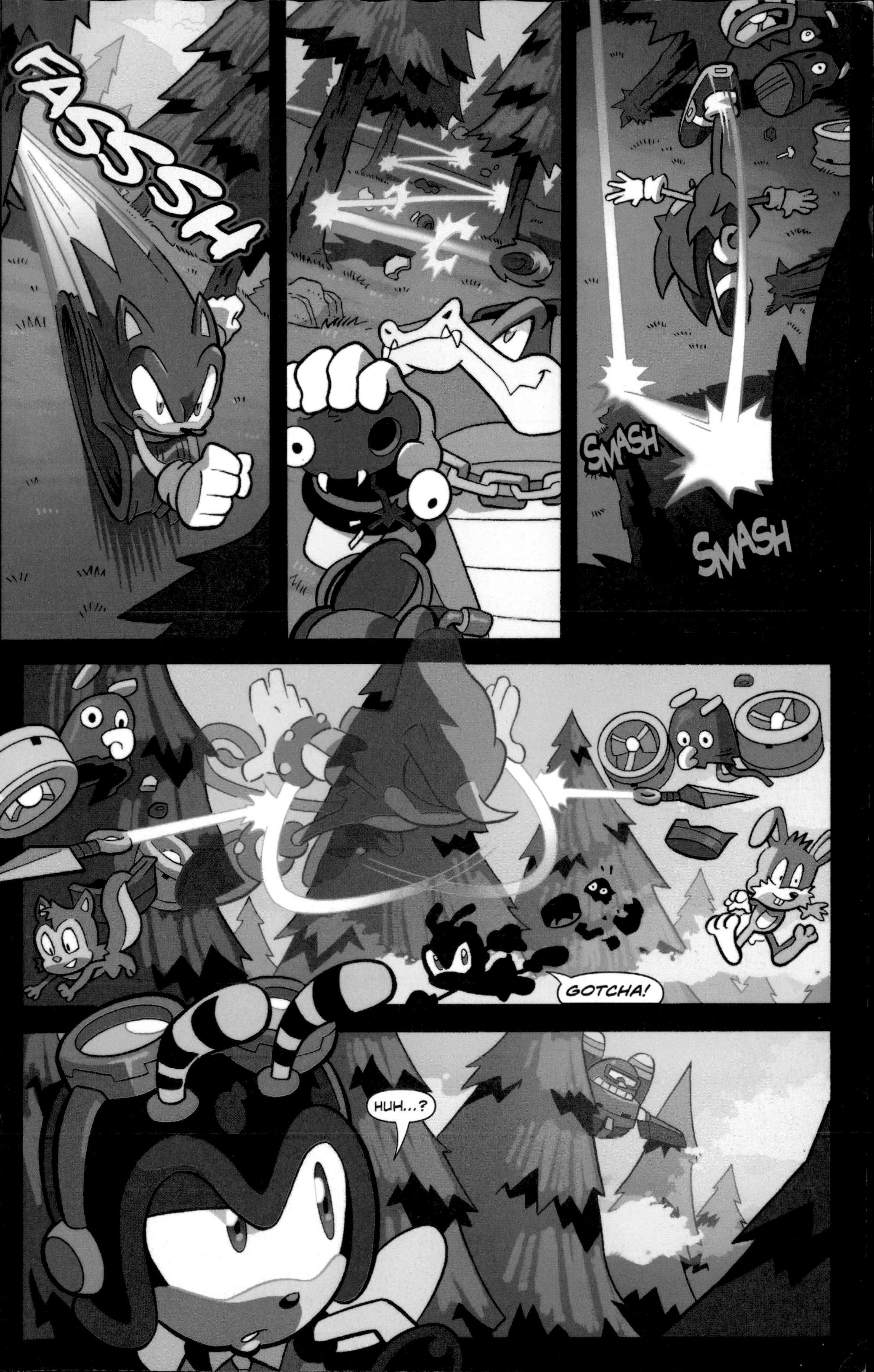
FASSSH
SMASH
SMASH
GOTCHA!
HUH...?

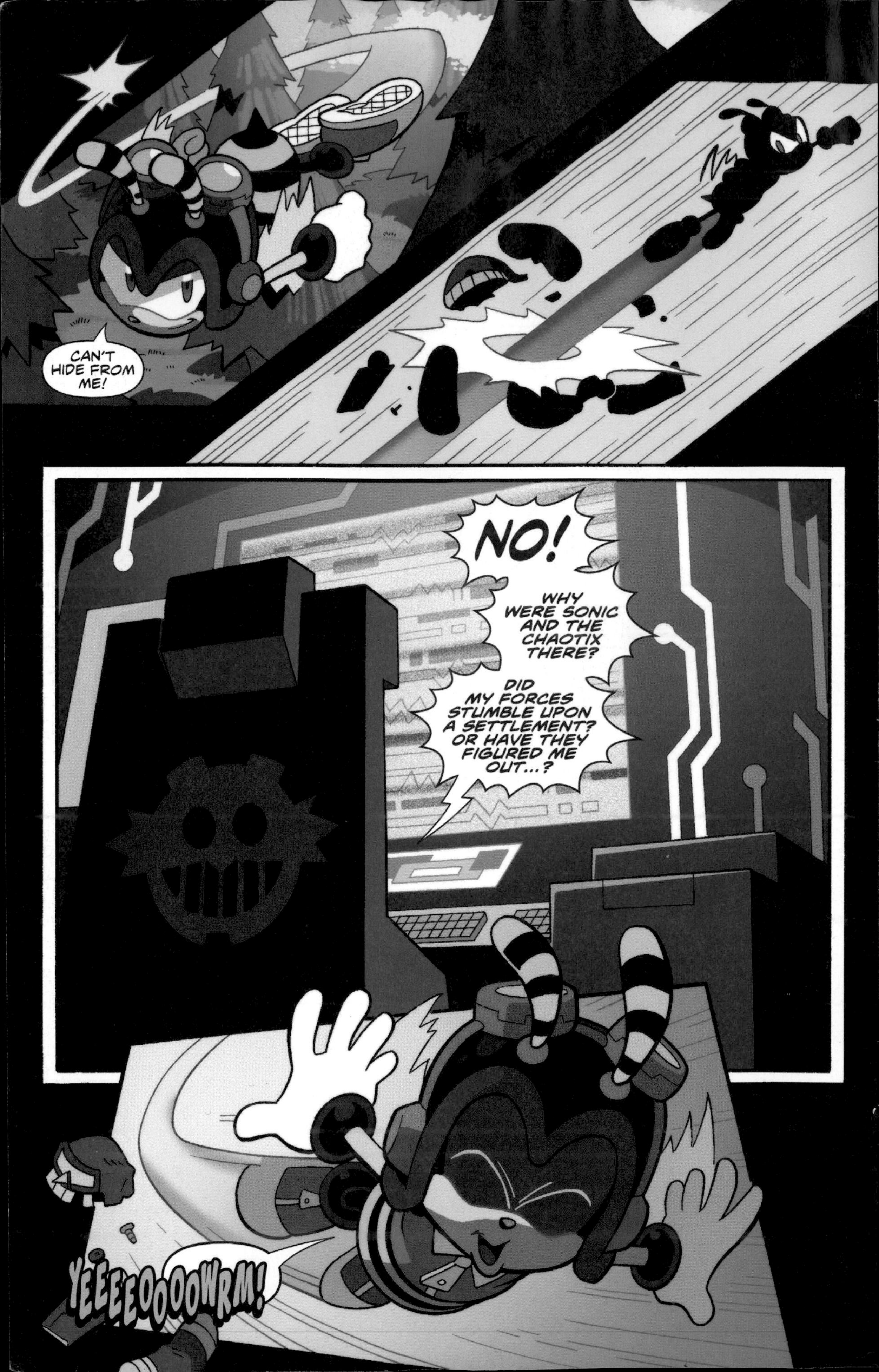
CAN'T HIDE FROM ME!
NO!
WHY WERE SONIC AND THE CHAOTIX THERE?
DID MY FORCES STUMBLE UPON A SETTLEMENT? OR HAVE THEY FIGURED ME OUT...?
YEEEEOOOOWRM!

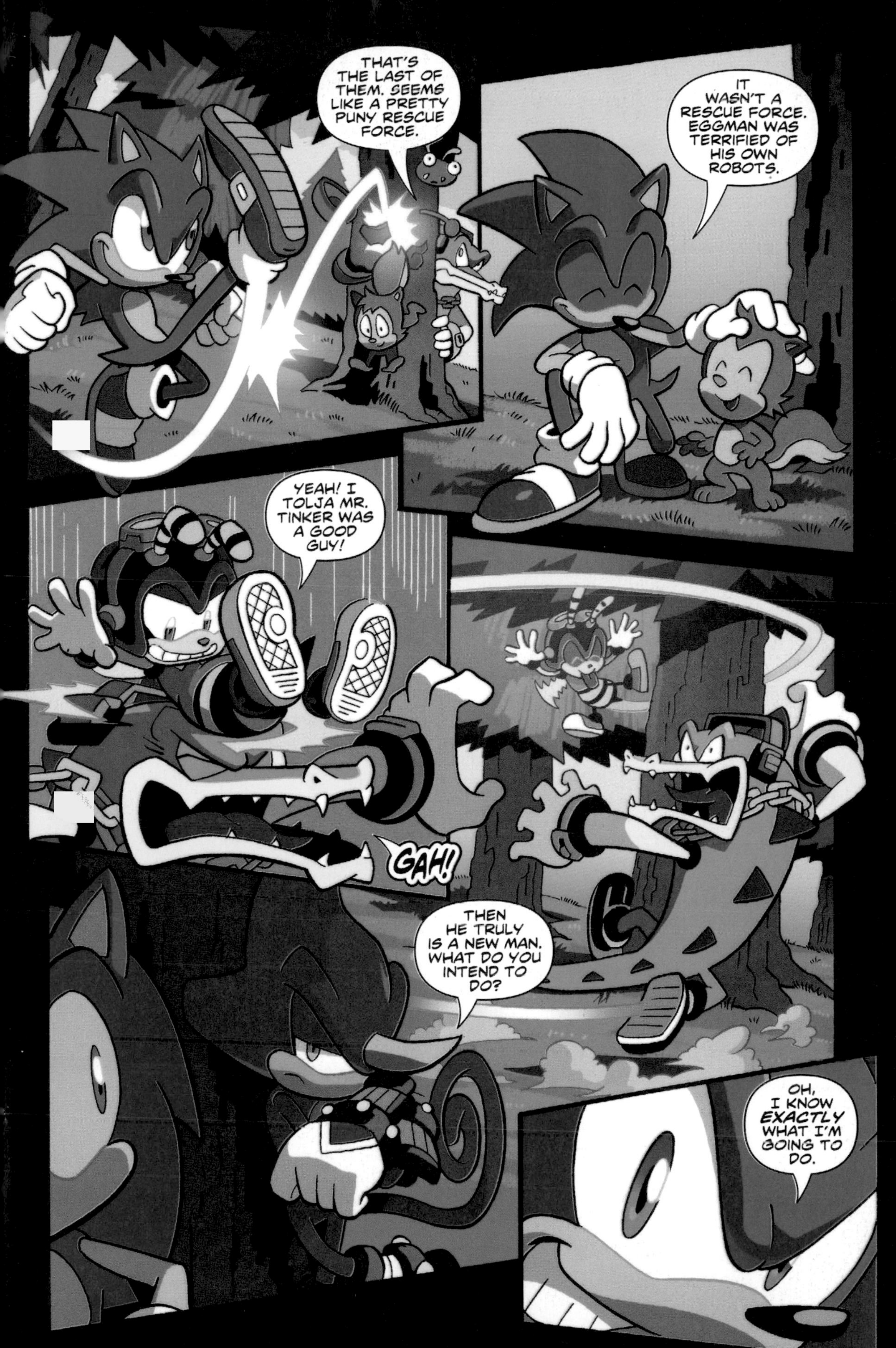
THAT'S THE LAST OF THEM. SEEMS LIKE A PRETTY PUNY RESCUE FORCE.
IT WASN'T A RESCUE FORCE. EGGMAN WAS TERRIFIED OF HIS OWN ROBOTS.
YEAH! I TOLJA MR. TINKER WAS A GOOD GUY!
GAH!
THEN HE TRULY IS A NEW MAN. WHAT DO YOU INTEND TO DO?
OH, I KNOW *EXACTLY* WHAT I'M GOING TO DO.

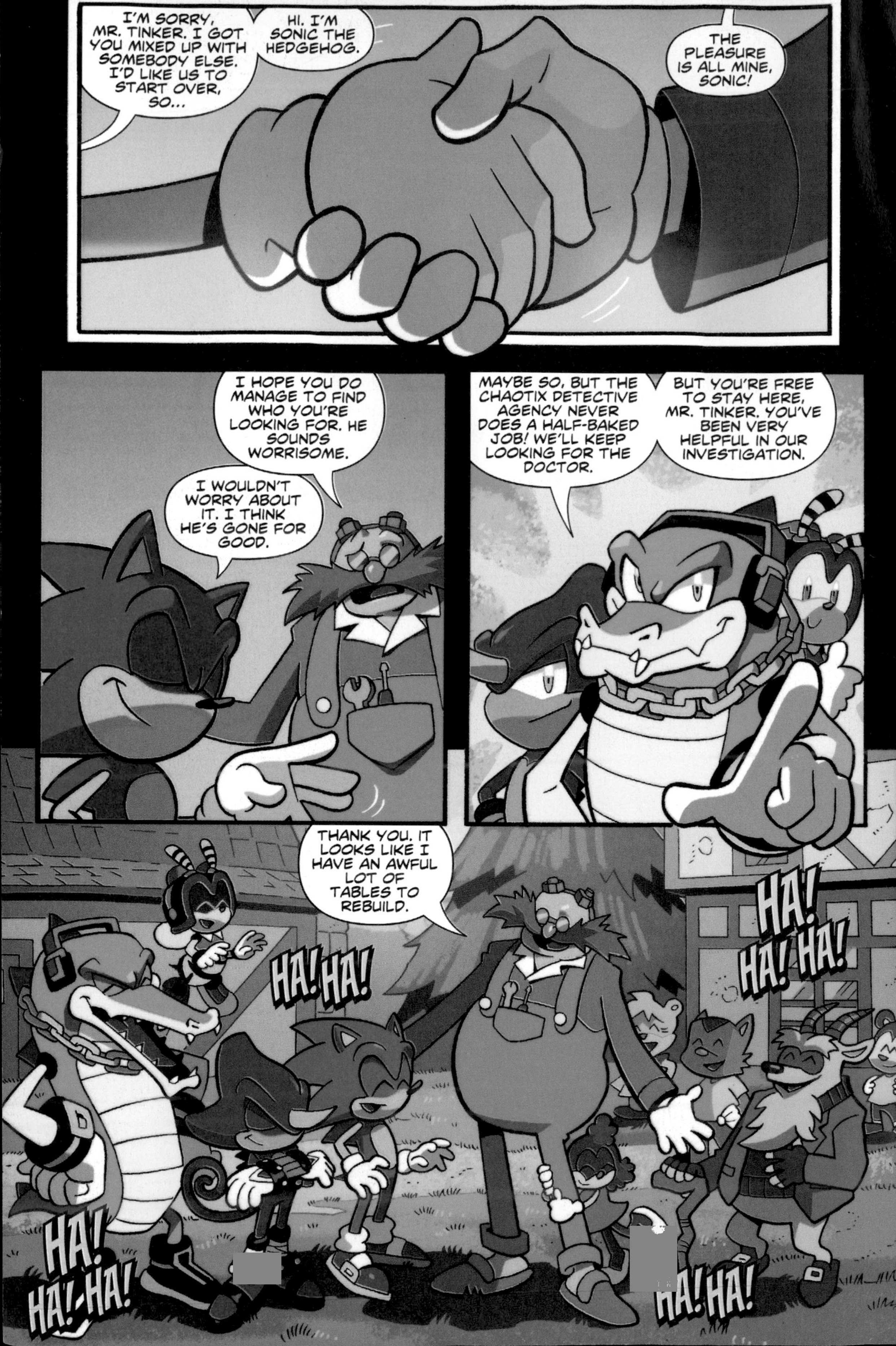
I'M SORRY, MR. TINKER. I GOT YOU MIXED UP WITH SOMEBODY ELSE. I'D LIKE US TO START OVER, SO...
HI. I'M SONIC THE HEDGEHOG.
THE PLEASURE IS ALL MINE, SONIC!
I HOPE YOU DO MANAGE TO FIND WHO YOU'RE LOOKING FOR. HE SOUNDS WORRISOME.
I WOULDN'T WORRY ABOUT IT. I THINK HE'S GONE FOR GOOD.
MAYBE SO, BUT THE CHAOTIX DETECTIVE AGENCY NEVER DOES A HALF-BAKED JOB! WE'LL KEEP LOOKING FOR THE DOCTOR.
BUT YOU'RE FREE TO STAY HERE, MR. TINKER. YOU'VE BEEN VERY HELPFUL IN OUR INVESTIGATION.
THANK YOU. IT LOOKS LIKE I HAVE AN AWFUL LOT OF TABLES TO REBUILD.
HA! HA!
HA! HA! HA!
HA! HA!-HA!
HA! HA!

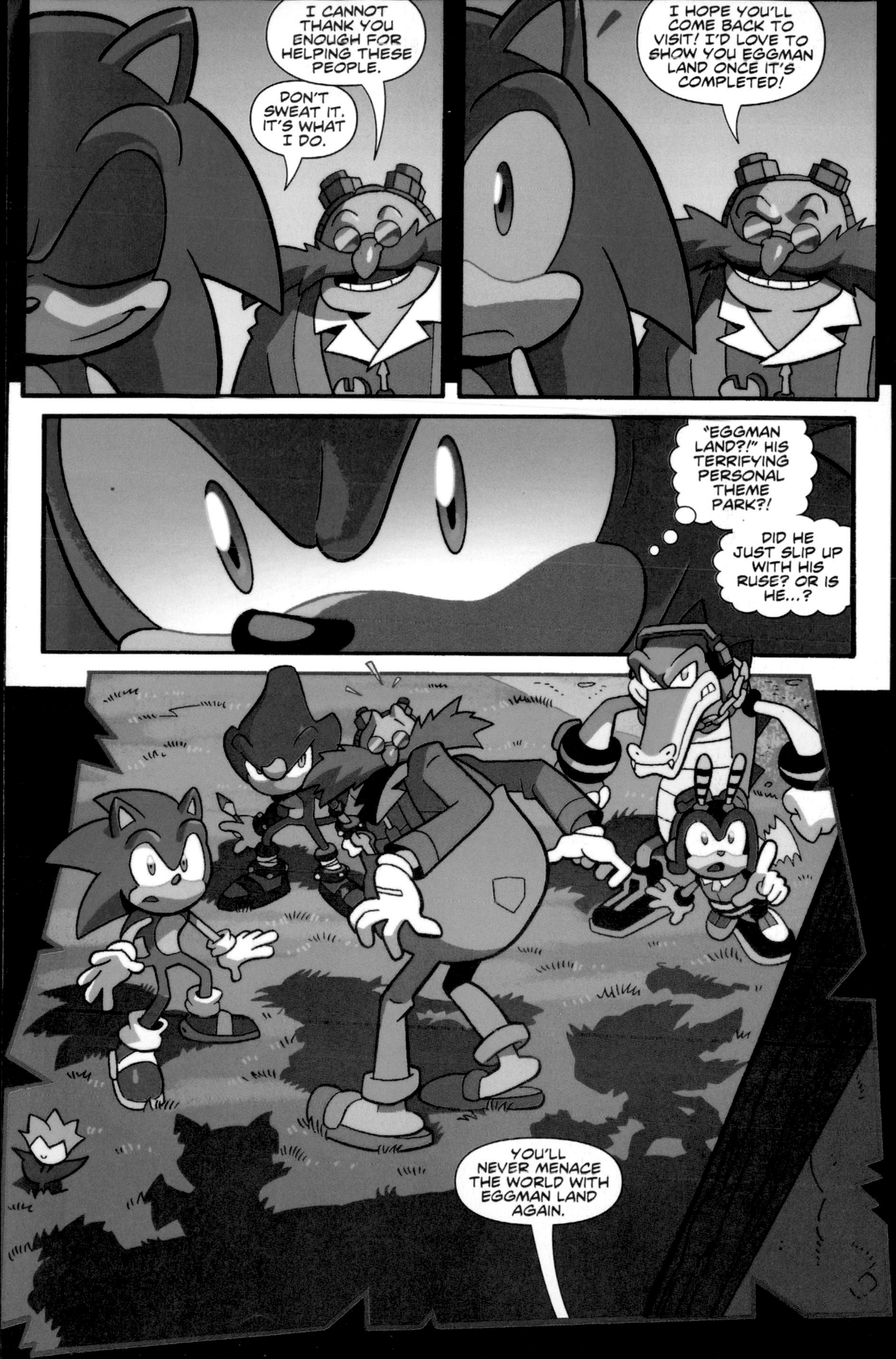
I CANNOT THANK YOU ENOUGH FOR HELPING THESE PEOPLE.
DON'T SWEAT IT. IT'S WHAT I DO.
I HOPE YOU'LL COME BACK TO VISIT! I'D LOVE TO SHOW YOU EGGMAN LAND ONCE IT'S COMPLETED!
"EGGMAN LAND?!" HIS TERRIFYING PERSONAL THEME PARK?!
DID HE JUST SLIP UP WITH HIS RUSE? OR IS HE...?
YOU'LL NEVER MENACE THE WORLD WITH EGGMAN LAND AGAIN.

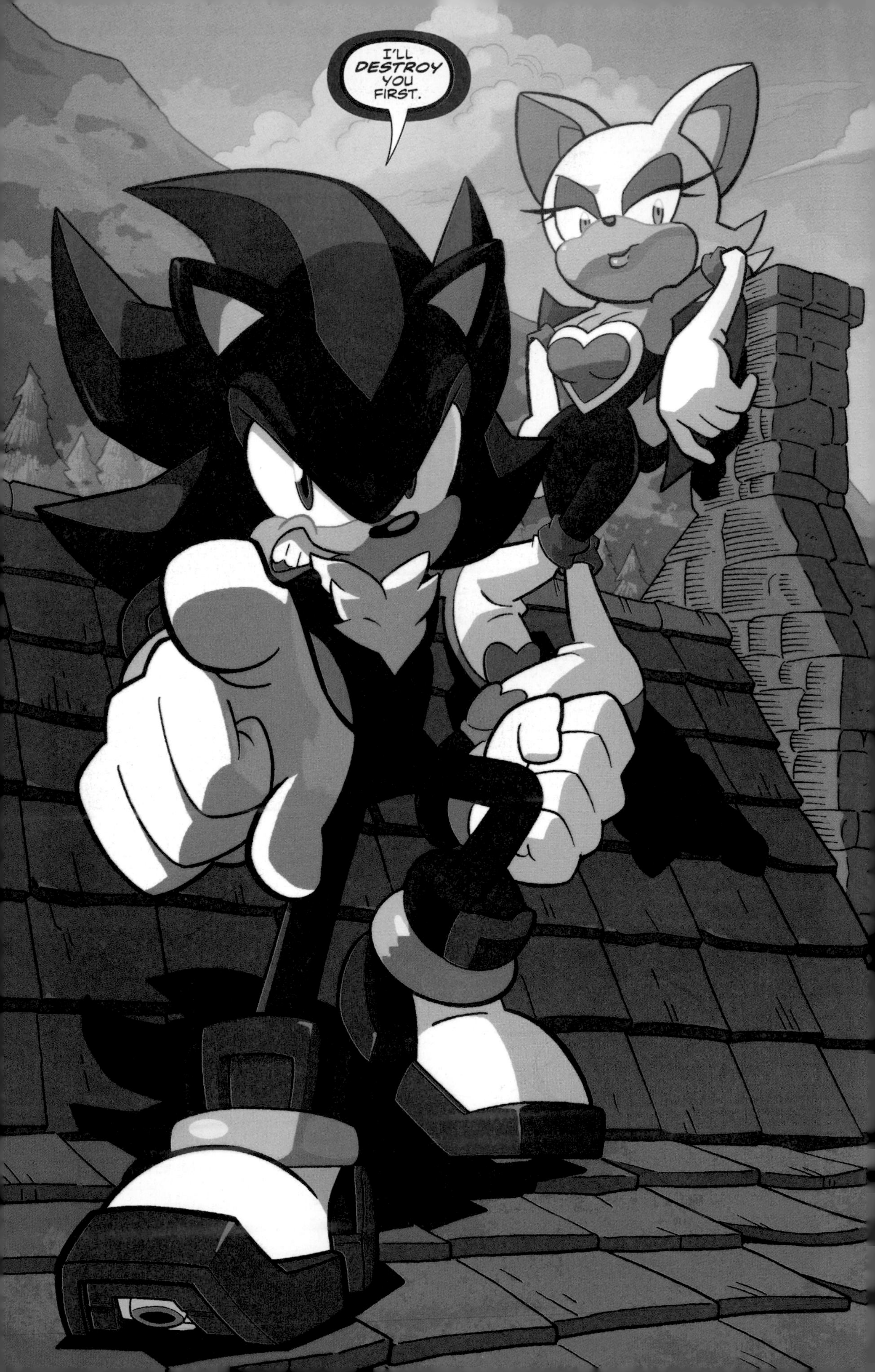
I'LL DESTROY YOU FIRST.

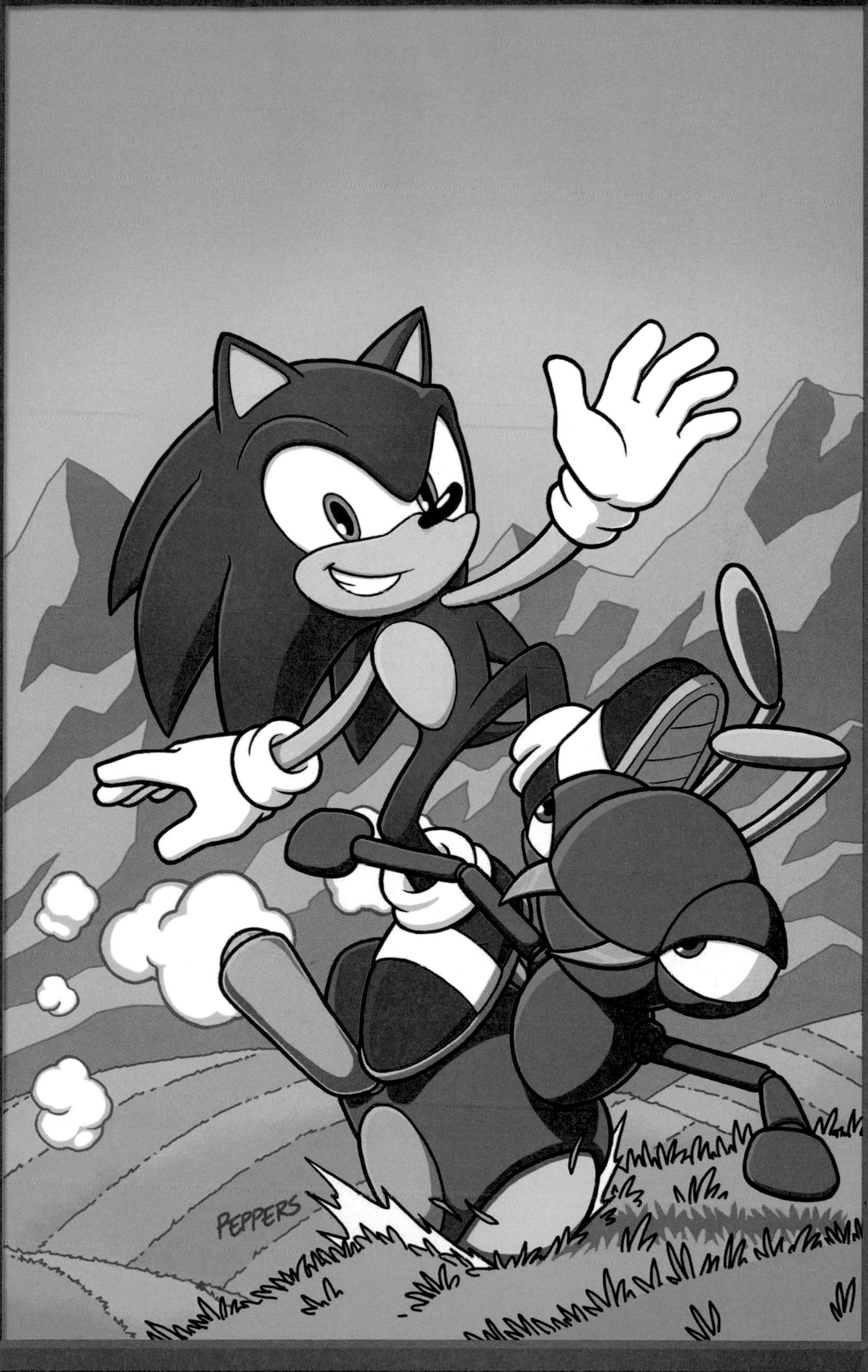
PEPPERS

ART BY **JAMAL PEPPERS**

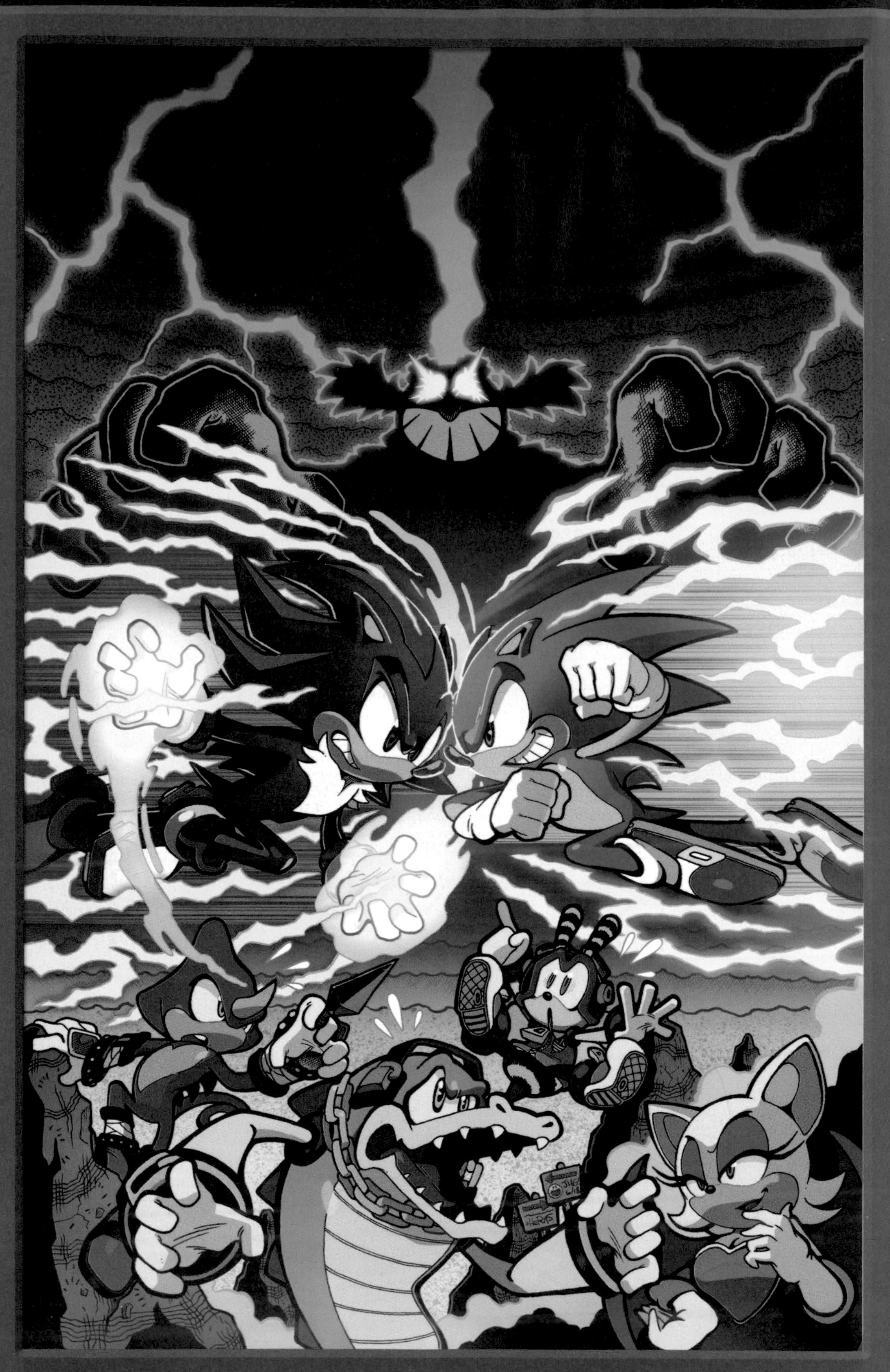

ART BY **JONATHAN GRAY** COLORS BY **MATT HERMS**

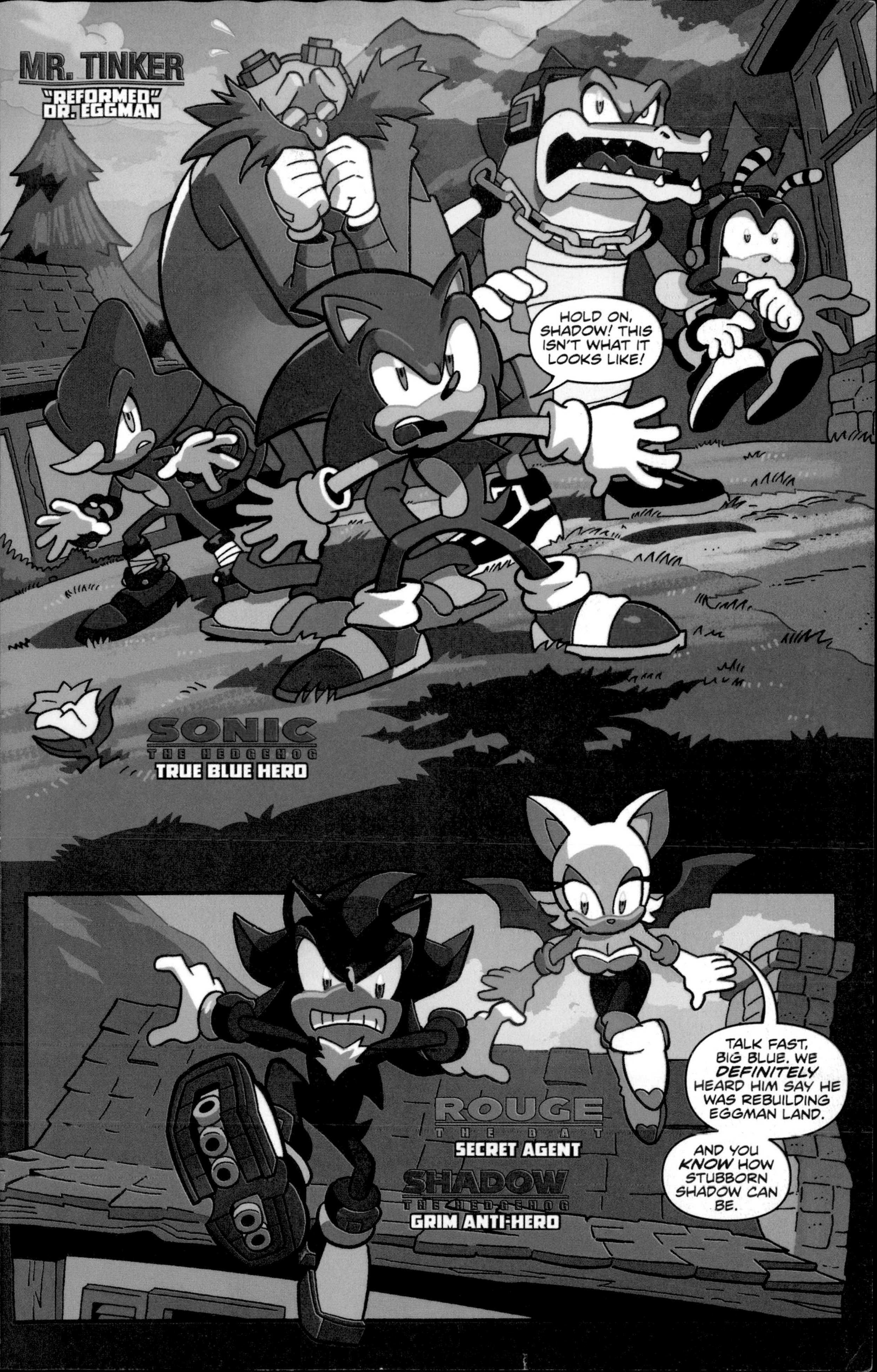
MR. TINKER
"REFORMED" DR. EGGMAN
HOLD ON, SHADOW! THIS ISN'T WHAT IT LOOKS LIKE!
SONIC THE HEDGEHOG
TRUE BLUE HERO
TALK FAST, BIG BLUE. WE DEFINITELY HEARD HIM SAY HE WAS REBUILDING EGGMAN LAND.
AND YOU KNOW HOW STUBBORN SHADOW CAN BE.
ROUGE THE BAT
SECRET AGENT
SHADOW THE HEDGEHOG
GRIM ANTI-HERO

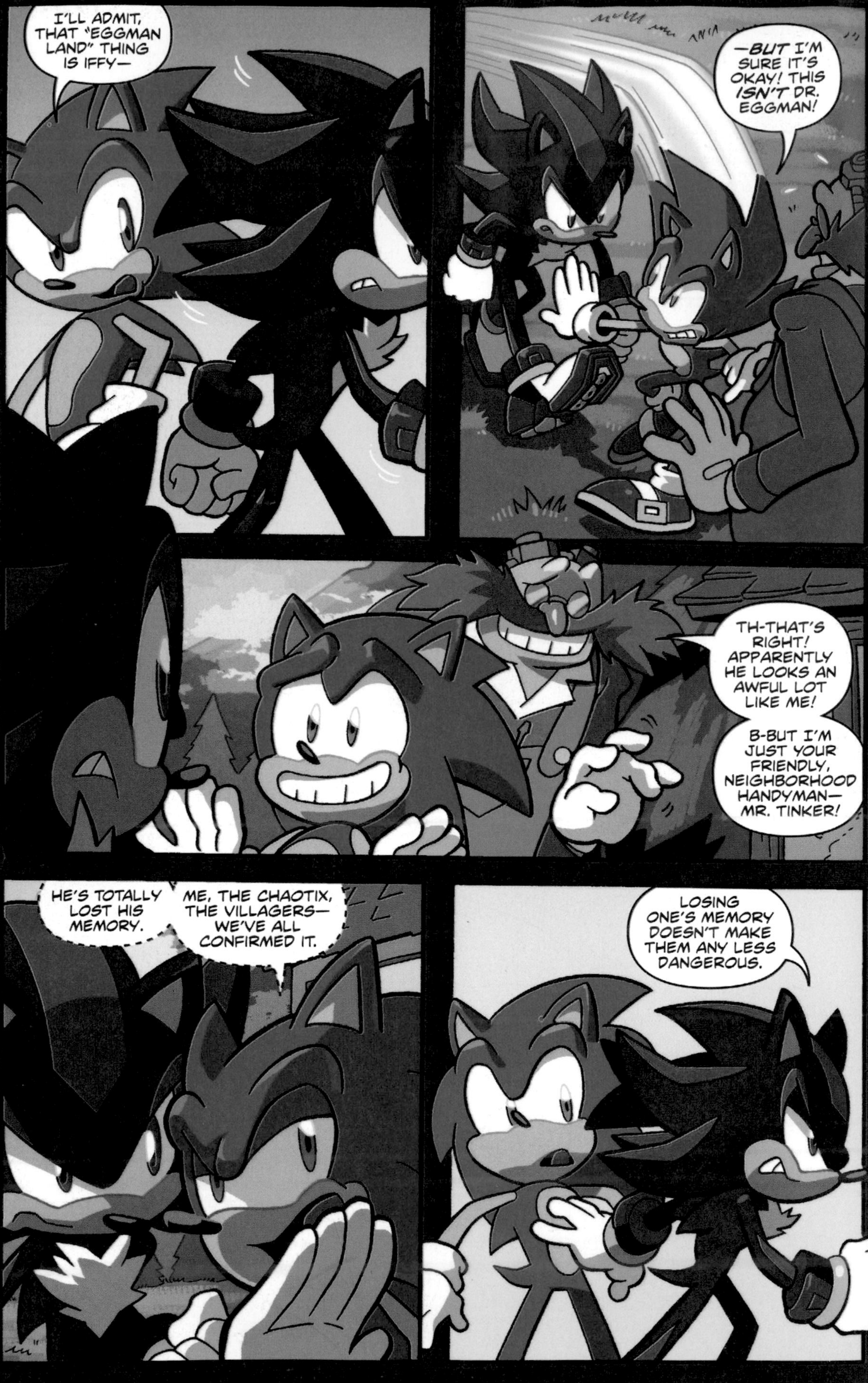
I'LL ADMIT, THAT "EGGMAN LAND" THING IS IFFY—
—BUT I'M SURE IT'S OKAY! THIS ISN'T DR. EGGMAN!
TH-THAT'S RIGHT! APPARENTLY HE LOOKS AN AWFUL LOT LIKE ME!
B-BUT I'M JUST YOUR FRIENDLY, NEIGHBORHOOD HANDYMAN—MR. TINKER!
HE'S TOTALLY LOST HIS MEMORY.
ME, THE CHAOTIX, THE VILLAGERS—WE'VE ALL CONFIRMED IT.
LOSING ONE'S MEMORY DOESN'T MAKE THEM ANY LESS DANGEROUS.

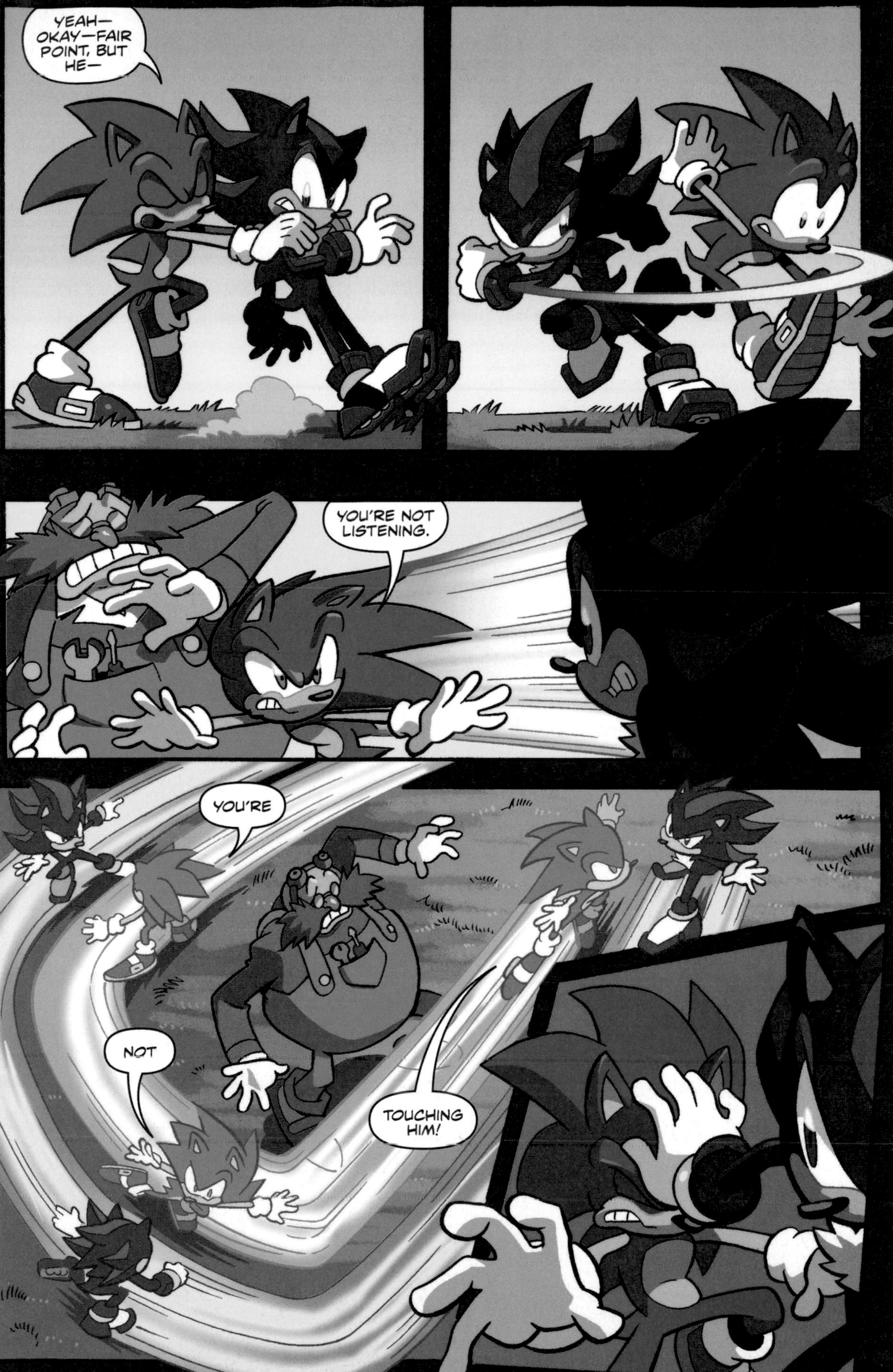
YEAH— OKAY—FAIR POINT, BUT HE—
YOU'RE NOT LISTENING.
YOU'RE
NOT
TOUCHING HIM!

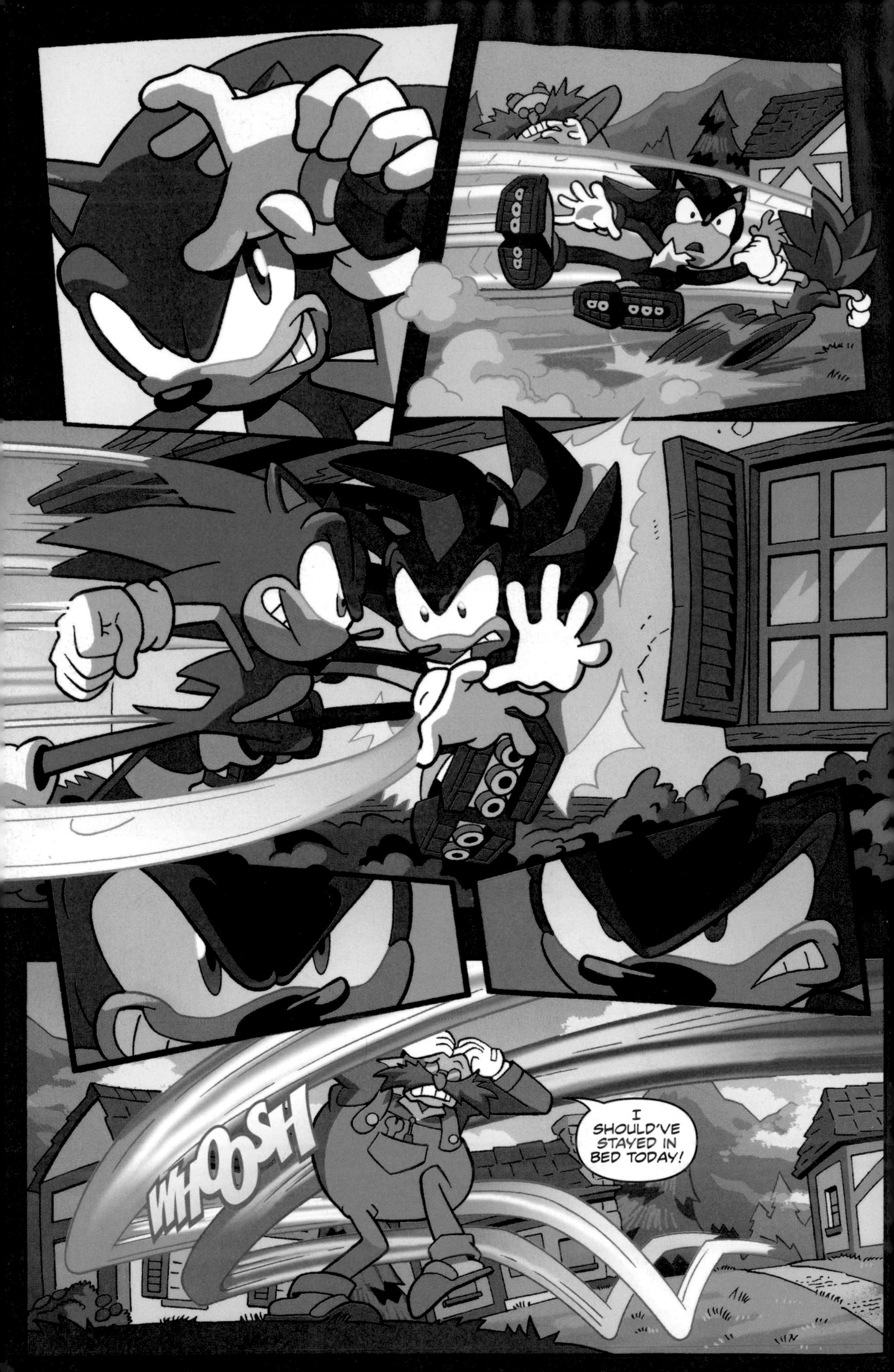
WHOOSH
I SHOULD'VE STAYED IN BED TODAY!

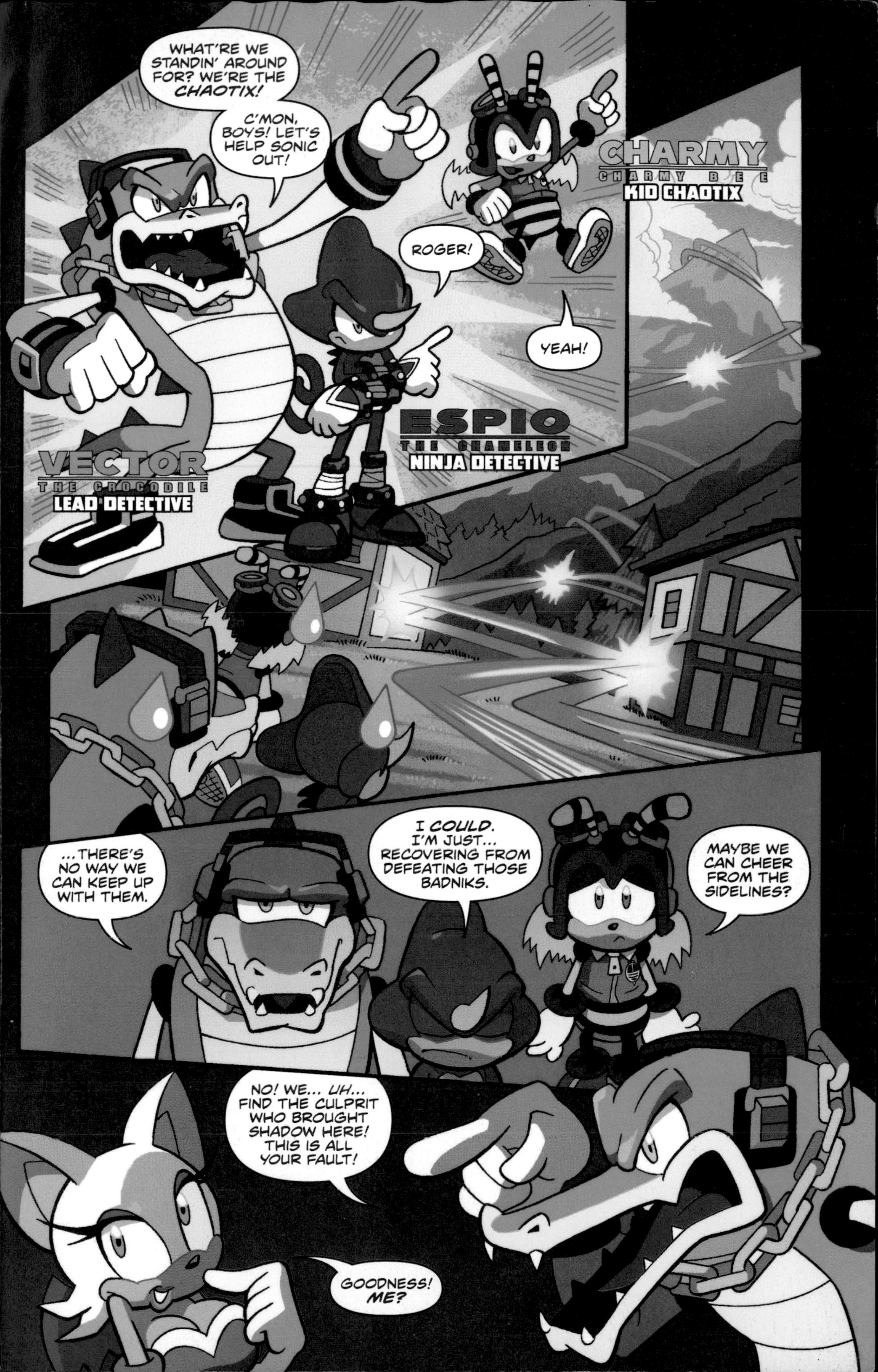
WHAT'RE WE STANDIN' AROUND FOR? WE'RE THE CHAOTIX!
C'MON, BOYS! LET'S HELP SONIC OUT!
ROGER!
YEAH!
CHARMY
CHARMY BEE
KID CHAOTIX
ESPIO
THE CHAMELEON
NINJA DETECTIVE
VECTOR
THE CROCODILE
LEAD DETECTIVE
...THERE'S NO WAY WE CAN KEEP UP WITH THEM.
I COULD. I'M JUST... RECOVERING FROM DEFEATING THOSE BADNIKS.
MAYBE WE CAN CHEER FROM THE SIDELINES?
NO! WE... UH... FIND THE CULPRIT WHO BROUGHT SHADOW HERE! THIS IS ALL YOUR FAULT!
GOODNESS! ME?

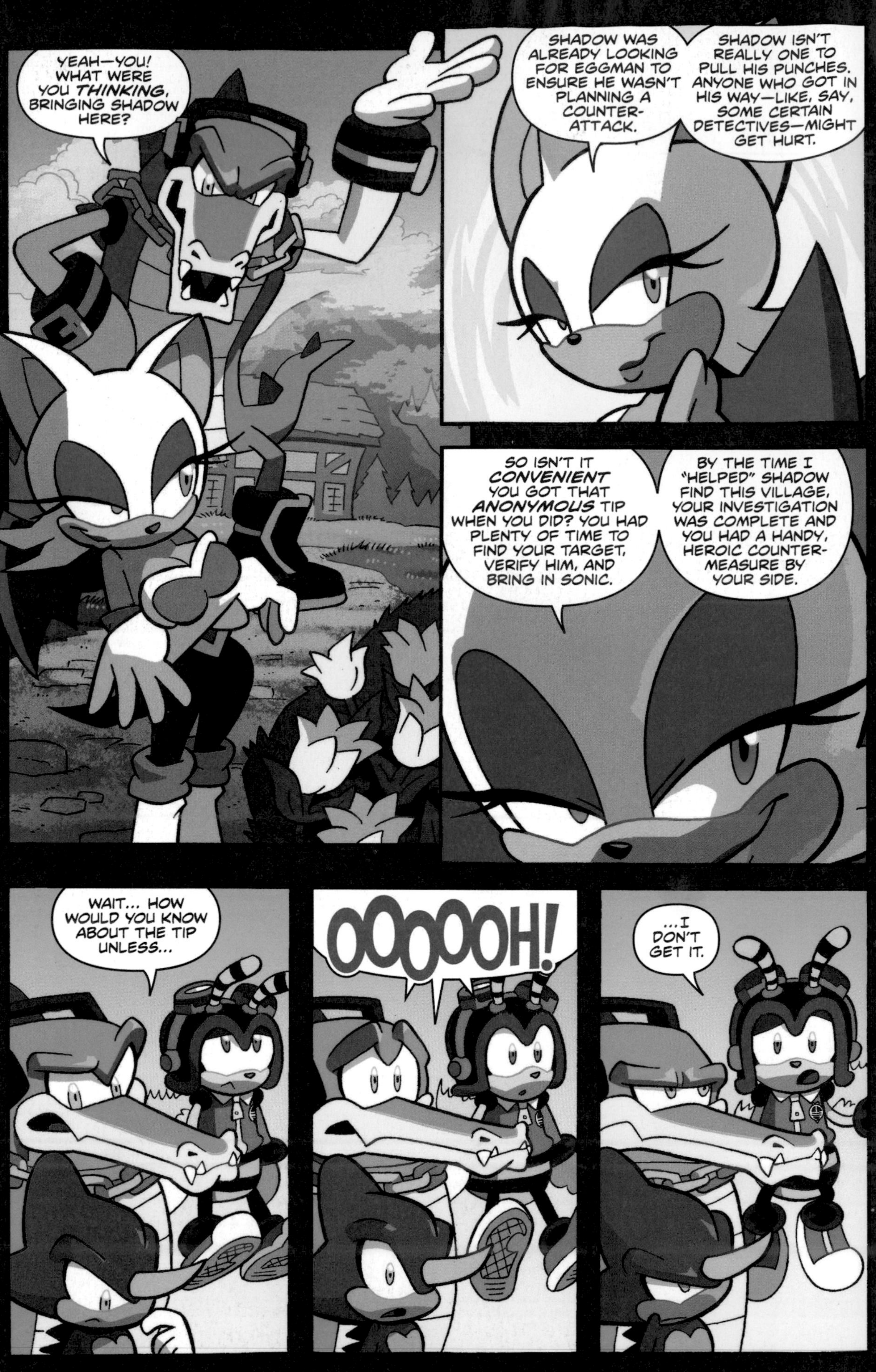
YEAH—YOU! WHAT WERE YOU *THINKING*, BRINGING SHADOW HERE?
SHADOW WAS ALREADY LOOKING FOR EGGMAN TO ENSURE HE WASN'T PLANNING A COUNTER-ATTACK.
SHADOW ISN'T REALLY ONE TO PULL HIS PUNCHES. ANYONE WHO GOT IN HIS WAY—LIKE, SAY, SOME CERTAIN DETECTIVES—MIGHT GET HURT.
SO ISN'T IT *CONVENIENT* YOU GOT THAT *ANONYMOUS* TIP WHEN YOU DID? YOU HAD PLENTY OF TIME TO FIND YOUR TARGET, VERIFY HIM, AND BRING IN SONIC.
BY THE TIME I "HELPED" SHADOW FIND THIS VILLAGE, YOUR INVESTIGATION WAS COMPLETE AND YOU HAD A HANDY, HEROIC COUNTER-MEASURE BY YOUR SIDE.
WAIT... HOW WOULD YOU KNOW ABOUT THE TIP UNLESS...
OOOOOH!
...I DON'T GET IT.

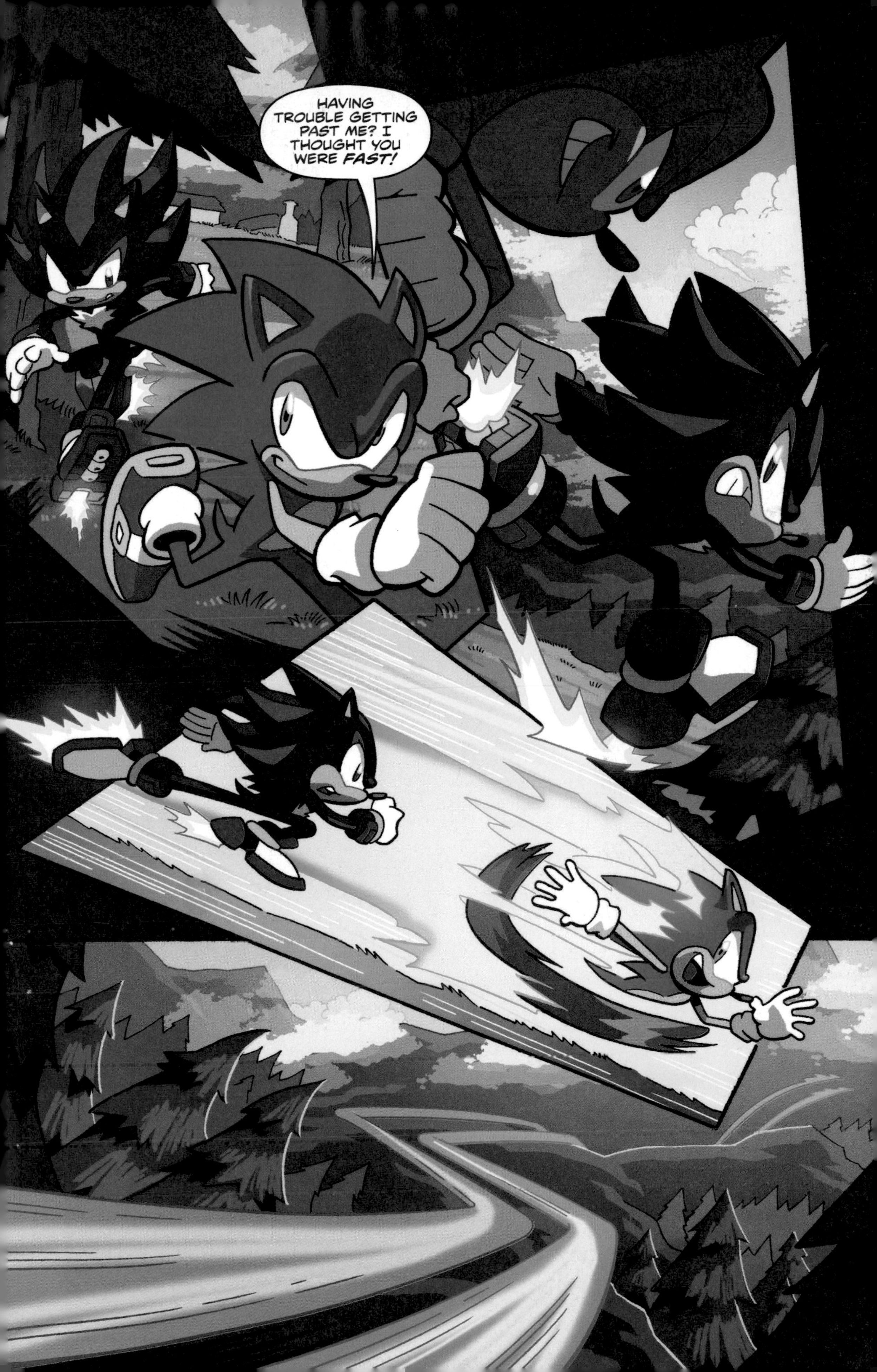
HAVING TROUBLE GETTING PAST ME? I THOUGHT YOU WERE *FAST!*

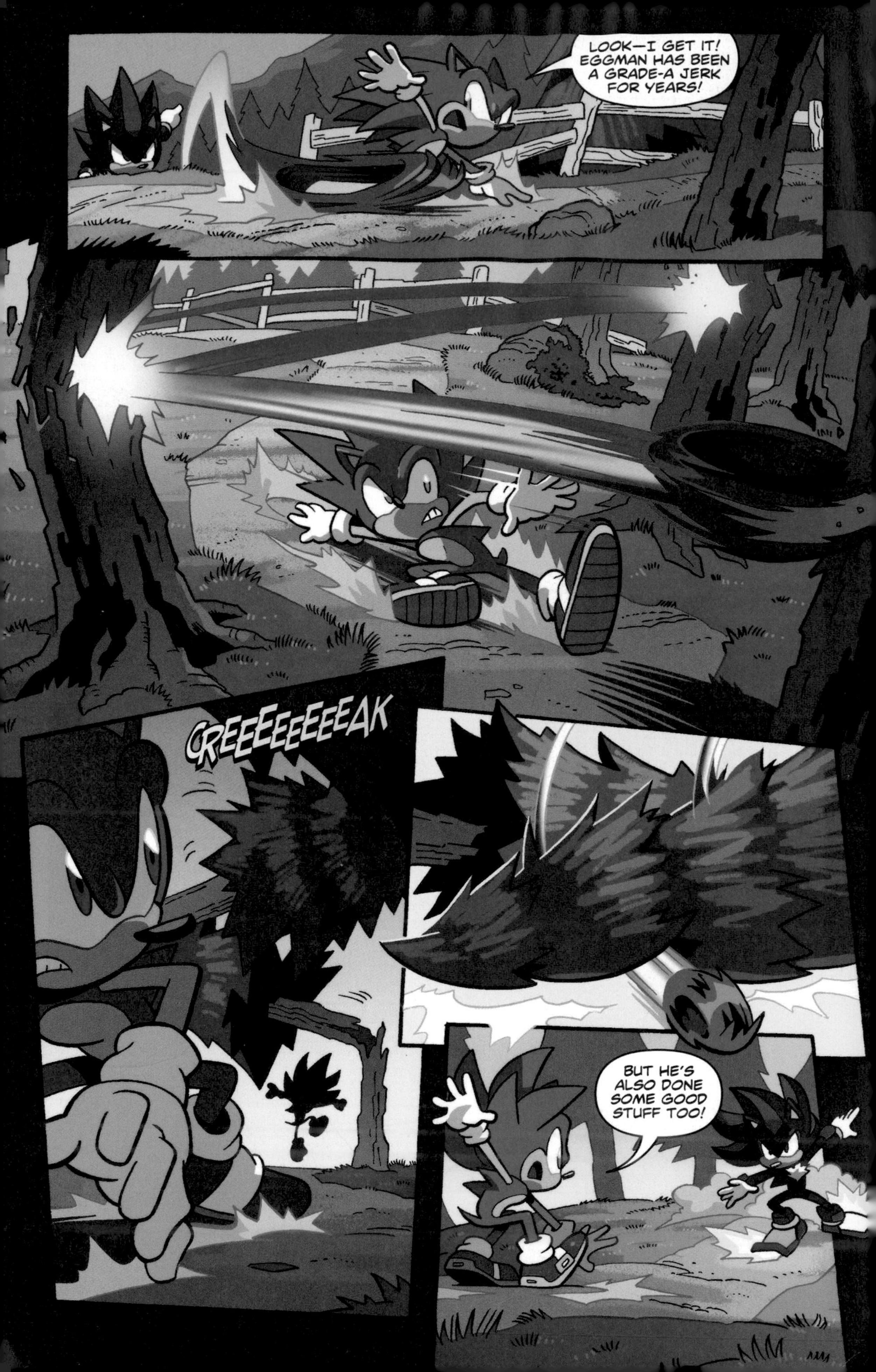
LOOK—I GET IT! EGGMAN HAS BEEN A GRADE-A JERK FOR YEARS!
CREEEEEEEEEAK
BUT HE'S ALSO DONE SOME GOOD STUFF TOO!

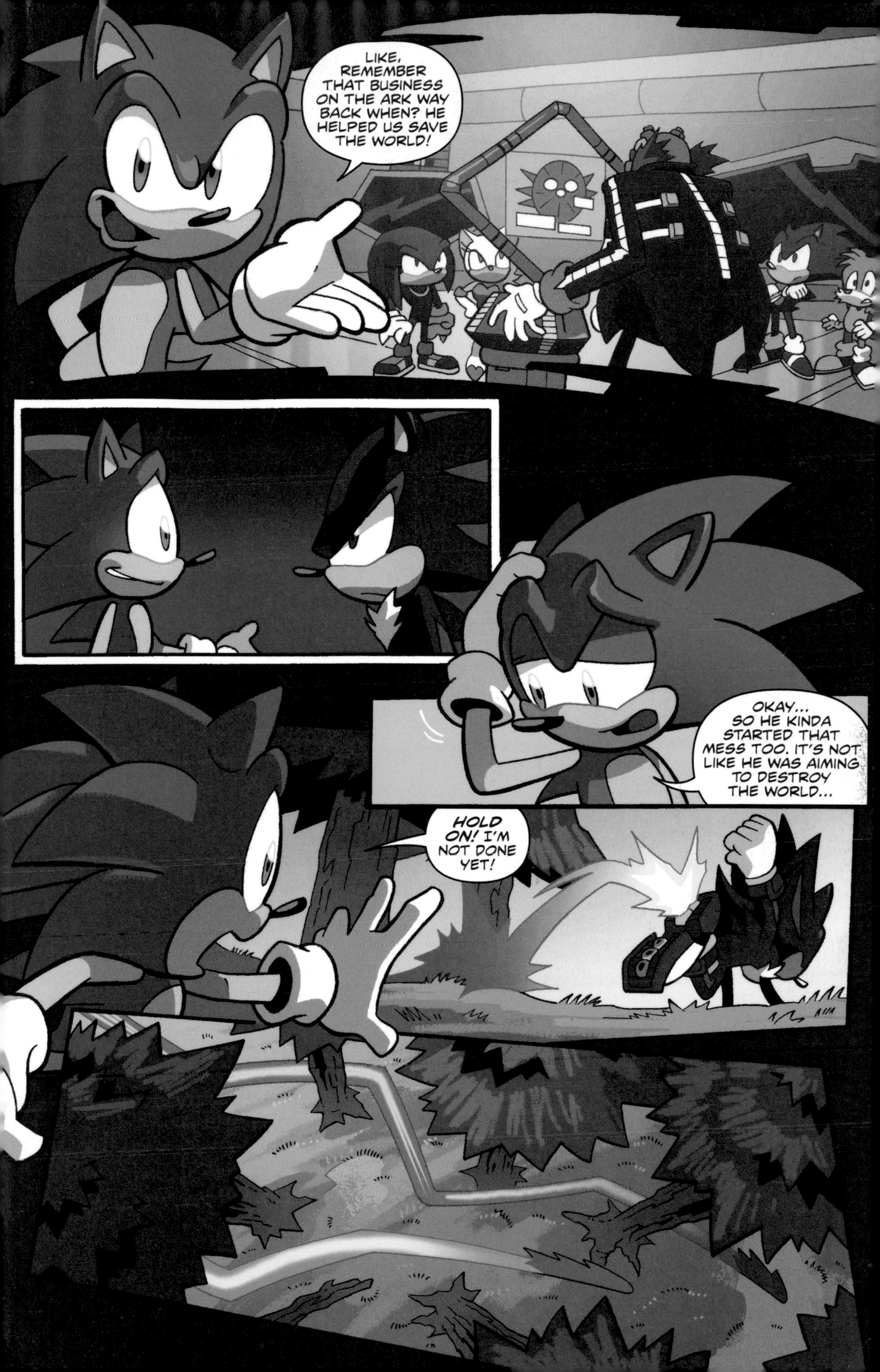
LIKE, REMEMBER THAT BUSINESS ON THE ARK WAY BACK WHEN? HE HELPED US SAVE THE WORLD!
OKAY... SO HE KINDA STARTED THAT MESS TOO. IT'S NOT LIKE HE WAS AIMING TO DESTROY THE WORLD...
HOLD ON! I'M NOT DONE YET!

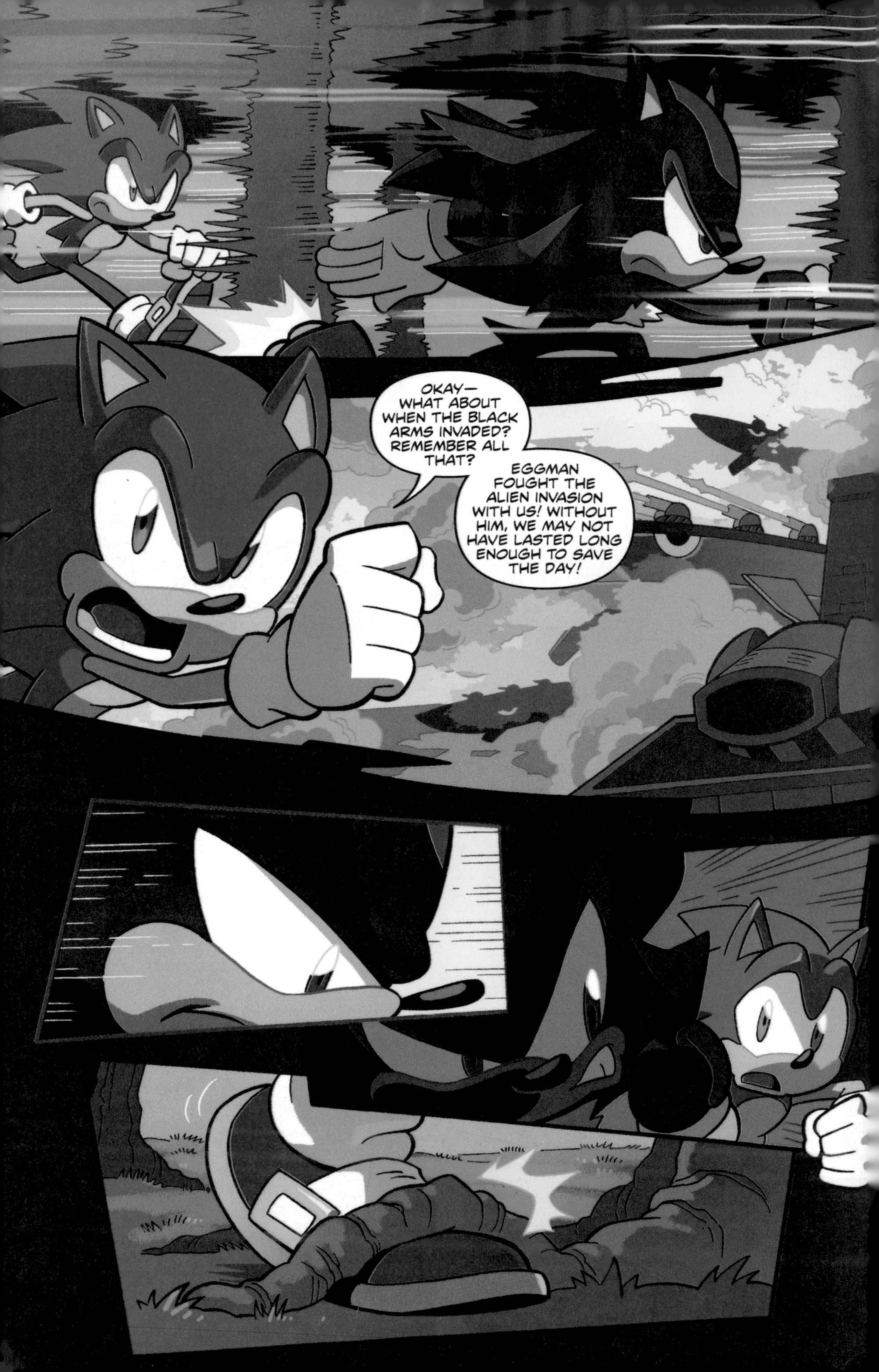
OKAY— WHAT ABOUT WHEN THE BLACK ARMS INVADED? REMEMBER ALL THAT?
EGGMAN FOUGHT THE ALIEN INVASION WITH US! WITHOUT HIM, WE MAY NOT HAVE LASTED LONG ENOUGH TO SAVE THE DAY!

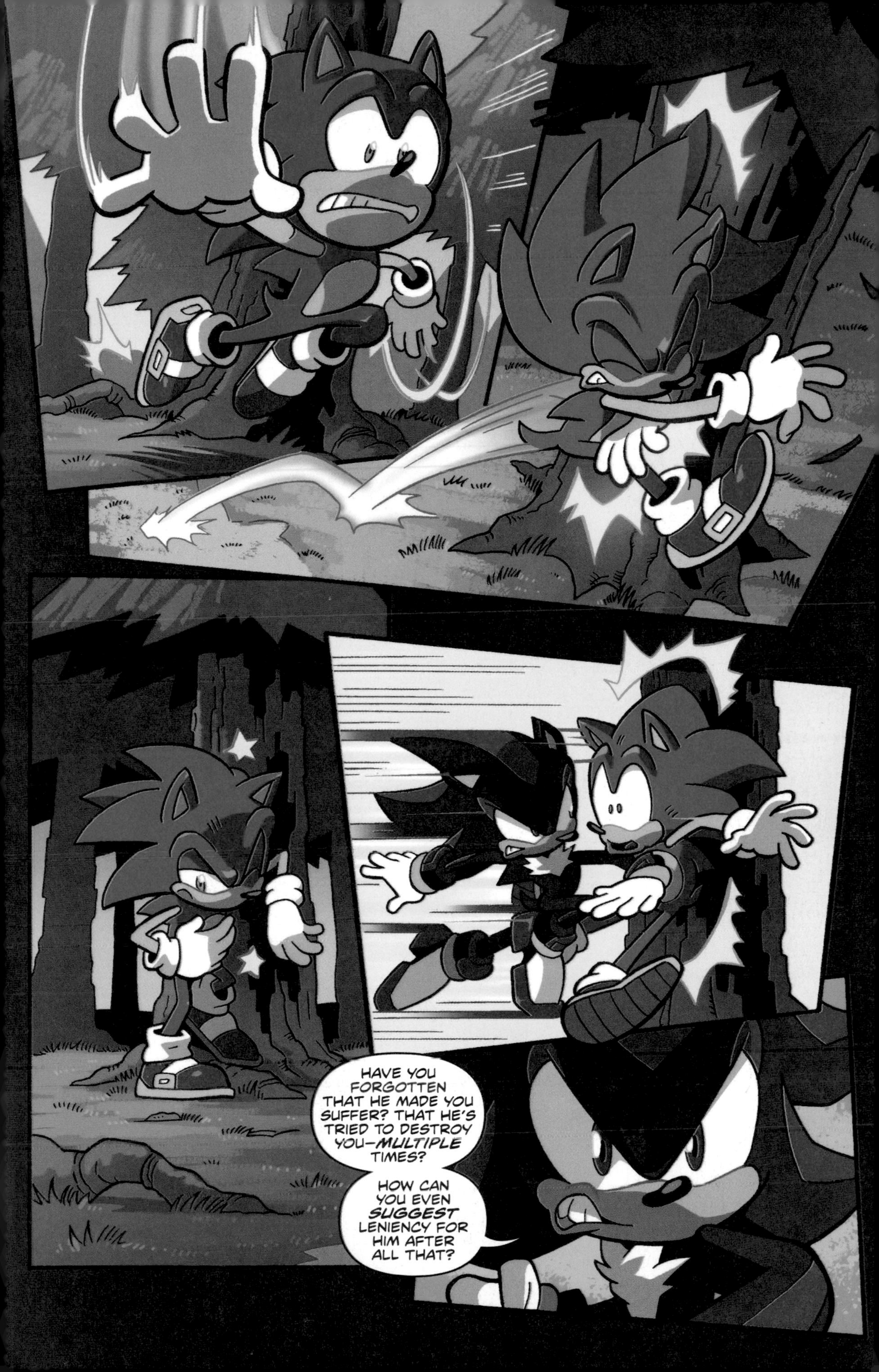
HAVE YOU FORGOTTEN THAT HE MADE YOU SUFFER? THAT HE'S TRIED TO DESTROY YOU—MULTIPLE TIMES?
HOW CAN YOU EVEN SUGGEST LENIENCY FOR HIM AFTER ALL THAT?

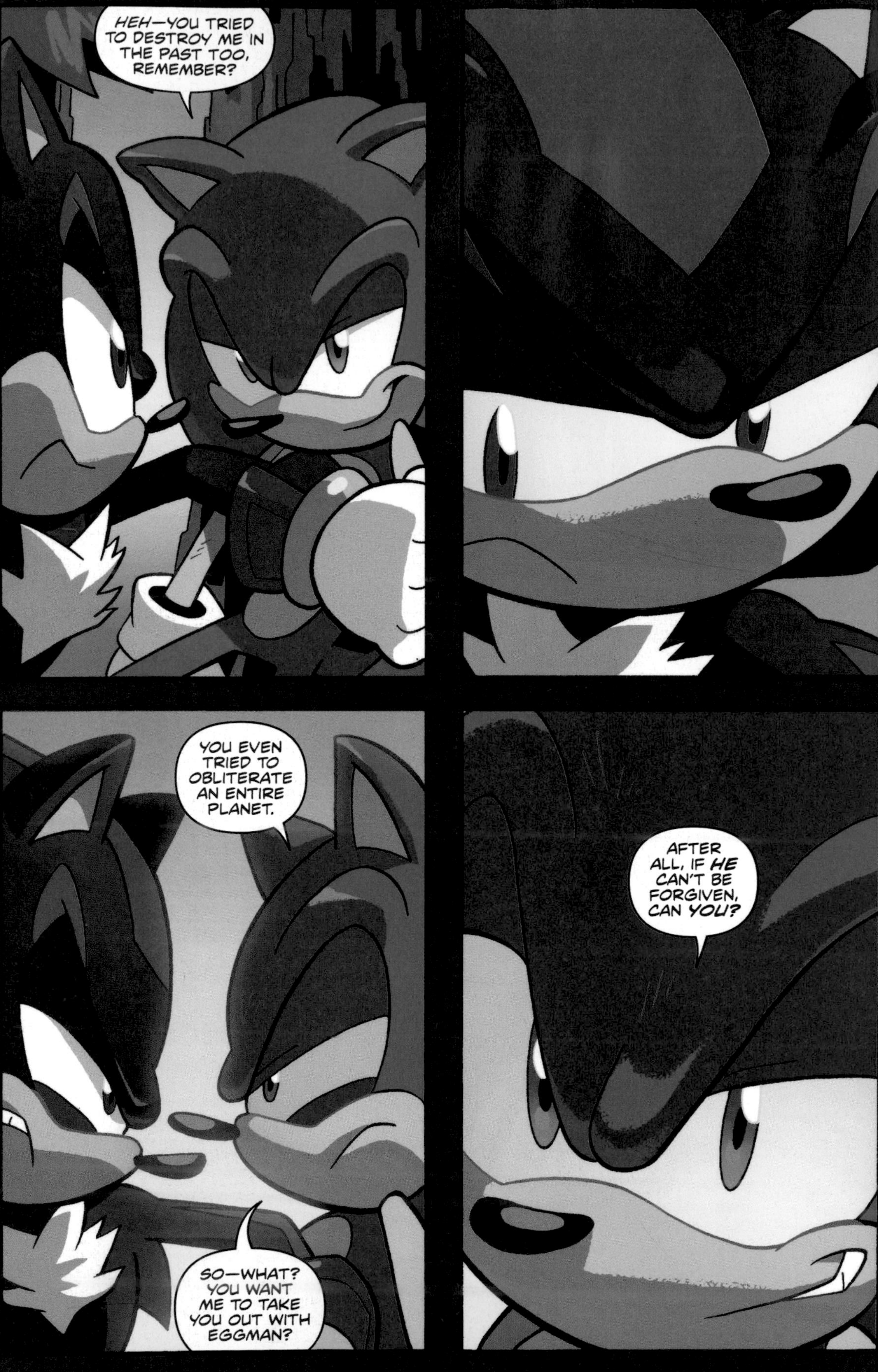
HEH—YOU TRIED TO DESTROY ME IN THE PAST TOO, REMEMBER?
YOU EVEN TRIED TO OBLITERATE AN ENTIRE PLANET.
SO—WHAT? YOU WANT ME TO TAKE YOU OUT WITH EGGMAN?
AFTER ALL, IF HE CAN'T BE FORGIVEN, CAN YOU?

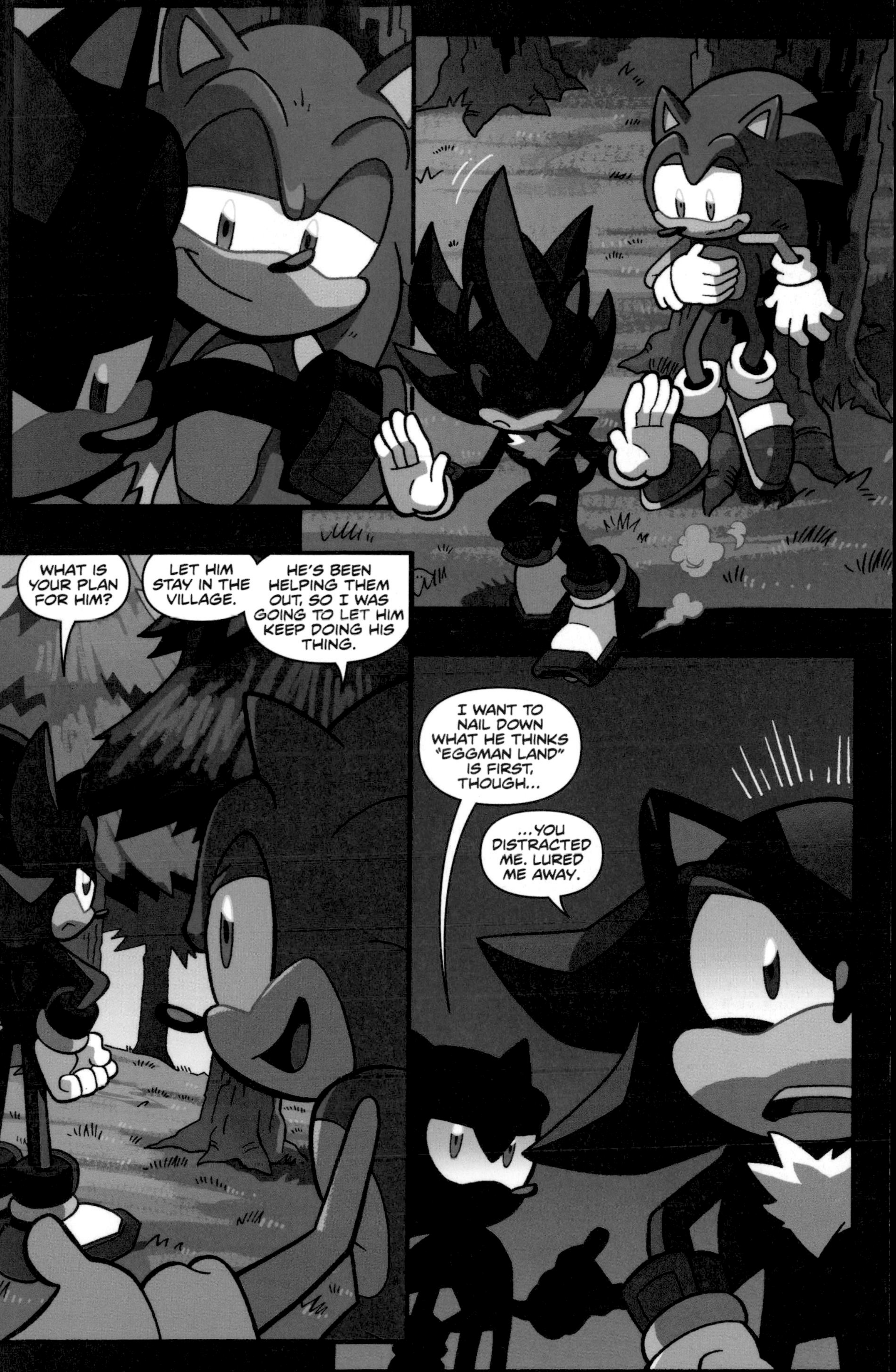
WHAT IS YOUR PLAN FOR HIM?
LET HIM STAY IN THE VILLAGE.
HE'S BEEN HELPING THEM OUT, SO I WAS GOING TO LET HIM KEEP DOING HIS THING.
I WANT TO NAIL DOWN WHAT HE THINKS "EGGMAN LAND" IS FIRST, THOUGH...
...YOU DISTRACTED ME. LURED ME AWAY.

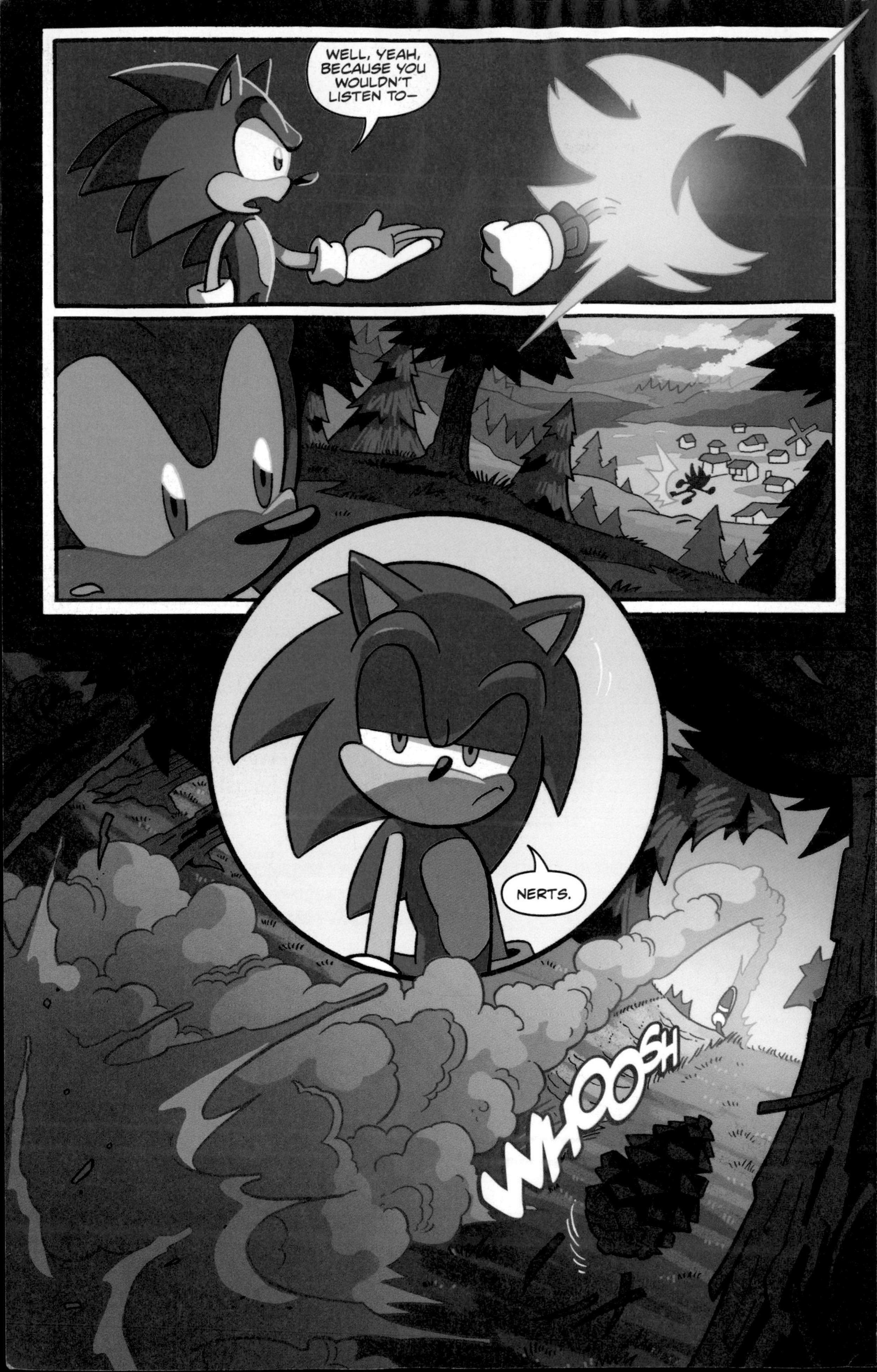
WELL, YEAH, BECAUSE YOU WOULDN'T LISTEN TO—
NERTS.
WHOOSH

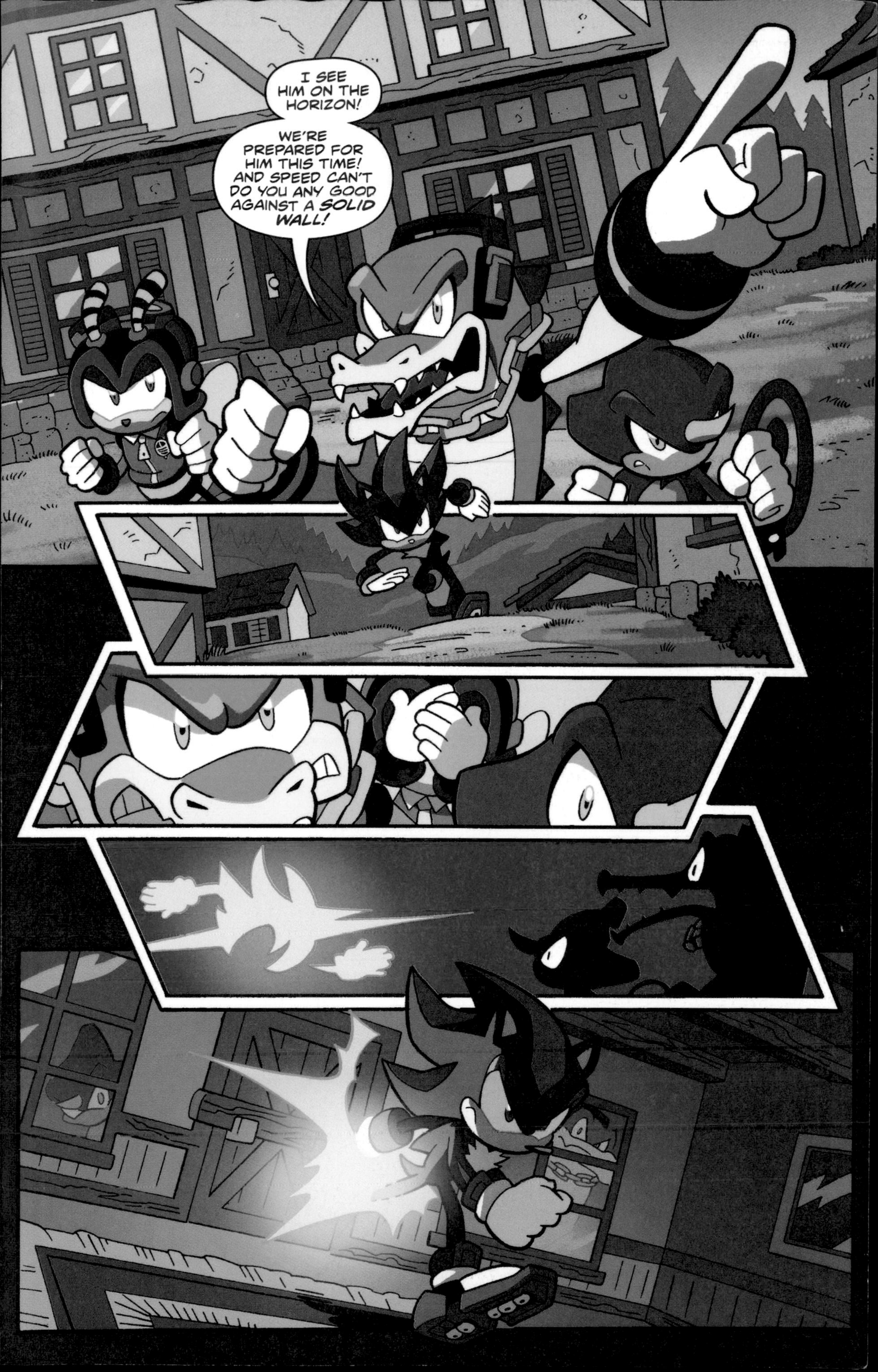
I SEE HIM ON THE HORIZON!
WE'RE PREPARED FOR HIM THIS TIME! AND SPEED CAN'T DO YOU ANY GOOD AGAINST A *SOLID WALL!*

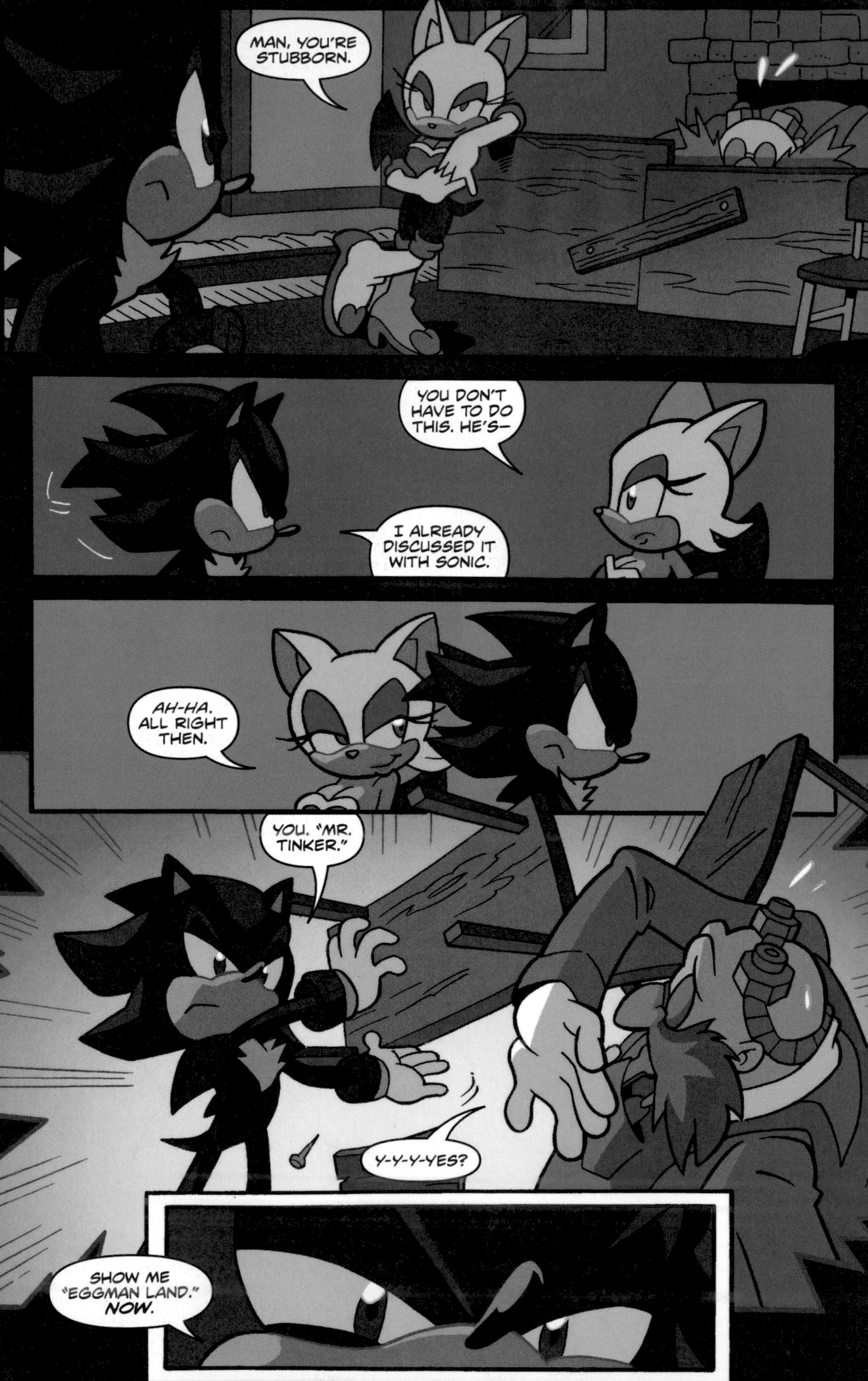
MAN, YOU'RE STUBBORN.
YOU DON'T HAVE TO DO THIS. HE'S—
I ALREADY DISCUSSED IT WITH SONIC.
AH-HA. ALL RIGHT THEN.
YOU. "MR. TINKER."
Y-Y-Y-YES?
SHOW ME "EGGMAN LAND." NOW.

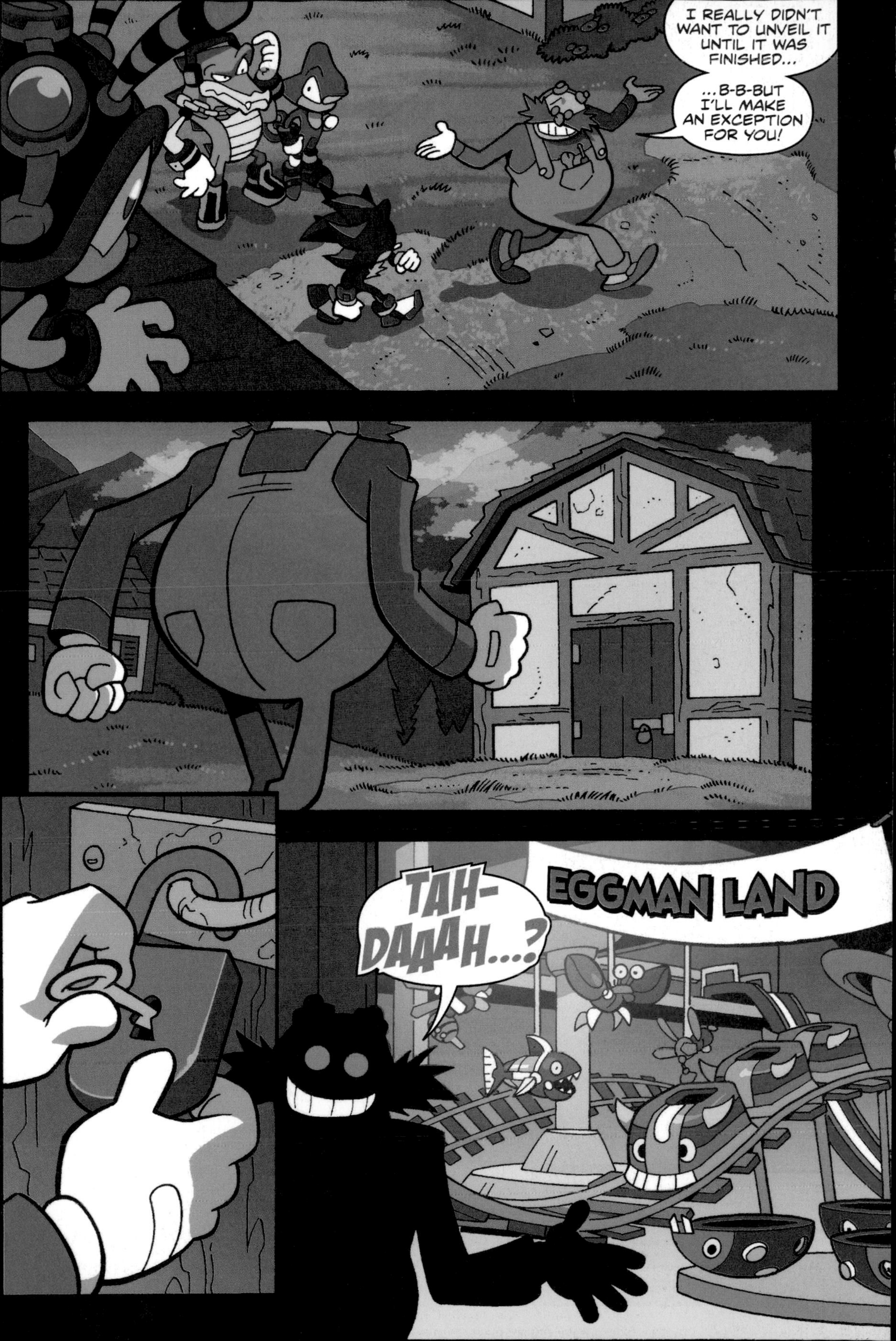
I REALLY DIDN'T WANT TO UNVEIL IT UNTIL IT WAS FINISHED...
...B-B-BUT I'LL MAKE AN EXCEPTION FOR YOU!
EGGMAN LAND
TAH-DAAAH...?

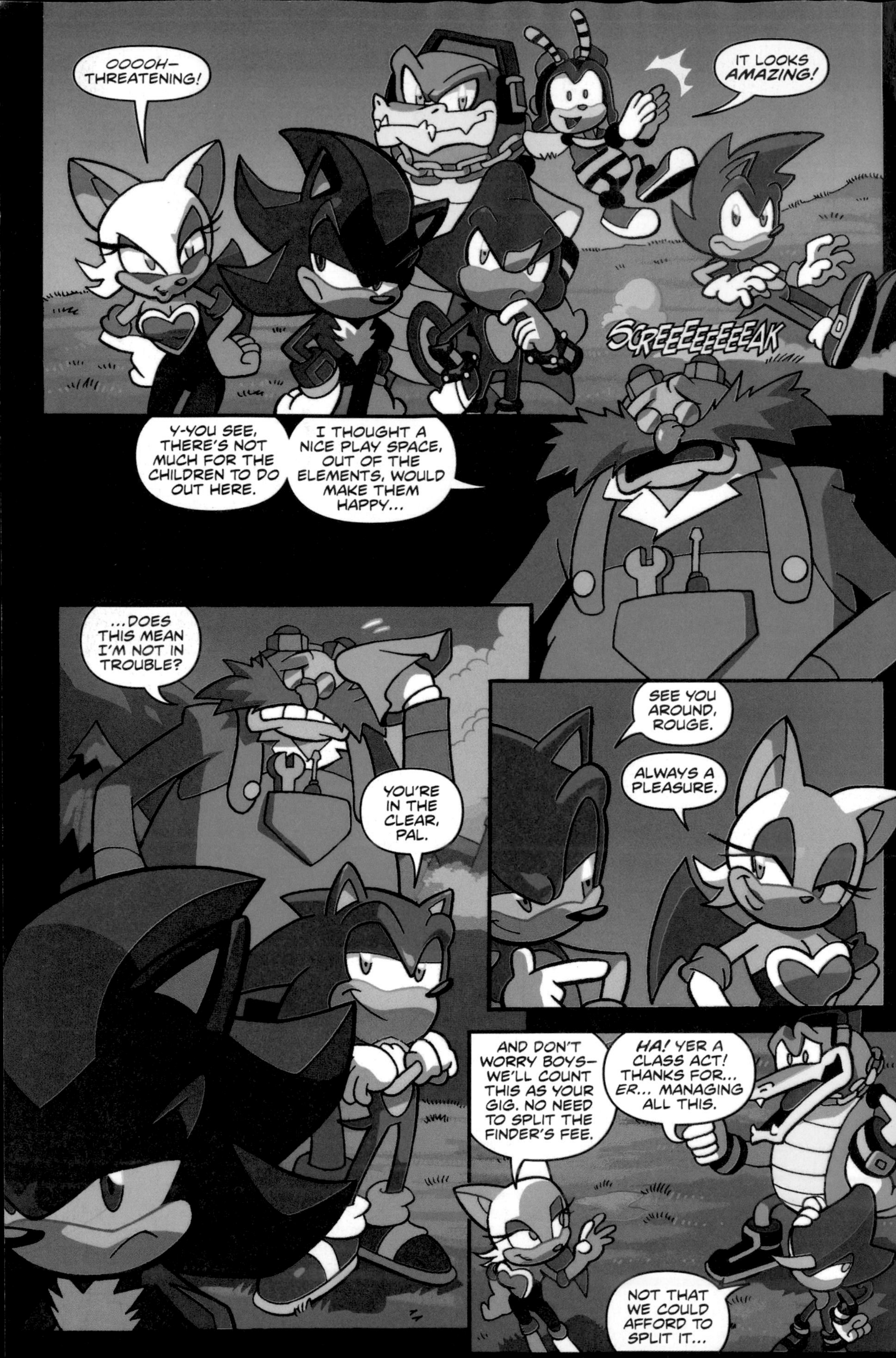
OOOOH—THREATENING!
IT LOOKS AMAZING!
SCREEEEEEEEEAK
Y-YOU SEE, THERE'S NOT MUCH FOR THE CHILDREN TO DO OUT HERE.
I THOUGHT A NICE PLAY SPACE, OUT OF THE ELEMENTS, WOULD MAKE THEM HAPPY...
...DOES THIS MEAN I'M NOT IN TROUBLE?
YOU'RE IN THE CLEAR, PAL.
SEE YOU AROUND, ROUGE.
ALWAYS A PLEASURE.
AND DON'T WORRY BOYS—WE'LL COUNT THIS AS YOUR GIG. NO NEED TO SPLIT THE FINDER'S FEE.
HA! YER A CLASS ACT! THANKS FOR... ER... MANAGING ALL THIS.
NOT THAT WE COULD AFFORD TO SPLIT IT...

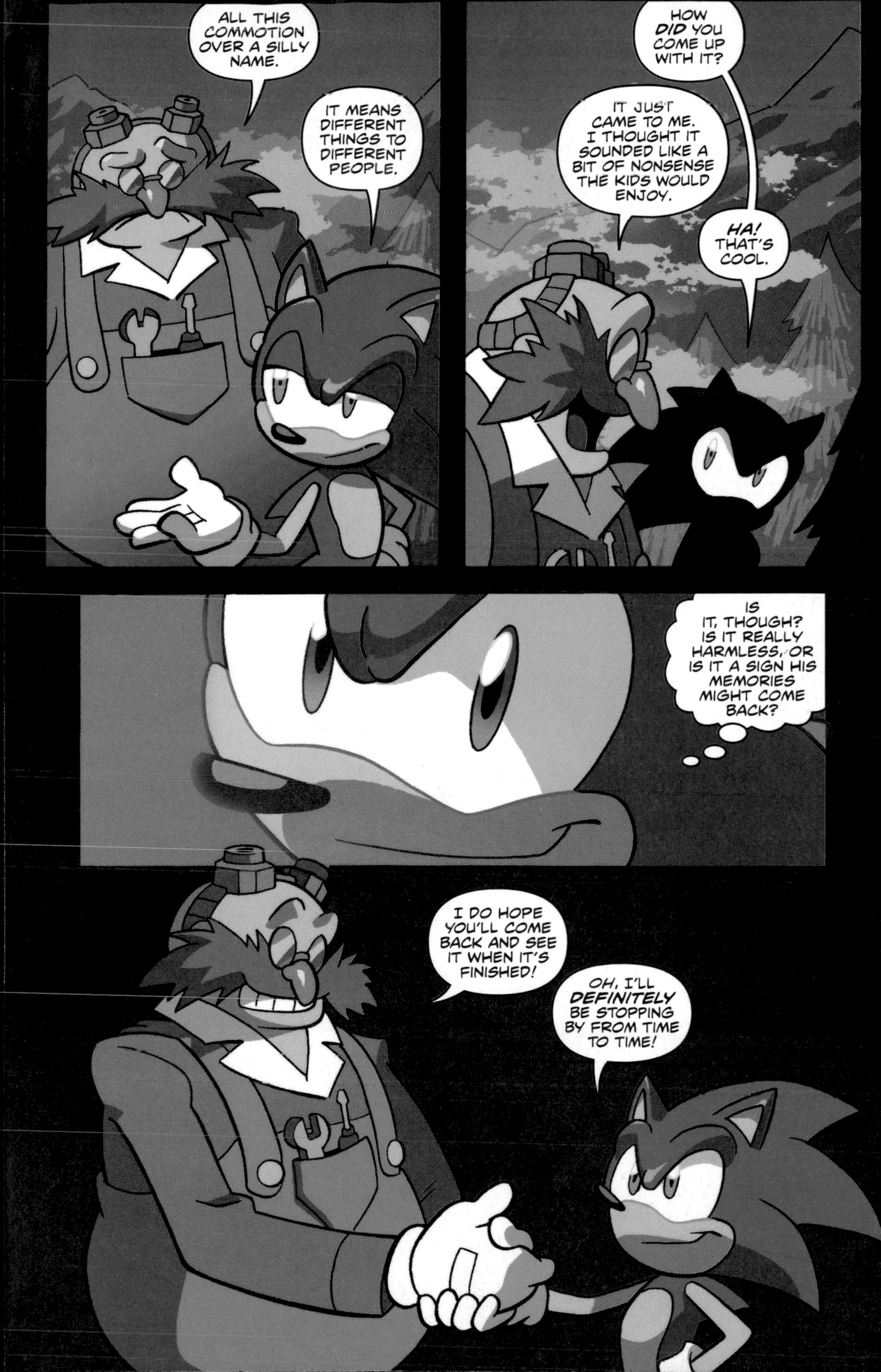
ALL THIS COMMOTION OVER A SILLY NAME.
IT MEANS DIFFERENT THINGS TO DIFFERENT PEOPLE.
HOW *DID* YOU COME UP WITH IT?
IT JUST CAME TO ME. I THOUGHT IT SOUNDED LIKE A BIT OF NONSENSE THE KIDS WOULD ENJOY.
HA! THAT'S COOL.
IS IT, THOUGH? IS IT REALLY HARMLESS, OR IS IT A SIGN HIS MEMORIES MIGHT COME BACK?
I DO HOPE YOU'LL COME BACK AND SEE IT WHEN IT'S FINISHED!
OH, I'LL *DEFINITELY* BE STOPPING BY FROM TIME TO TIME!

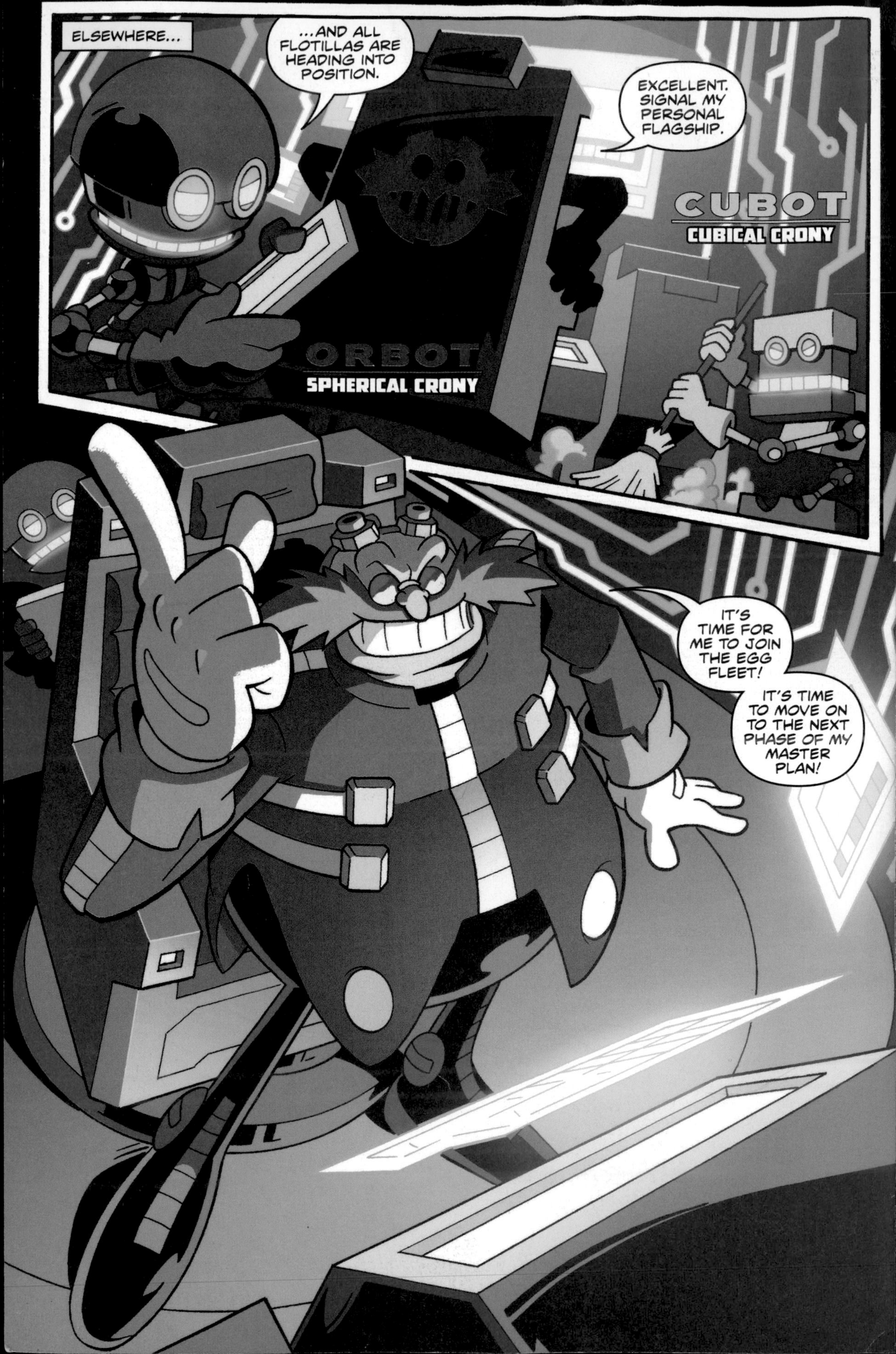
ELSEWHERE...
...AND ALL FLOTILLAS ARE HEADING INTO POSITION.
EXCELLENT. SIGNAL MY PERSONAL FLAGSHIP.
CUBOT
CUBICAL CRONY
ORBOT
SPHERICAL CRONY
IT'S TIME FOR ME TO JOIN THE EGG FLEET!
IT'S TIME TO MOVE ON TO THE NEXT PHASE OF MY MASTER PLAN!

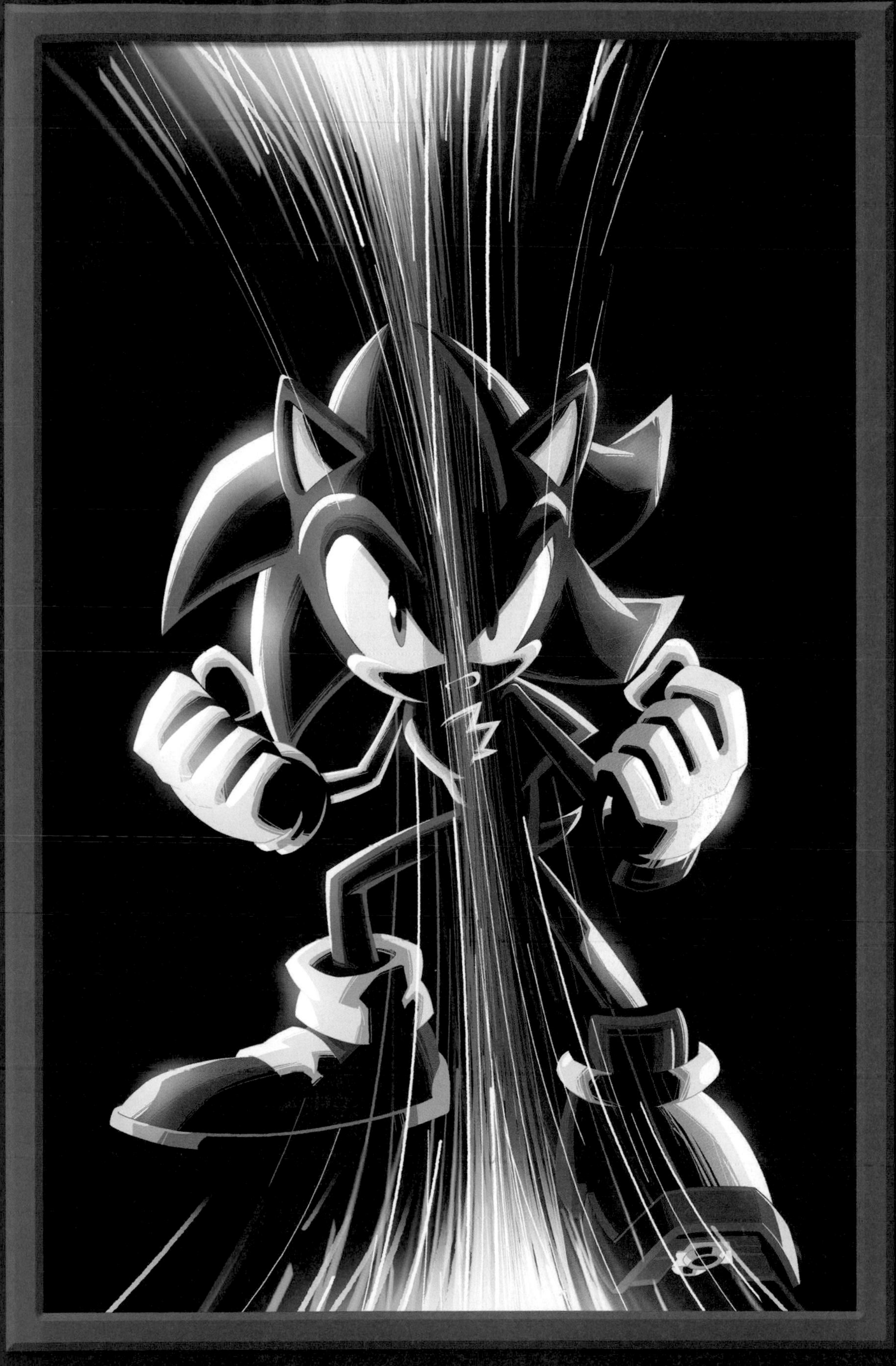

ART BY TRACY YARDLEY

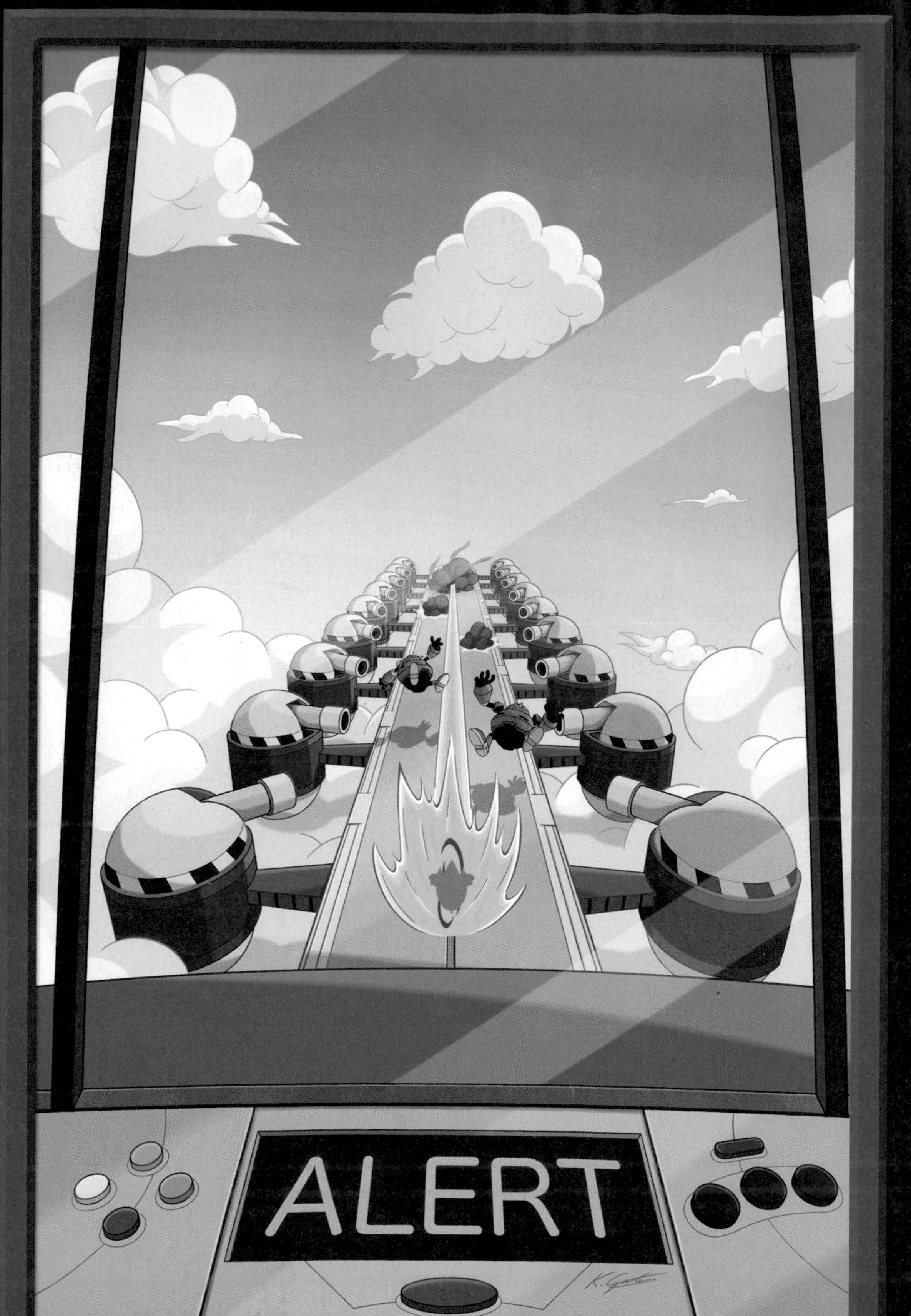
ALERT
K. Gates

ART BY KIERAN GATES

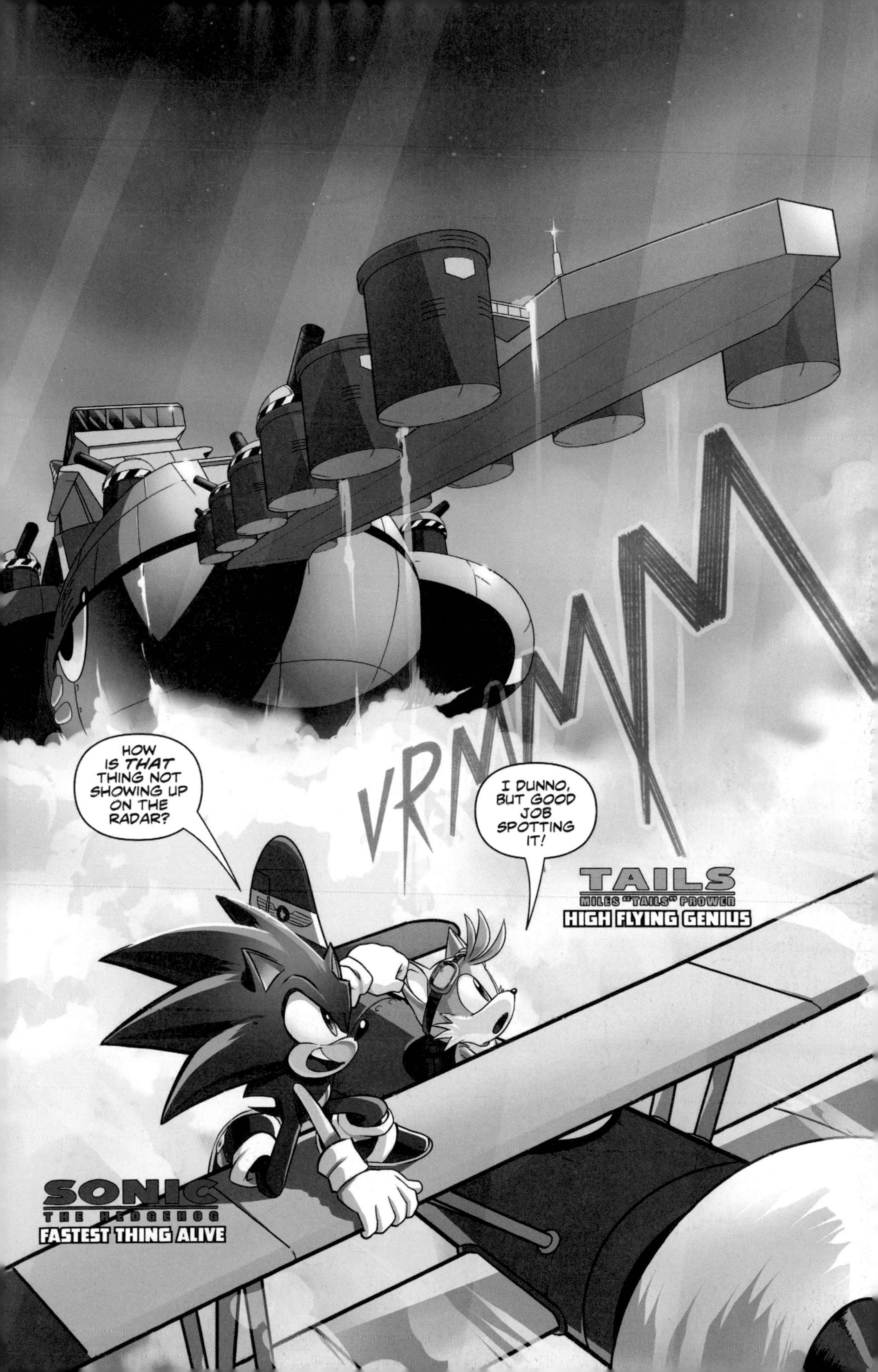
VRMMMM
HOW IS *THAT* THING NOT SHOWING UP ON THE RADAR?
I DUNNO, BUT GOOD JOB SPOTTING IT!
TAILS
MILES "TAILS" PROWER
HIGH FLYING GENIUS
SONIC
THE HEDGEHOG
FASTEST THING ALIVE

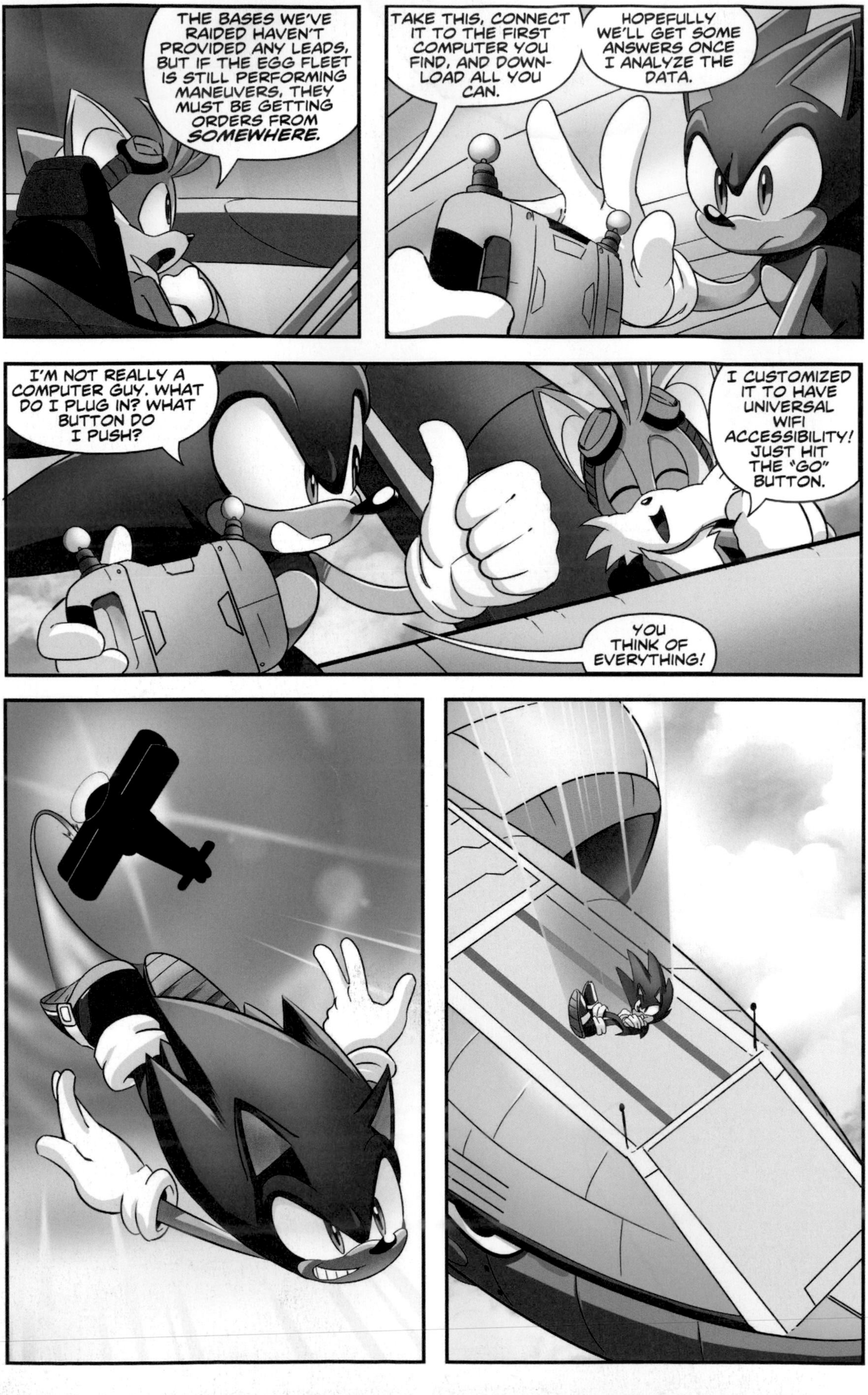
THE BASES WE'VE RAIDED HAVEN'T PROVIDED ANY LEADS, BUT IF THE EGG FLEET IS STILL PERFORMING MANEUVERS, THEY MUST BE GETTING ORDERS FROM SOMEWHERE.
TAKE THIS, CONNECT IT TO THE FIRST COMPUTER YOU FIND, AND DOWN-LOAD ALL YOU CAN.
HOPEFULLY WE'LL GET SOME ANSWERS ONCE I ANALYZE THE DATA.
I'M NOT REALLY A COMPUTER GUY. WHAT DO I PLUG IN? WHAT BUTTON DO I PUSH?
I CUSTOMIZED IT TO HAVE UNIVERSAL WIFI ACCESSIBILITY! JUST HIT THE "GO" BUTTON.
YOU THINK OF EVERYTHING!

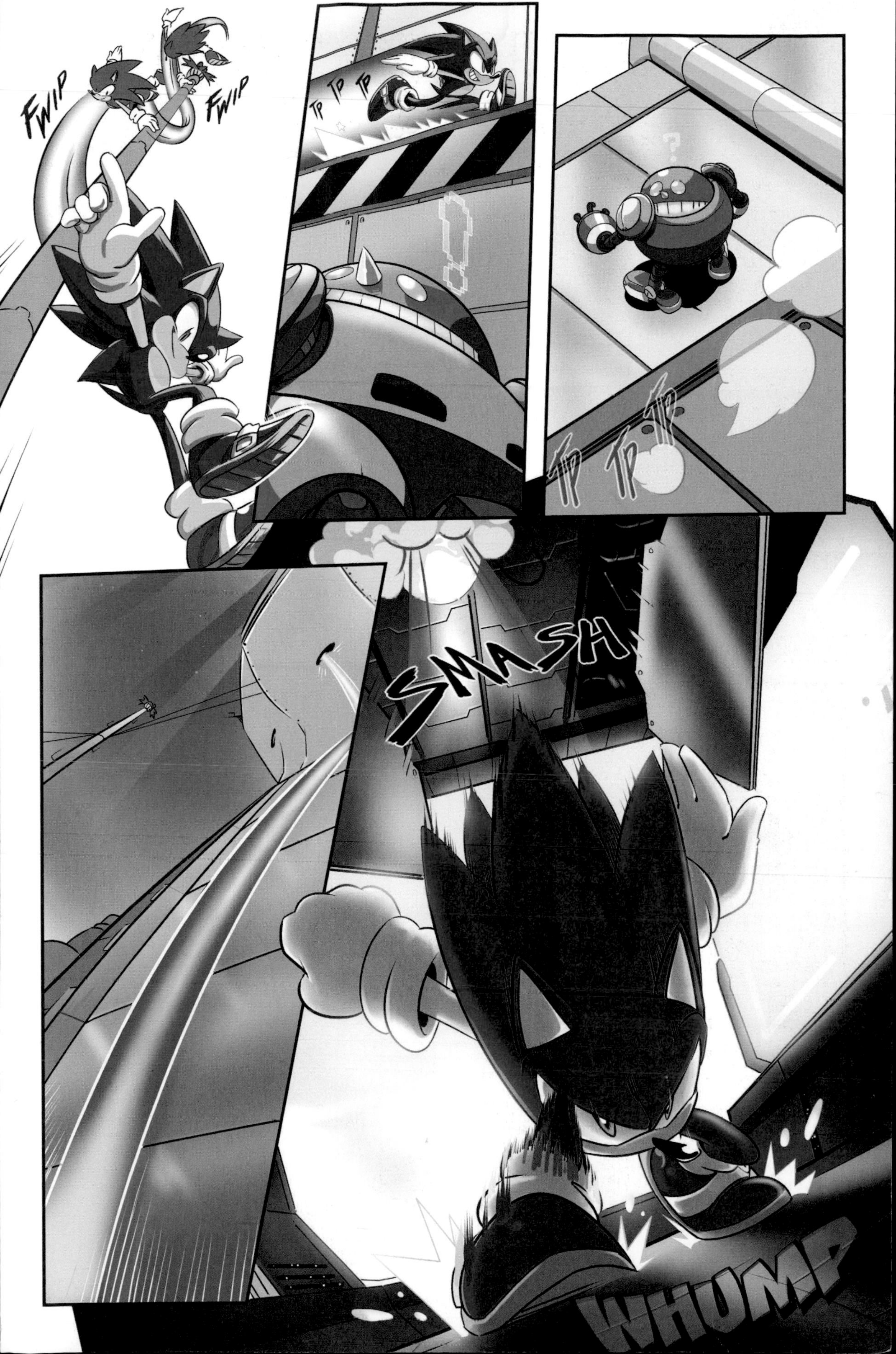
FWIP
FWIP
TP TP TP
?
TP TP TP
SMASH
WHUMP

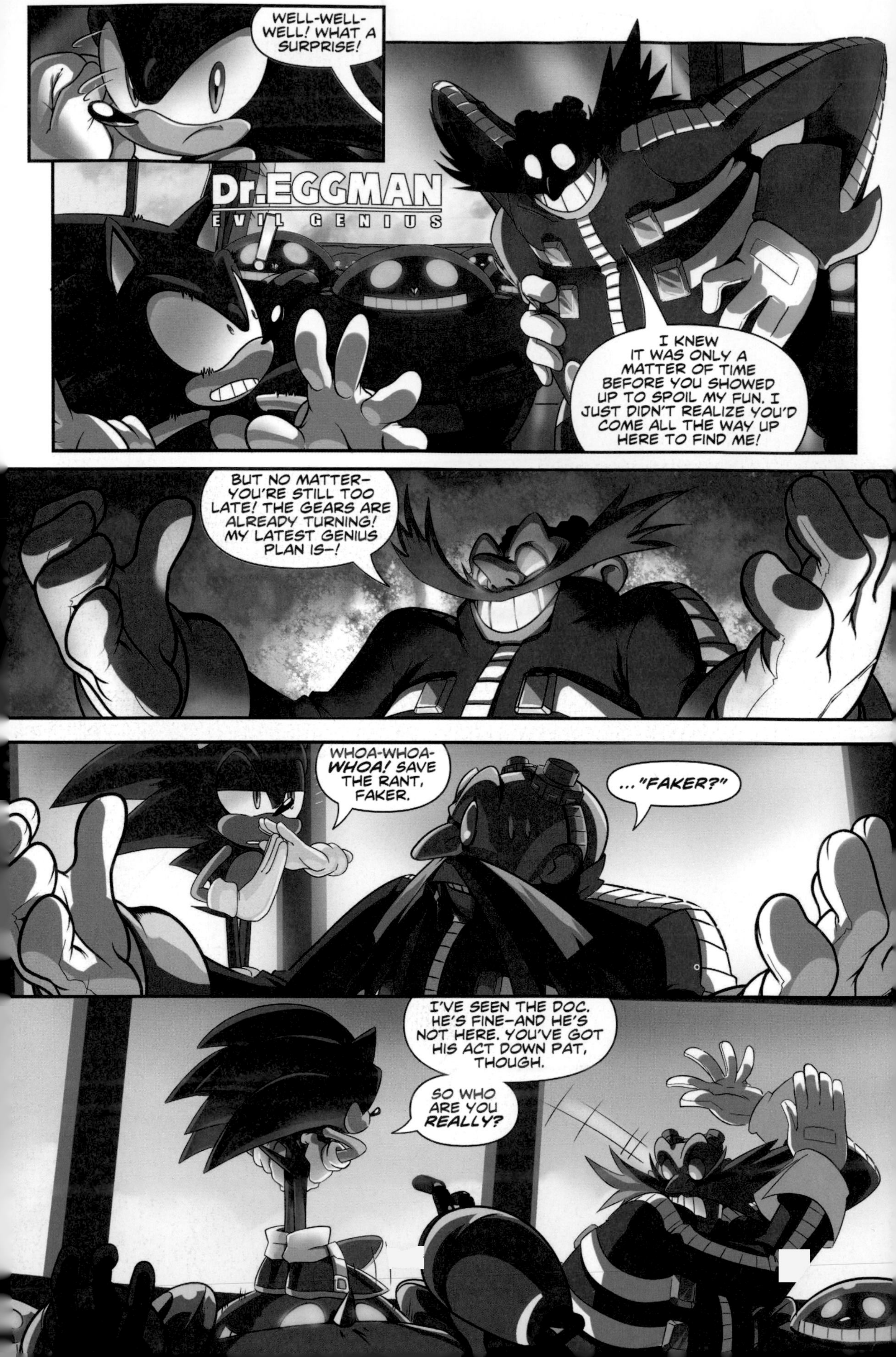

WELL-WELL-WELL! WHAT A SURPRISE!
Dr.EGGMAN
EVIL GENIUS
!
I KNEW IT WAS ONLY A MATTER OF TIME BEFORE YOU SHOWED UP TO SPOIL MY FUN. I JUST DIDN'T REALIZE YOU'D COME ALL THE WAY UP HERE TO FIND ME!
BUT NO MATTER–YOU'RE STILL TOO LATE! THE GEARS ARE ALREADY TURNING! MY LATEST GENIUS PLAN IS–!
WHOA-WHOA-*WHOA!* SAVE THE RANT, FAKER.
..."FAKER?"
I'VE SEEN THE DOC. HE'S FINE–AND HE'S NOT HERE. YOU'VE GOT HIS ACT DOWN PAT, THOUGH.
SO WHO ARE YOU *REALLY?*

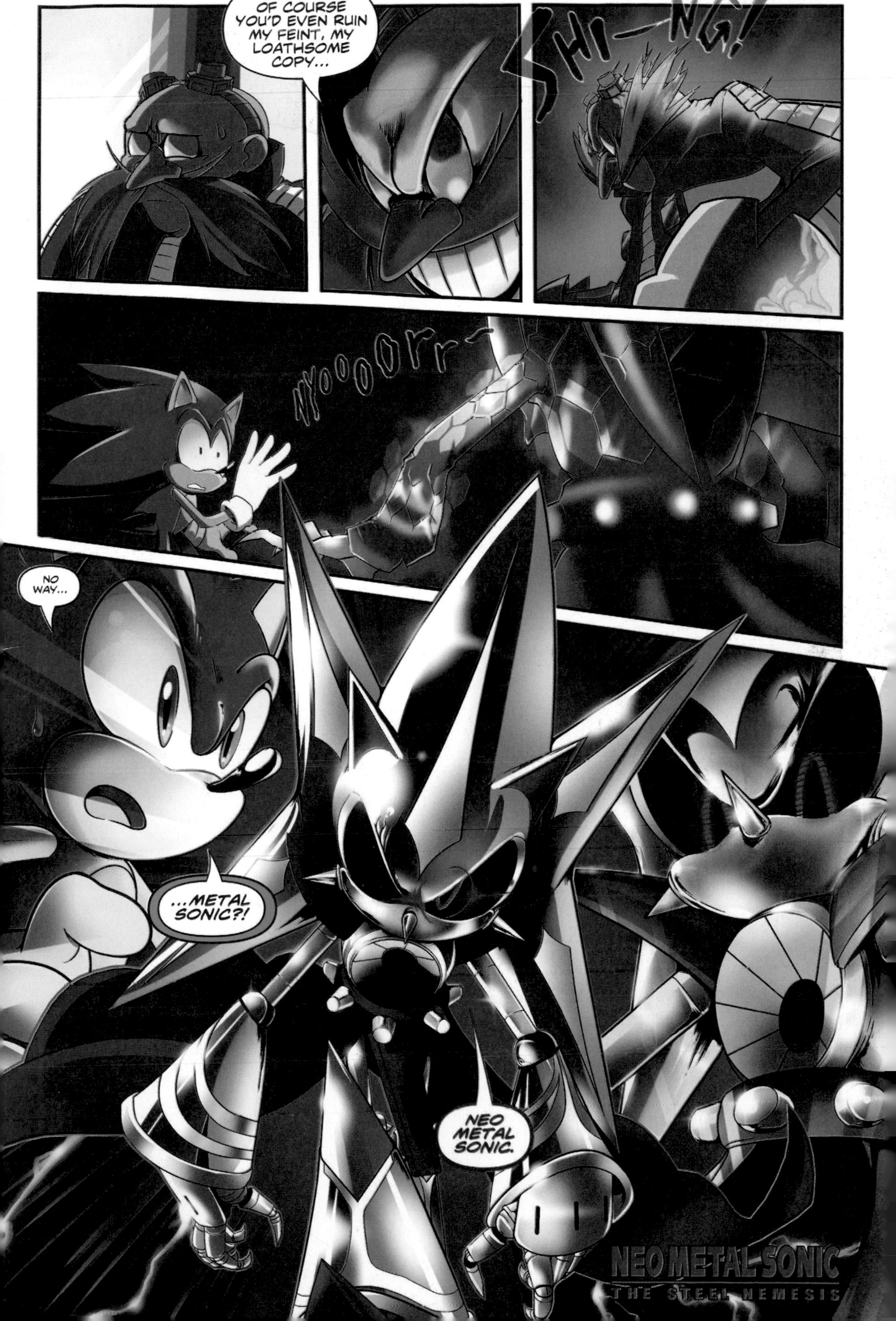
HMPH. OF COURSE YOU'D EVEN RUIN MY FEINT, MY LOATHSOME COPY...
SHI—NG!
NYOOOORrr~
NO WAY...
...METAL SONIC?!
NEO METAL SONIC.
NEO METAL SONIC
THE STEEL NEMESIS

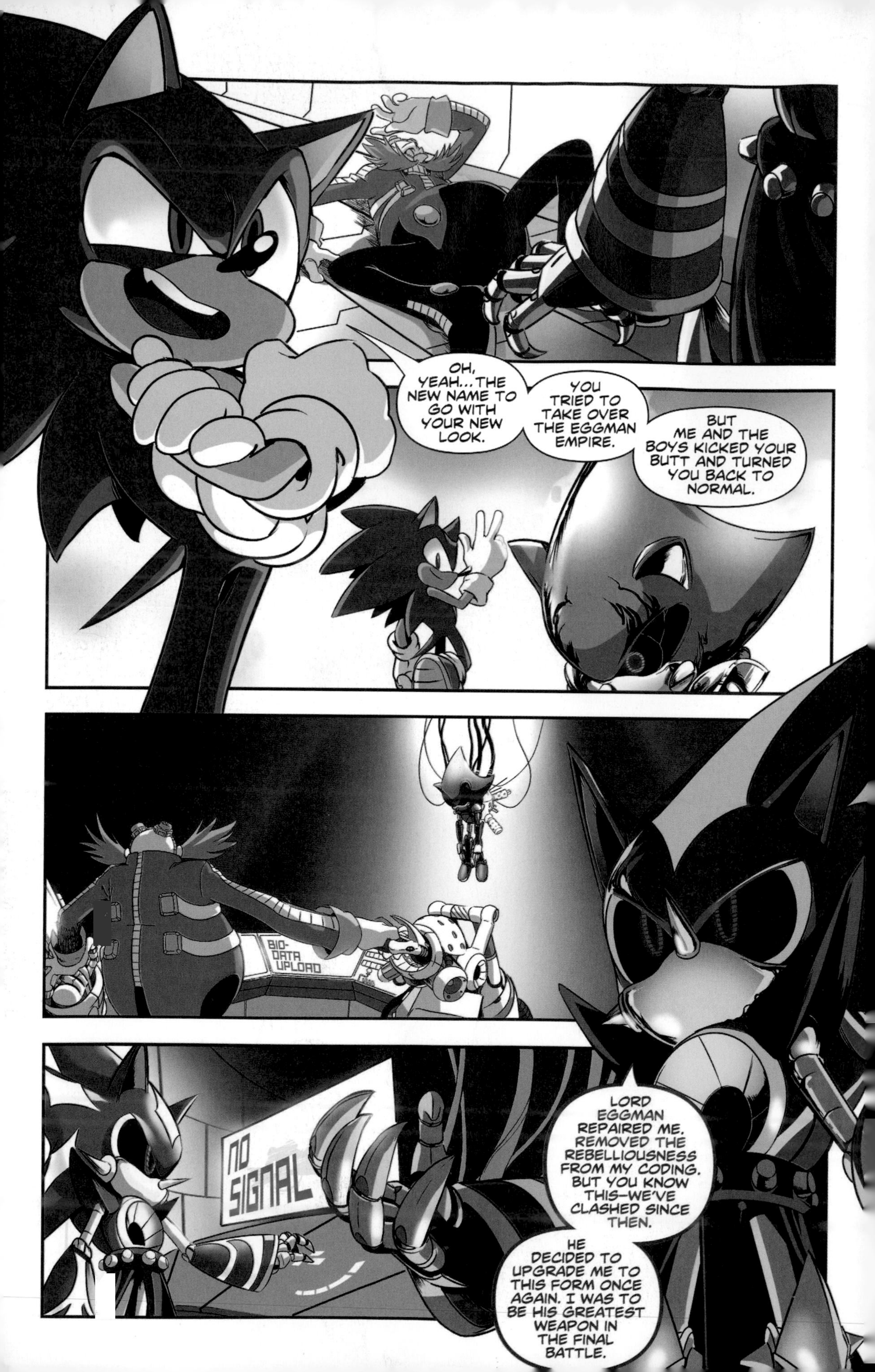
OH, YEAH... THE NEW NAME TO GO WITH YOUR NEW LOOK.
YOU TRIED TO TAKE OVER THE EGGMAN EMPIRE.
BUT ME AND THE BOYS KICKED YOUR BUTT AND TURNED YOU BACK TO NORMAL.
BIO-DATA UPLOAD
NO SIGNAL
LORD EGGMAN REPAIRED ME. REMOVED THE REBELLIOUSNESS FROM MY CODING. BUT YOU KNOW THIS—WE'VE CLASHED SINCE THEN.
HE DECIDED TO UPGRADE ME TO THIS FORM ONCE AGAIN. I WAS TO BE HIS GREATEST WEAPON IN THE FINAL BATTLE.

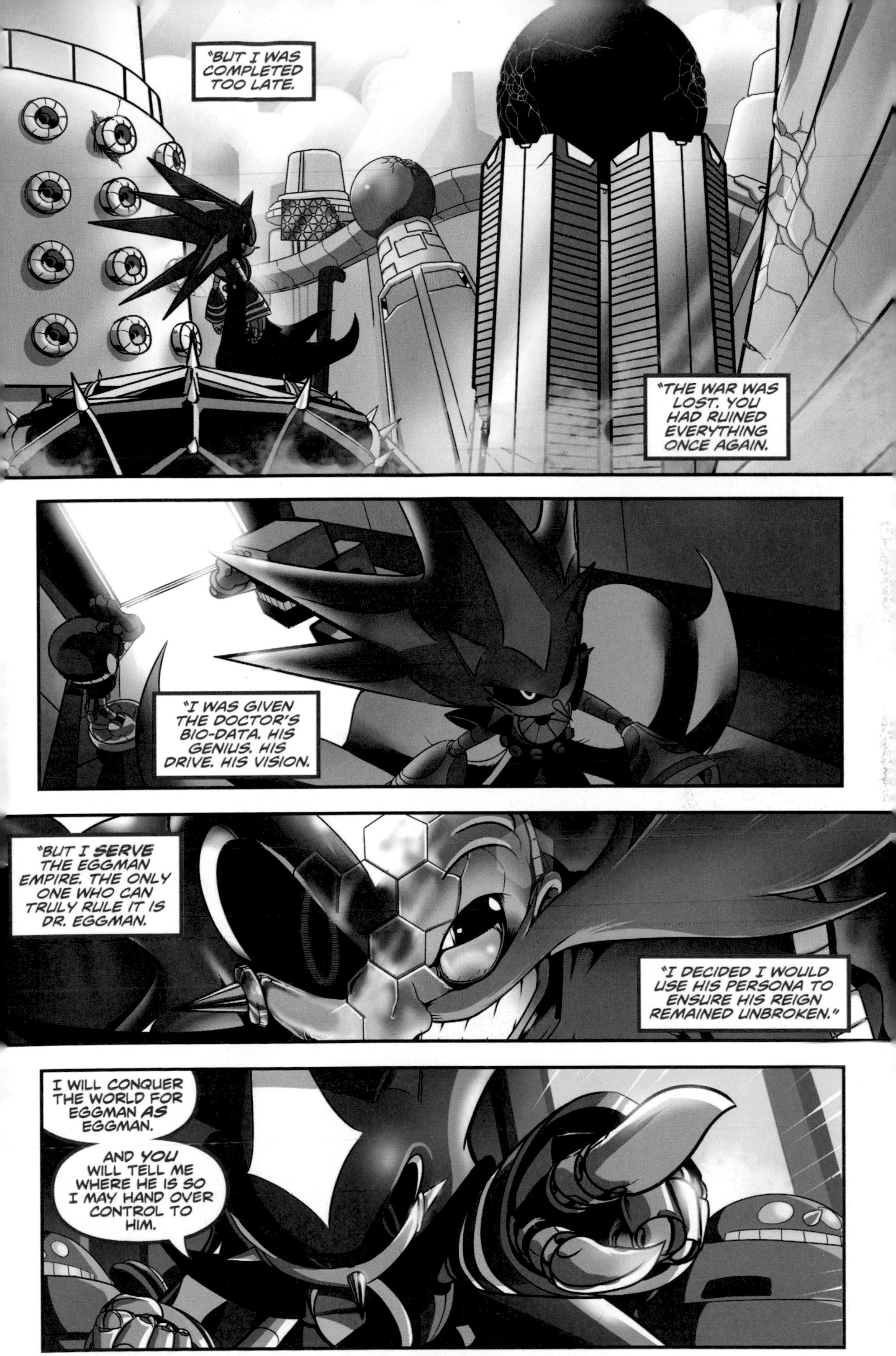
"BUT I WAS COMPLETED TOO LATE.
"THE WAR WAS LOST. YOU HAD RUINED EVERYTHING ONCE AGAIN.
"I WAS GIVEN THE DOCTOR'S BIO-DATA. HIS GENIUS. HIS DRIVE. HIS VISION.
"BUT I SERVE THE EGGMAN EMPIRE. THE ONLY ONE WHO CAN TRULY RULE IT IS DR. EGGMAN.
"I DECIDED I WOULD USE HIS PERSONA TO ENSURE HIS REIGN REMAINED UNBROKEN."
I WILL CONQUER THE WORLD FOR EGGMAN AS EGGMAN.
AND YOU WILL TELL ME WHERE HE IS SO I MAY HAND OVER CONTROL TO HIM.

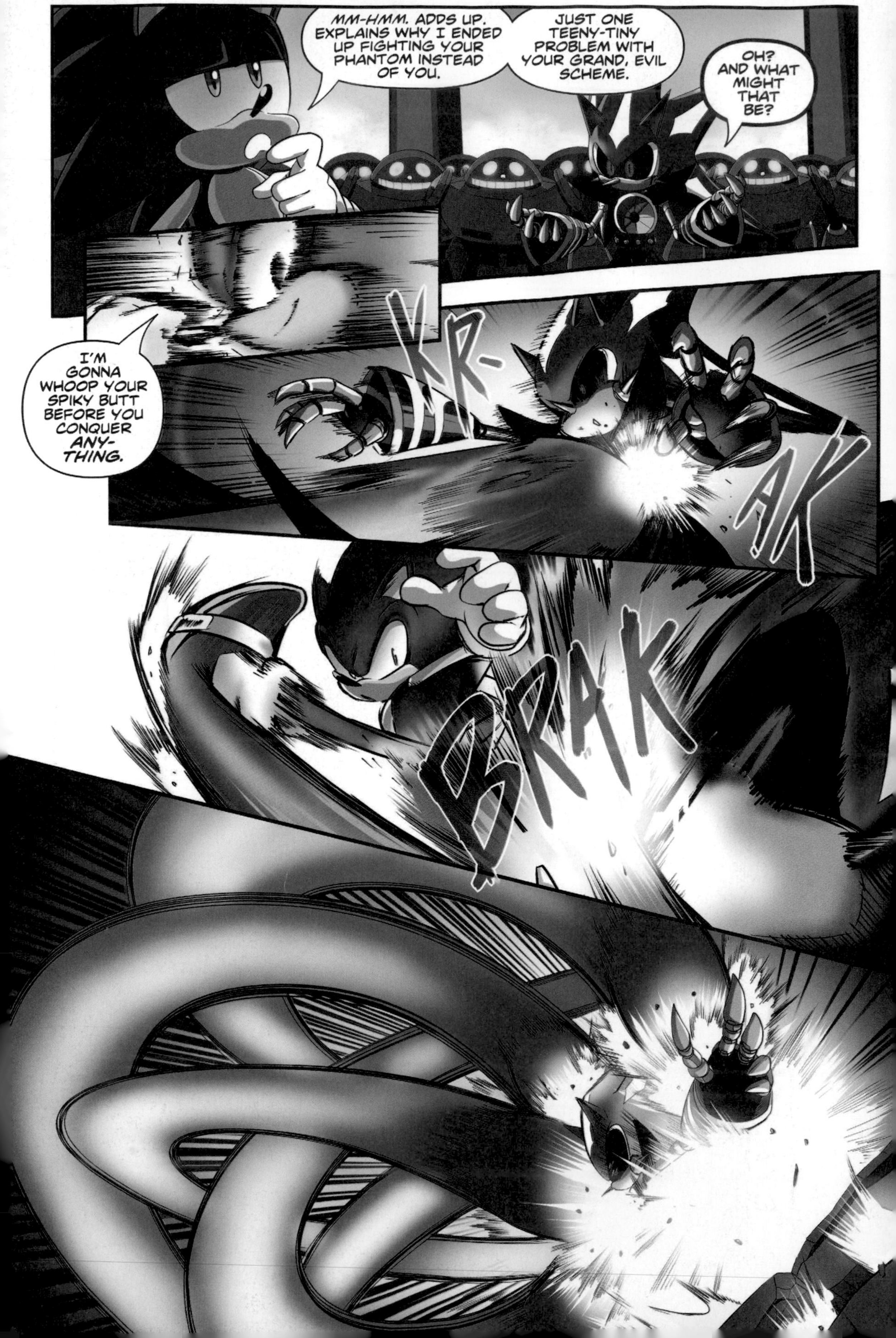
MM-HMM. ADDS UP. EXPLAINS WHY I ENDED UP FIGHTING YOUR PHANTOM INSTEAD OF YOU.
JUST ONE TEENY-TINY PROBLEM WITH YOUR GRAND, EVIL SCHEME.
OH? AND WHAT MIGHT THAT BE?
I'M GONNA WHOOP YOUR SPIKY BUTT BEFORE YOU CONQUER ANY-THING.
KR-
AK
BRAK

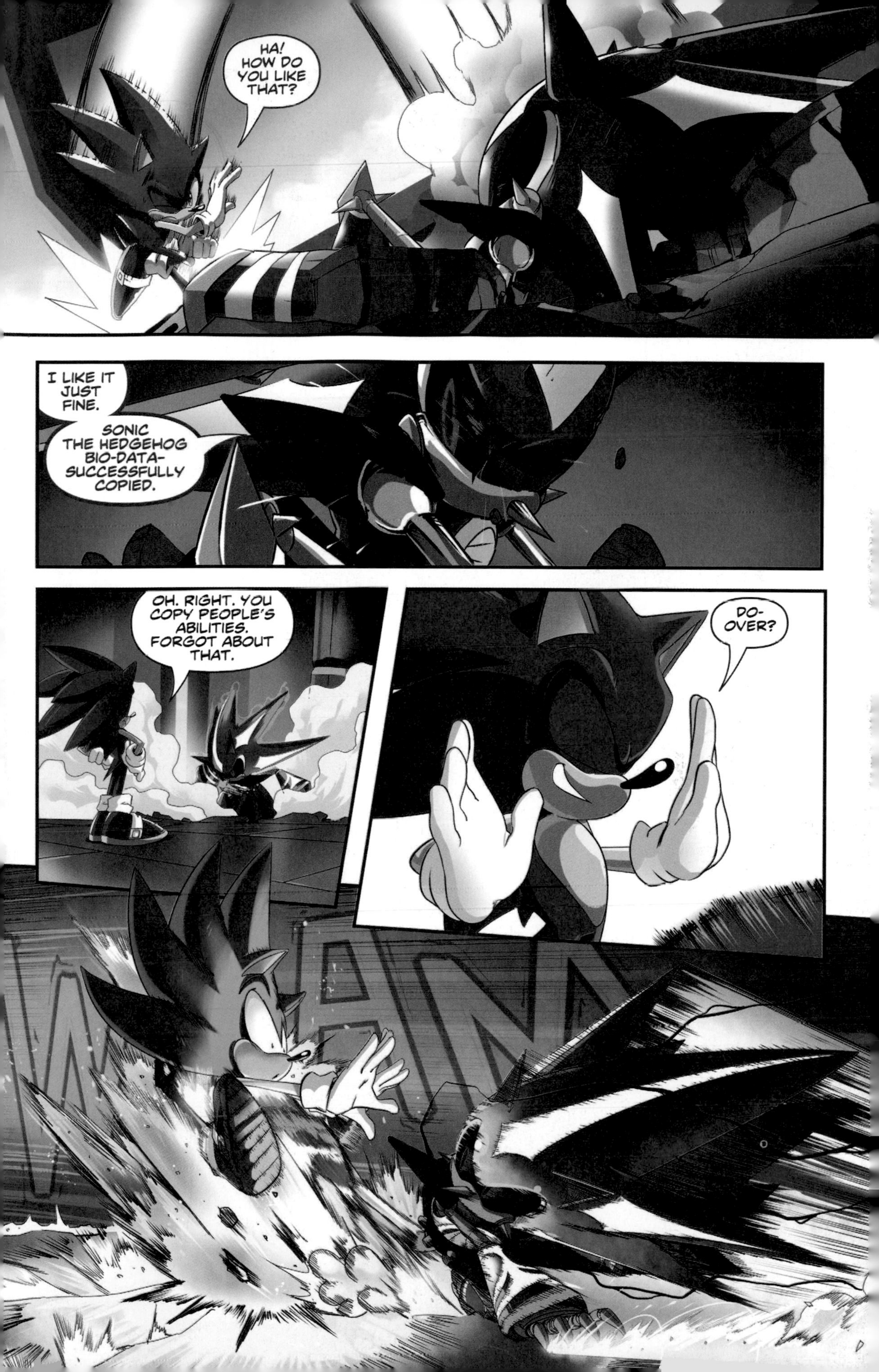
HA! HOW DO YOU LIKE THAT?
I LIKE IT JUST FINE.
SONIC THE HEDGEHOG BIO-DATA-SUCCESSFULLY COPIED.
OH. RIGHT. YOU COPY PEOPLE'S ABILITIES. FORGOT ABOUT THAT.
DO-OVER?

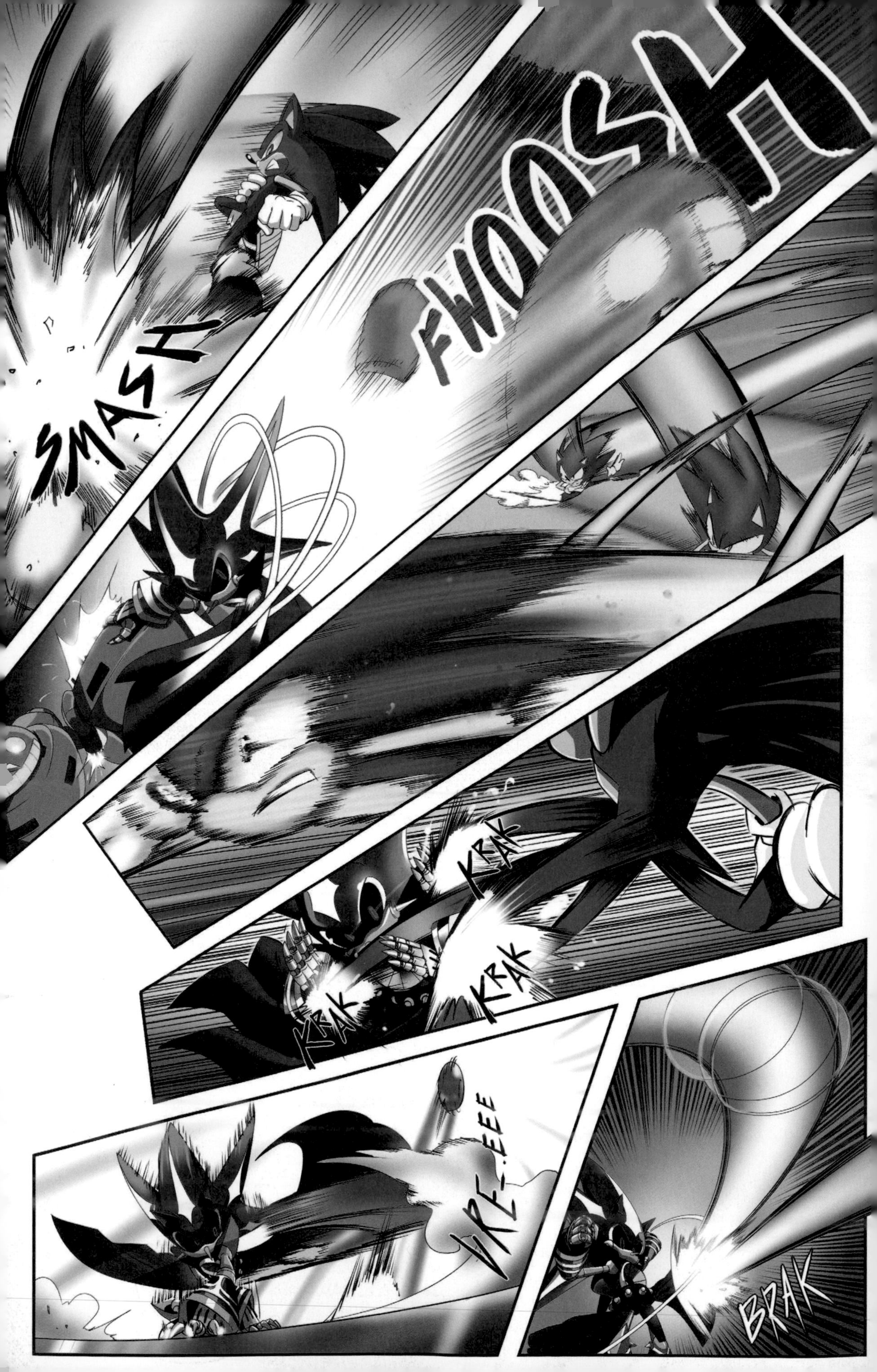
SMASH
FWOOSH
KRAK
KRAK
KRAK
VREEEEE
BRAK

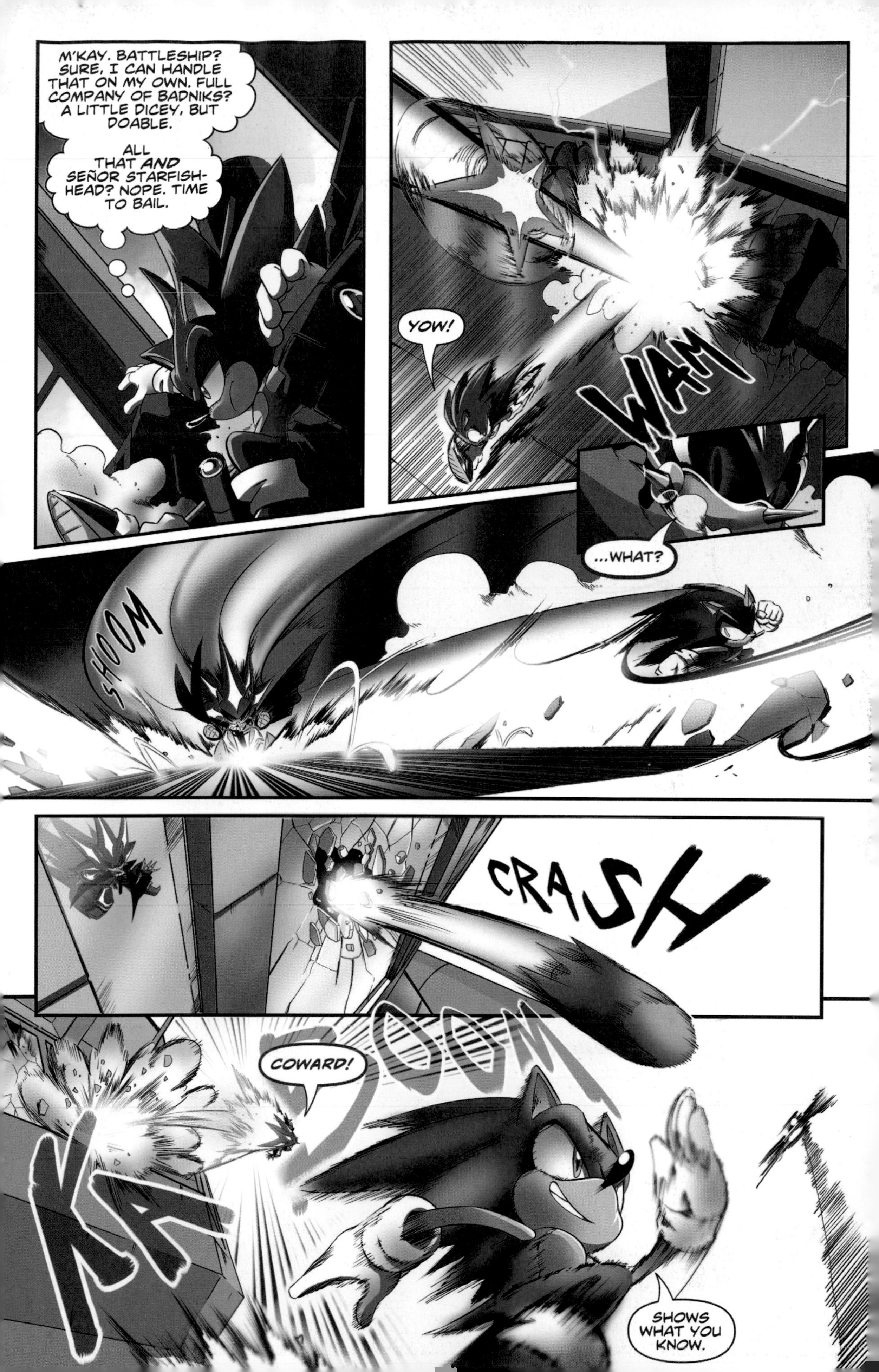
M'KAY. BATTLESHIP? SURE, I CAN HANDLE THAT ON MY OWN. FULL COMPANY OF BADNIKS? A LITTLE DICEY, BUT DOABLE.
ALL THAT AND SEÑOR STARFISH-HEAD? NOPE. TIME TO BAIL.
YOW!
WAM
...WHAT?
SHOOM
CRASH
COWARD!
KA-BOOM
SHOWS WHAT YOU KNOW.

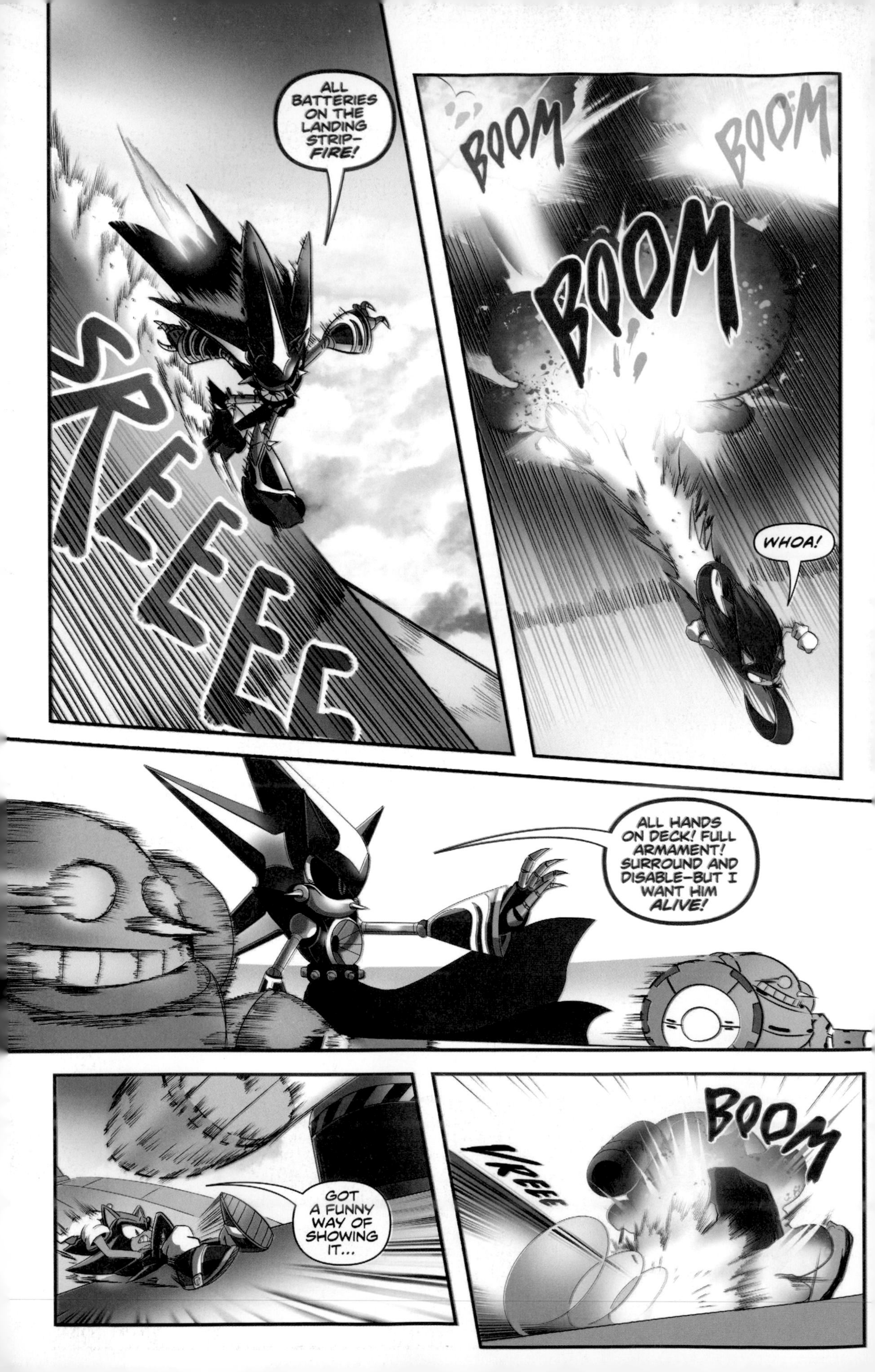

ALL BATTERIES ON THE LANDING STRIP- FIRE!
SREEEEE
BOOM
BOOM
BOOM
WHOA!
ALL HANDS ON DECK! FULL ARMAMENT! SURROUND AND DISABLE—BUT I WANT HIM ALIVE!
GOT A FUNNY WAY OF SHOWING IT...
VREEE
BOOM

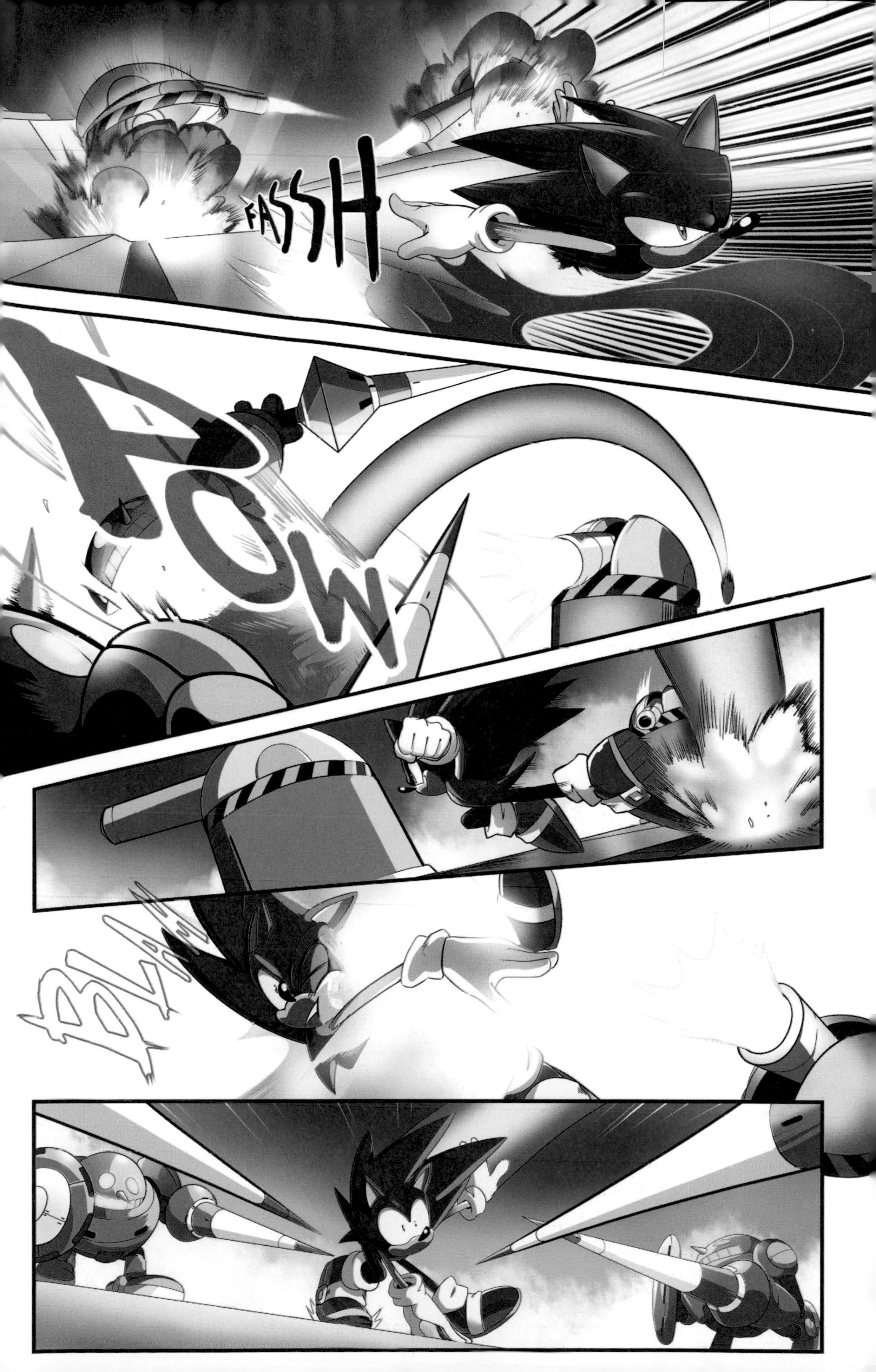
FASSH
POW

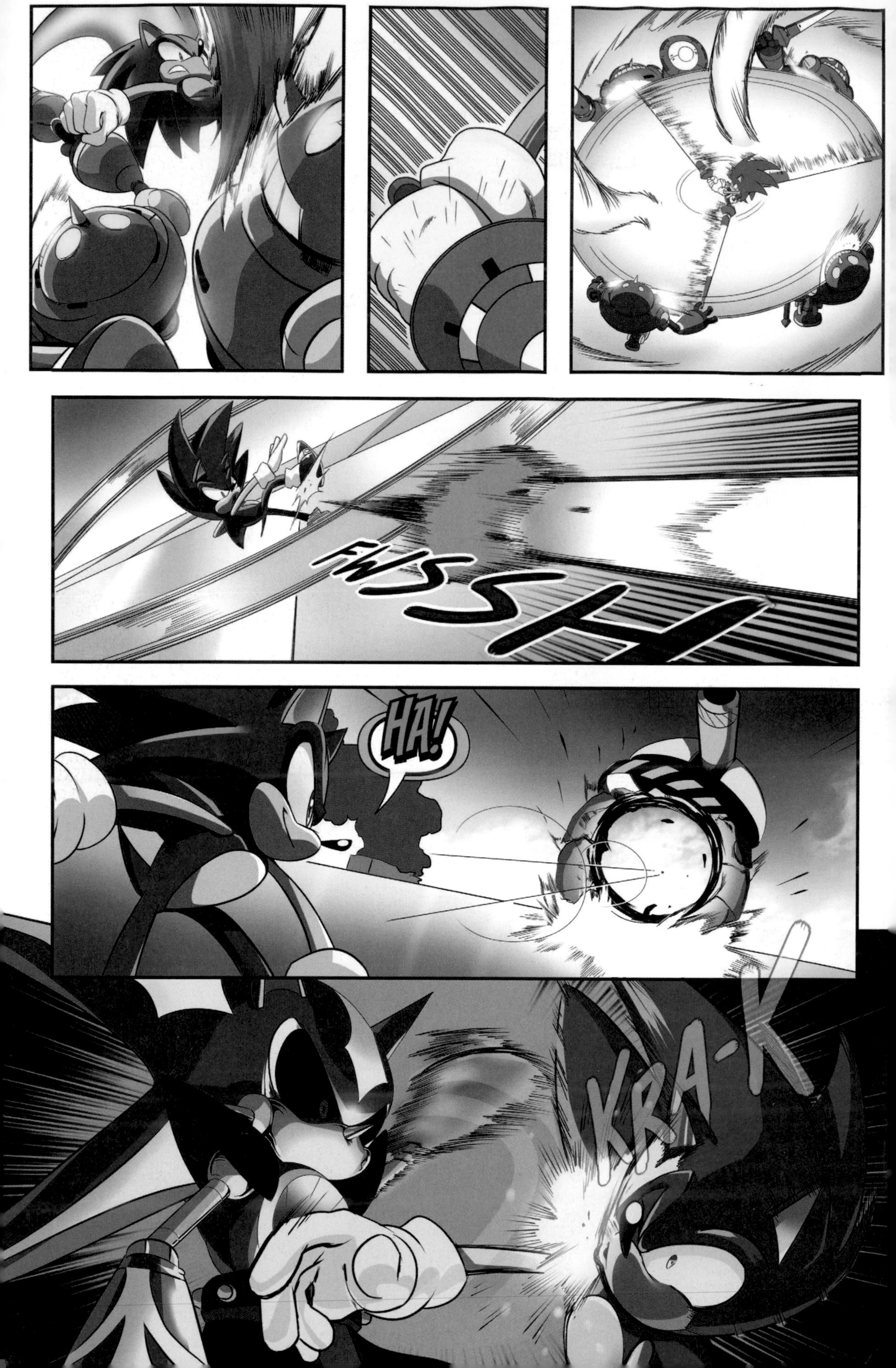
FWSSH
HA!
KRA-K

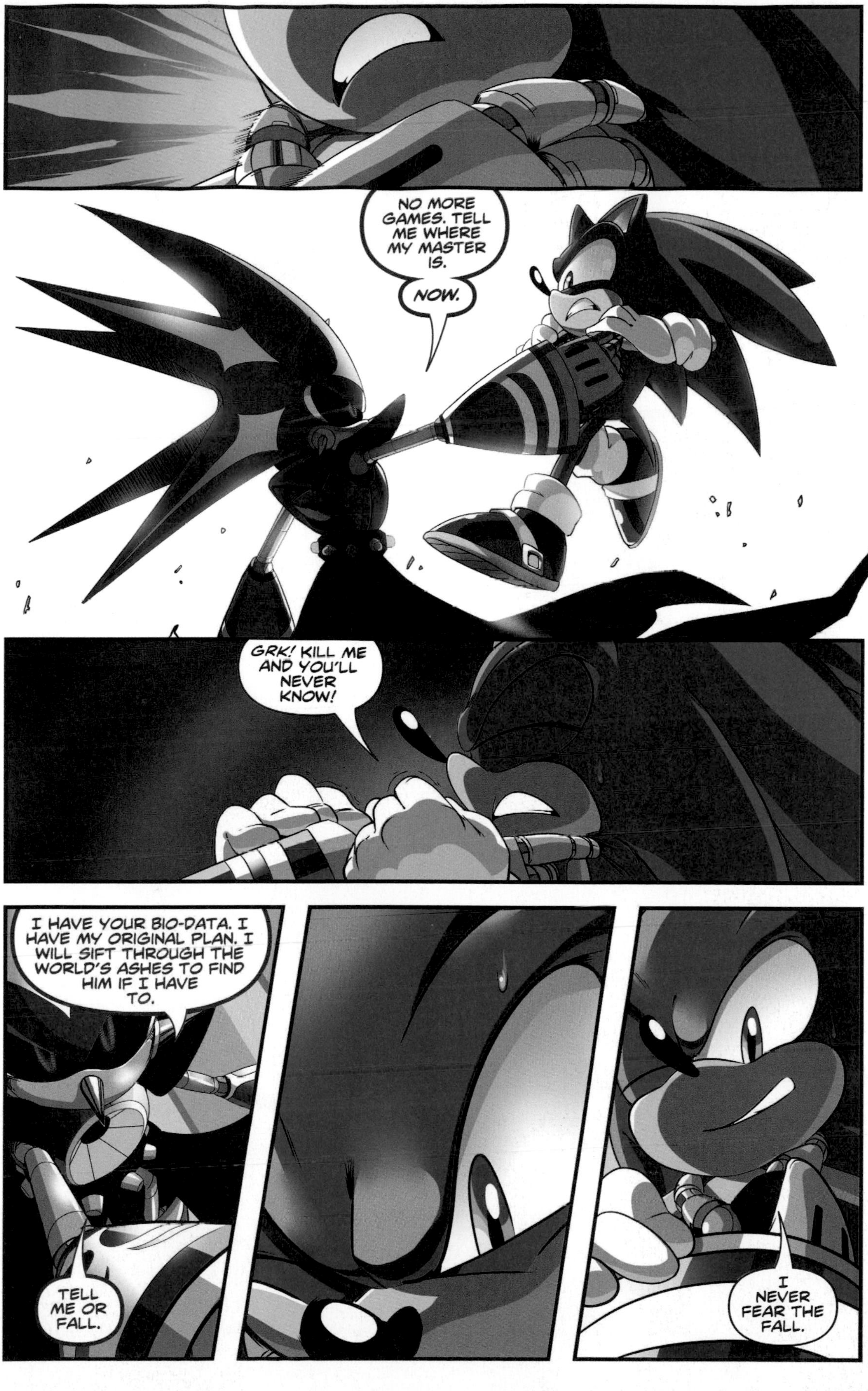
NO MORE GAMES. TELL ME WHERE MY MASTER IS.
NOW.
GRK! KILL ME AND YOU'LL NEVER KNOW!
I HAVE YOUR BIO-DATA. I HAVE MY ORIGINAL PLAN. I WILL SIFT THROUGH THE WORLD'S ASHES TO FIND HIM IF I HAVE TO.
TELL ME OR FALL.
I NEVER FEAR THE FALL.

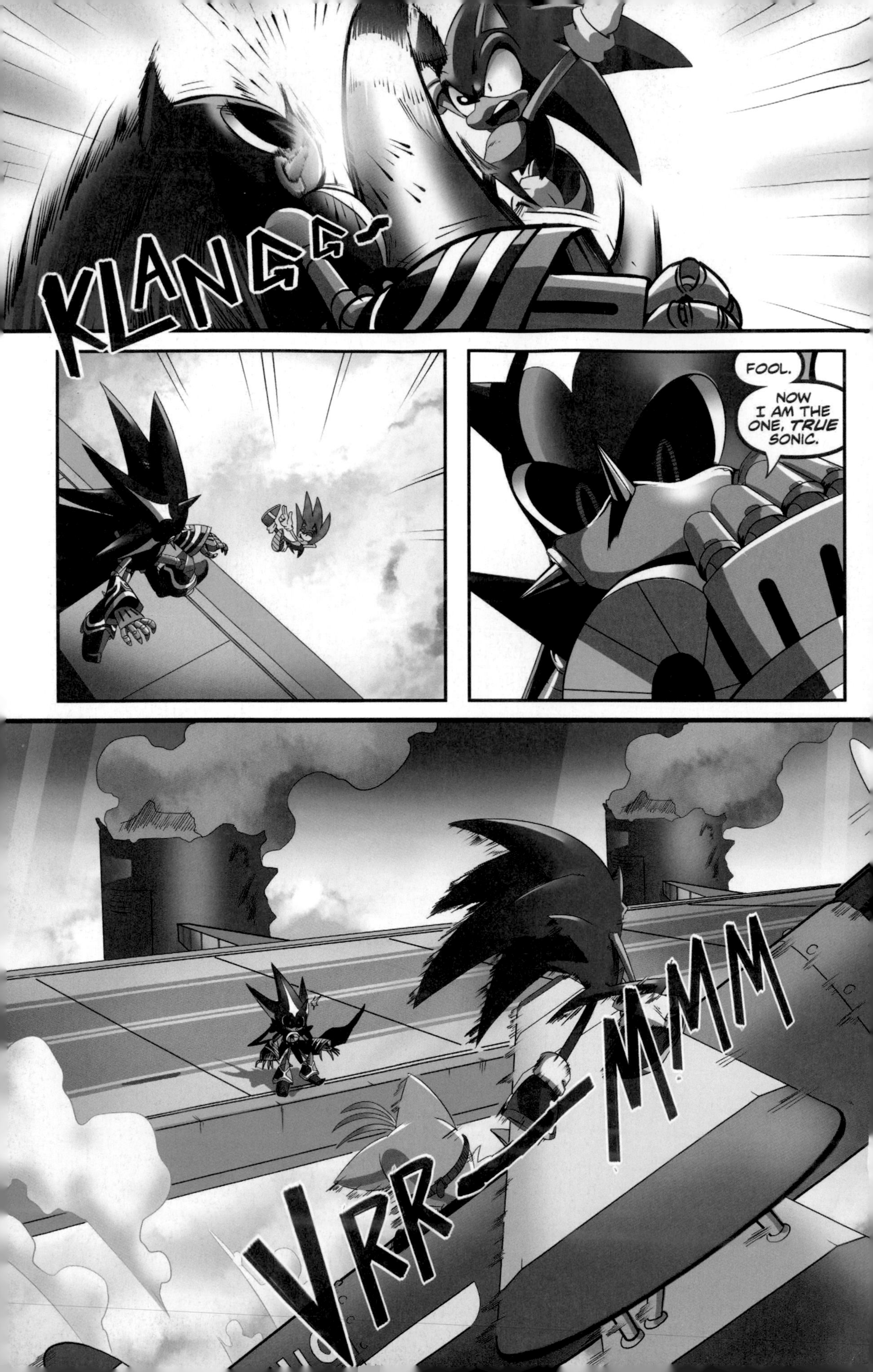
KLANGG-
FOOL.
NOW I AM THE ONE, *TRUE* SONIC.
VRR--MMM

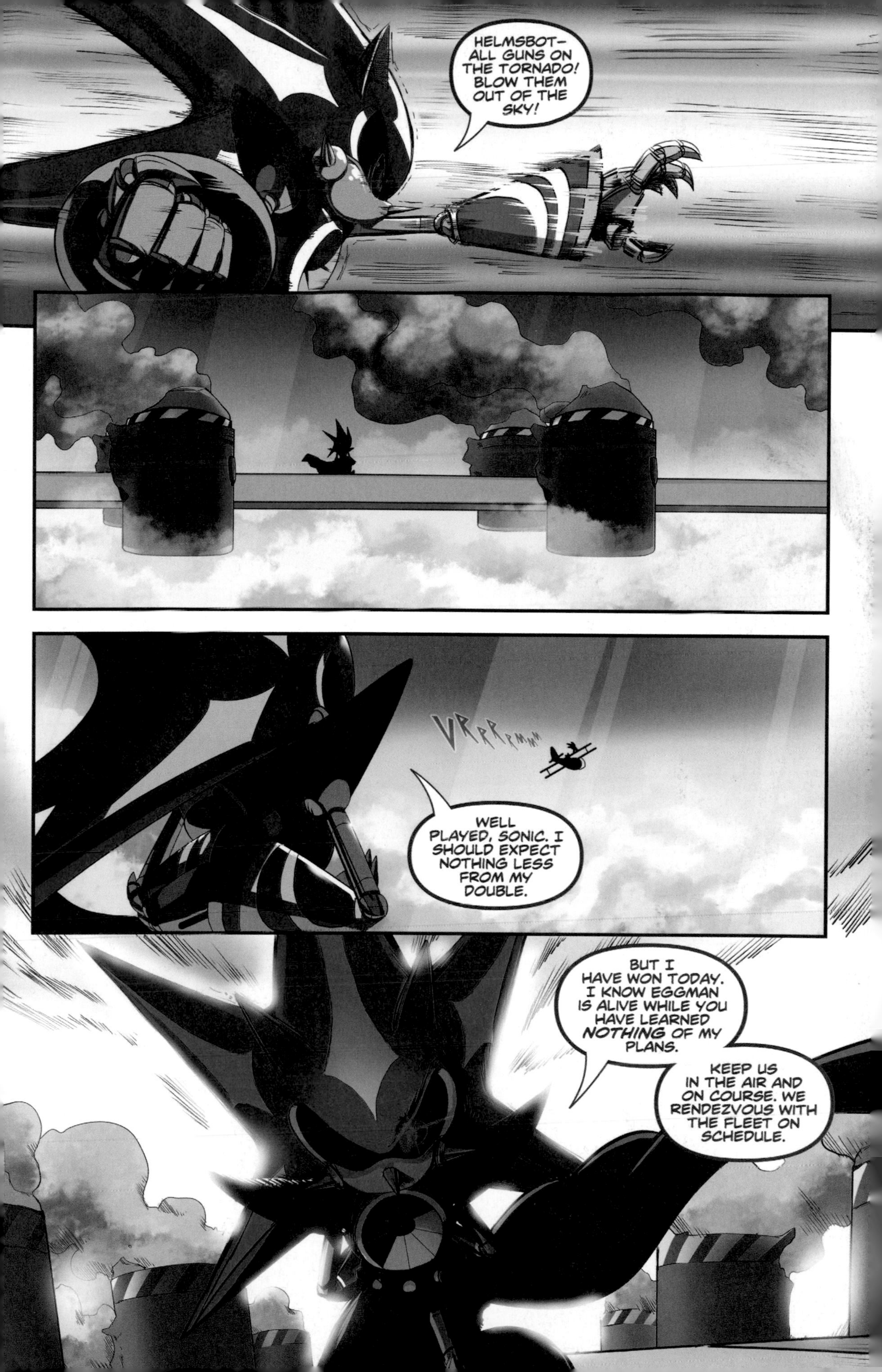
HELMSBOT— ALL GUNS ON THE TORNADO! BLOW THEM OUT OF THE SKY!
VRRRRMMM
WELL PLAYED, SONIC. I SHOULD EXPECT NOTHING LESS FROM MY DOUBLE.
BUT I HAVE WON TODAY. I KNOW EGGMAN IS ALIVE WHILE YOU HAVE LEARNED *NOTHING* OF MY PLANS.
KEEP US IN THE AIR AND ON COURSE. WE RENDEZVOUS WITH THE FLEET ON SCHEDULE.

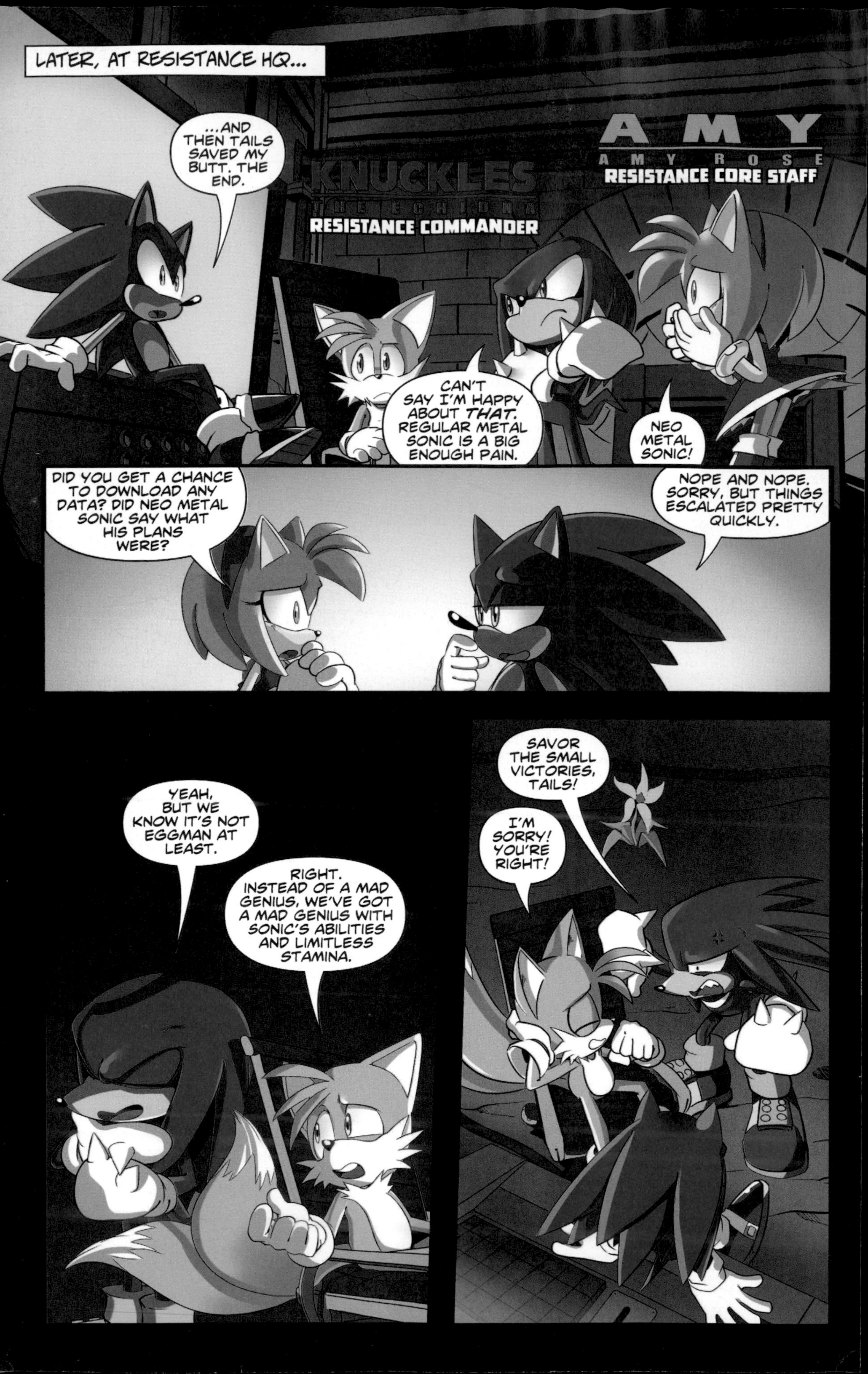
LATER, AT RESISTANCE HQ...
...AND THEN TAILS SAVED MY BUTT. THE END.
KNUCKLES THE ECHIDNA RESISTANCE COMMANDER
AMY AMY ROSE RESISTANCE CORE STAFF
CAN'T SAY I'M HAPPY ABOUT THAT. REGULAR METAL SONIC IS A BIG ENOUGH PAIN.
NEO METAL SONIC!
DID YOU GET A CHANCE TO DOWNLOAD ANY DATA? DID NEO METAL SONIC SAY WHAT HIS PLANS WERE?
NOPE AND NOPE. SORRY, BUT THINGS ESCALATED PRETTY QUICKLY.
YEAH, BUT WE KNOW IT'S NOT EGGMAN AT LEAST.
RIGHT. INSTEAD OF A MAD GENIUS, WE'VE GOT A MAD GENIUS WITH SONIC'S ABILITIES AND LIMITLESS STAMINA.
SAVOR THE SMALL VICTORIES, TAILS!
I'M SORRY! YOU'RE RIGHT!

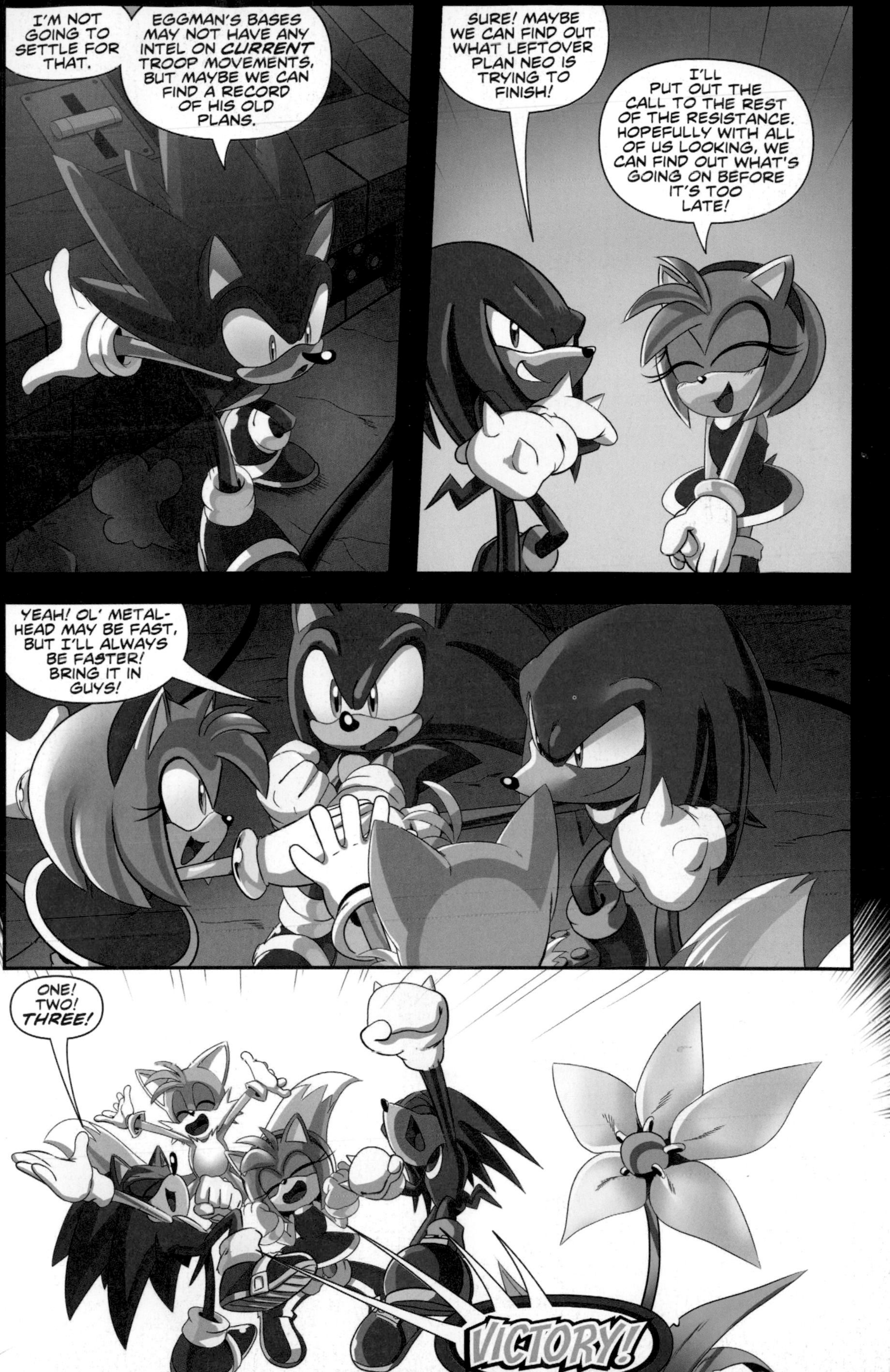
I'M NOT GOING TO SETTLE FOR THAT.
EGGMAN'S BASES MAY NOT HAVE ANY INTEL ON *CURRENT* TROOP MOVEMENTS, BUT MAYBE WE CAN FIND A RECORD OF HIS OLD PLANS.
SURE! MAYBE WE CAN FIND OUT WHAT LEFTOVER PLAN NEO IS TRYING TO FINISH!
I'LL PUT OUT THE CALL TO THE REST OF THE RESISTANCE. HOPEFULLY WITH ALL OF US LOOKING, WE CAN FIND OUT WHAT'S GOING ON BEFORE IT'S TOO LATE!
YEAH! OL' METAL-HEAD MAY BE FAST, BUT I'LL ALWAYS BE FASTER! BRING IT IN GUYS!
ONE! TWO! ***THREE!***
VICTORY!

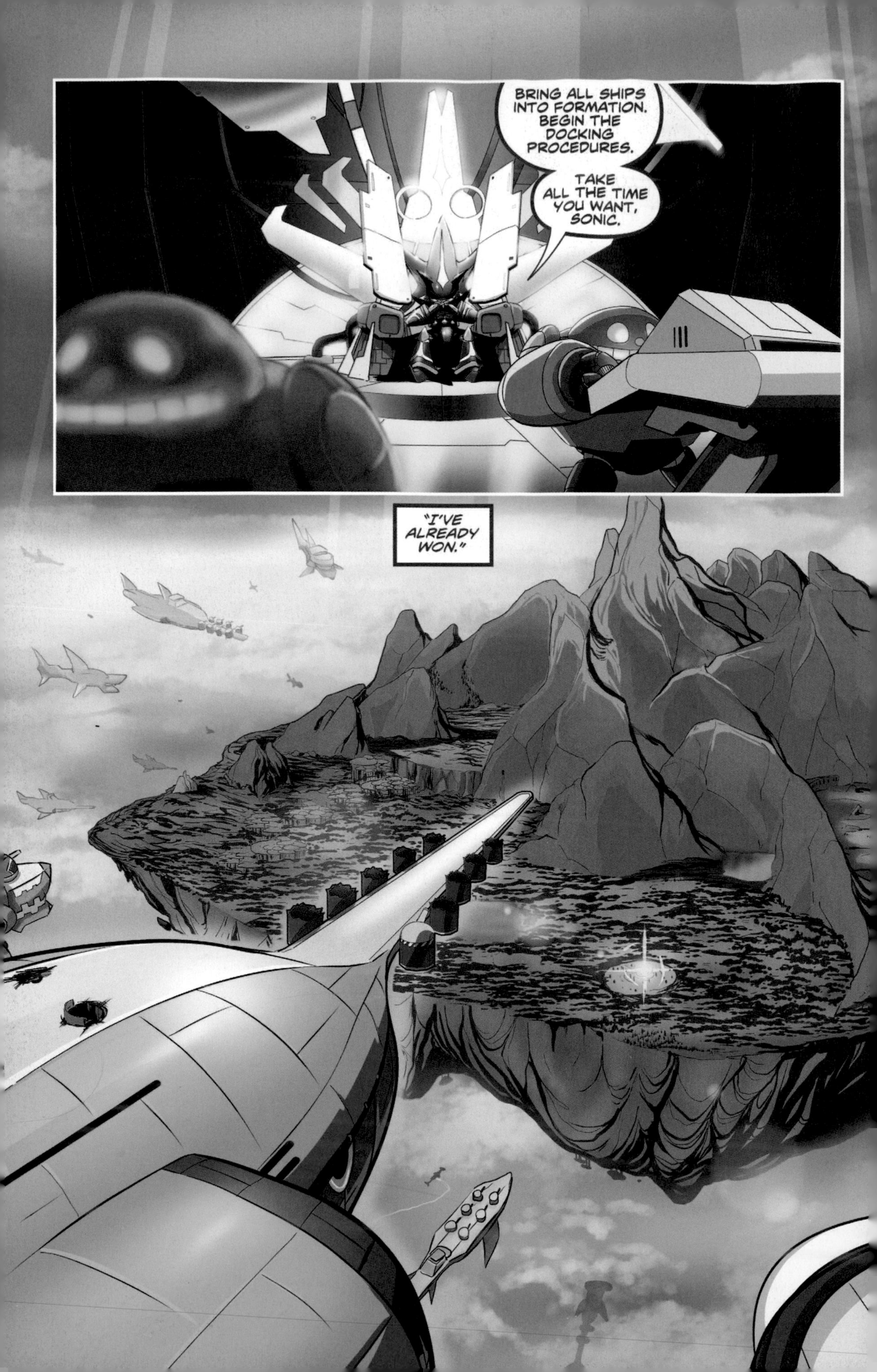
BRING ALL SHIPS INTO FORMATION. BEGIN THE DOCKING PROCEDURES.
TAKE ALL THE TIME YOU WANT, SONIC.
"I'VE ALREADY WON."

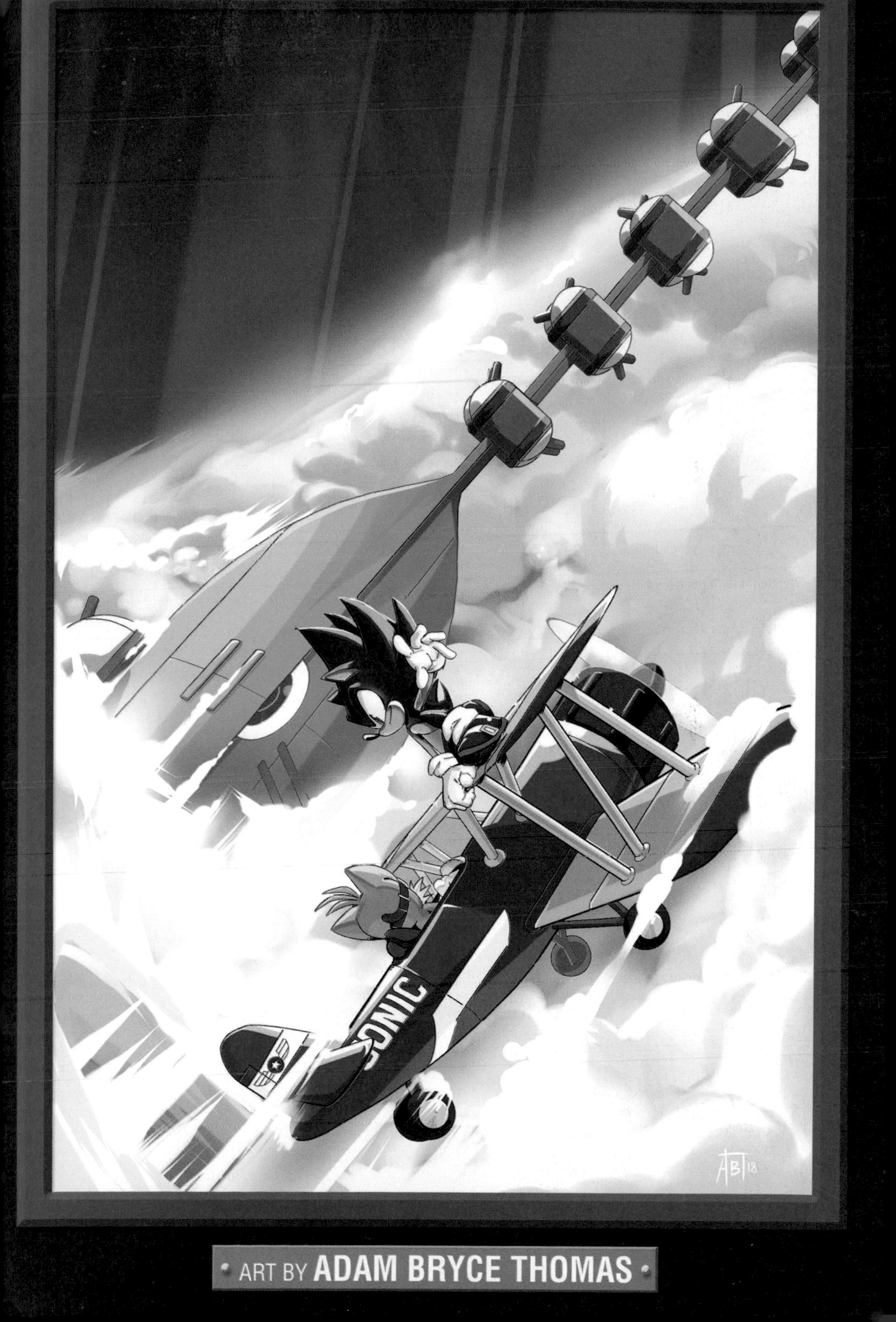
SONIC
ABT 18

ART BY **ADAM BRYCE THOMAS**

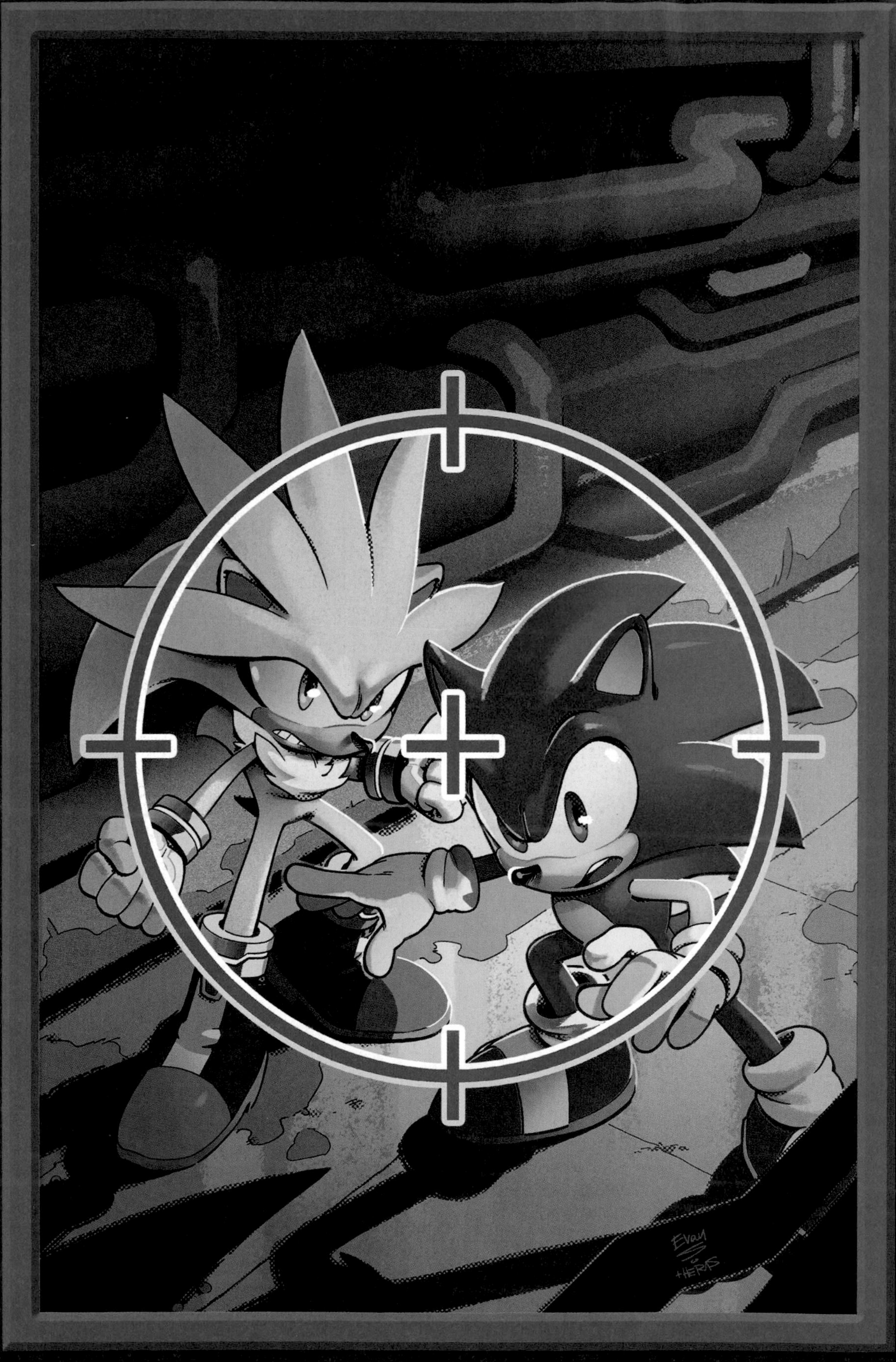

ART BY **EVAN STANLEY** COLORS BY **MATT HERMS**

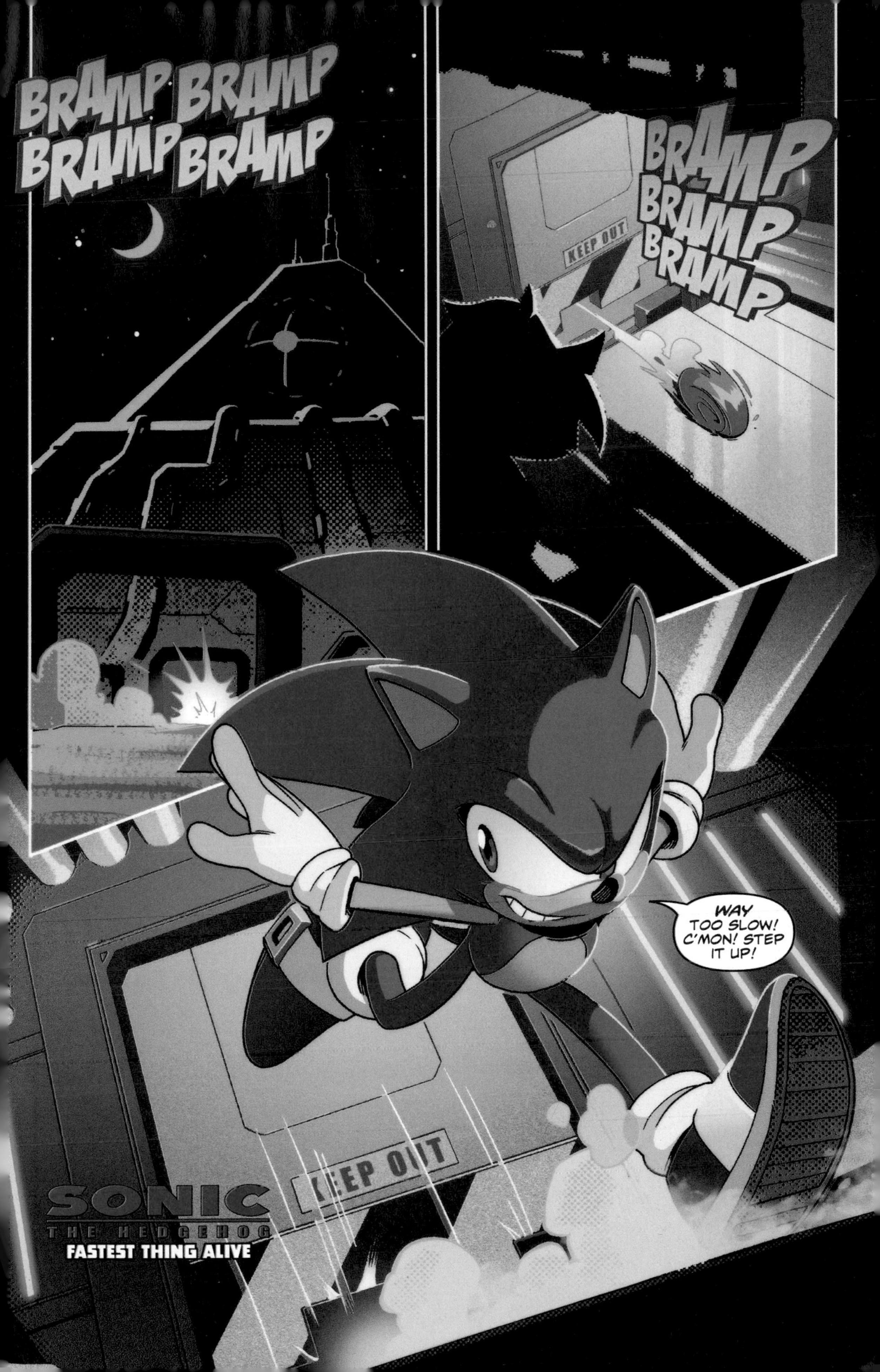
BRAMP BRAMP
BRAMP BRAMP
BRAMP
BRAMP
BRAMP
BRAMP
KEEP OUT
WAY TOO SLOW! C'MON! STEP IT UP!
KEEP OUT
SONIC
THE HEDGEHOG
FASTEST THING ALIVE

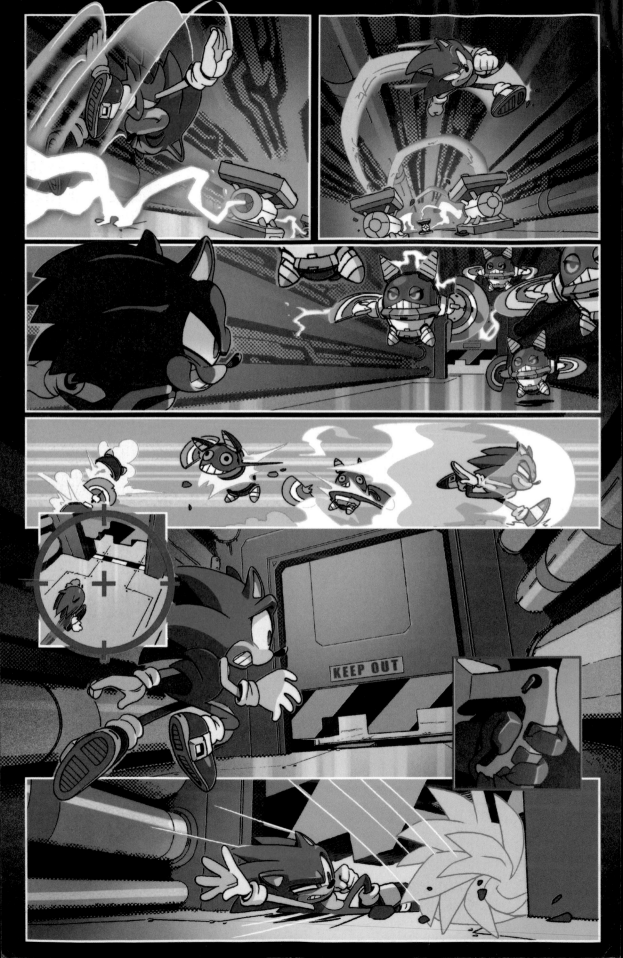

KEEP OUT

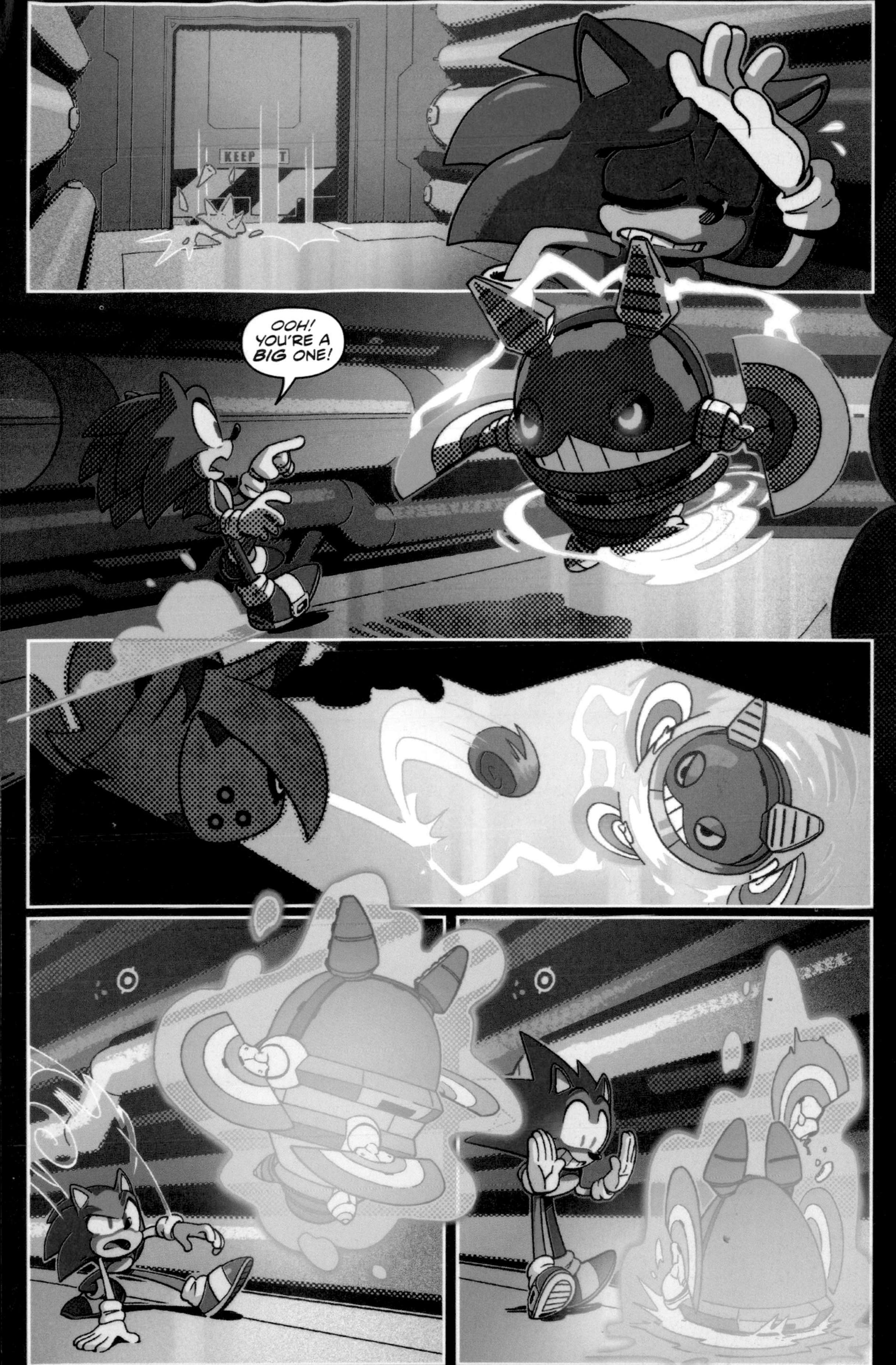
KEEP
OOH! YOU'RE A BIG ONE!

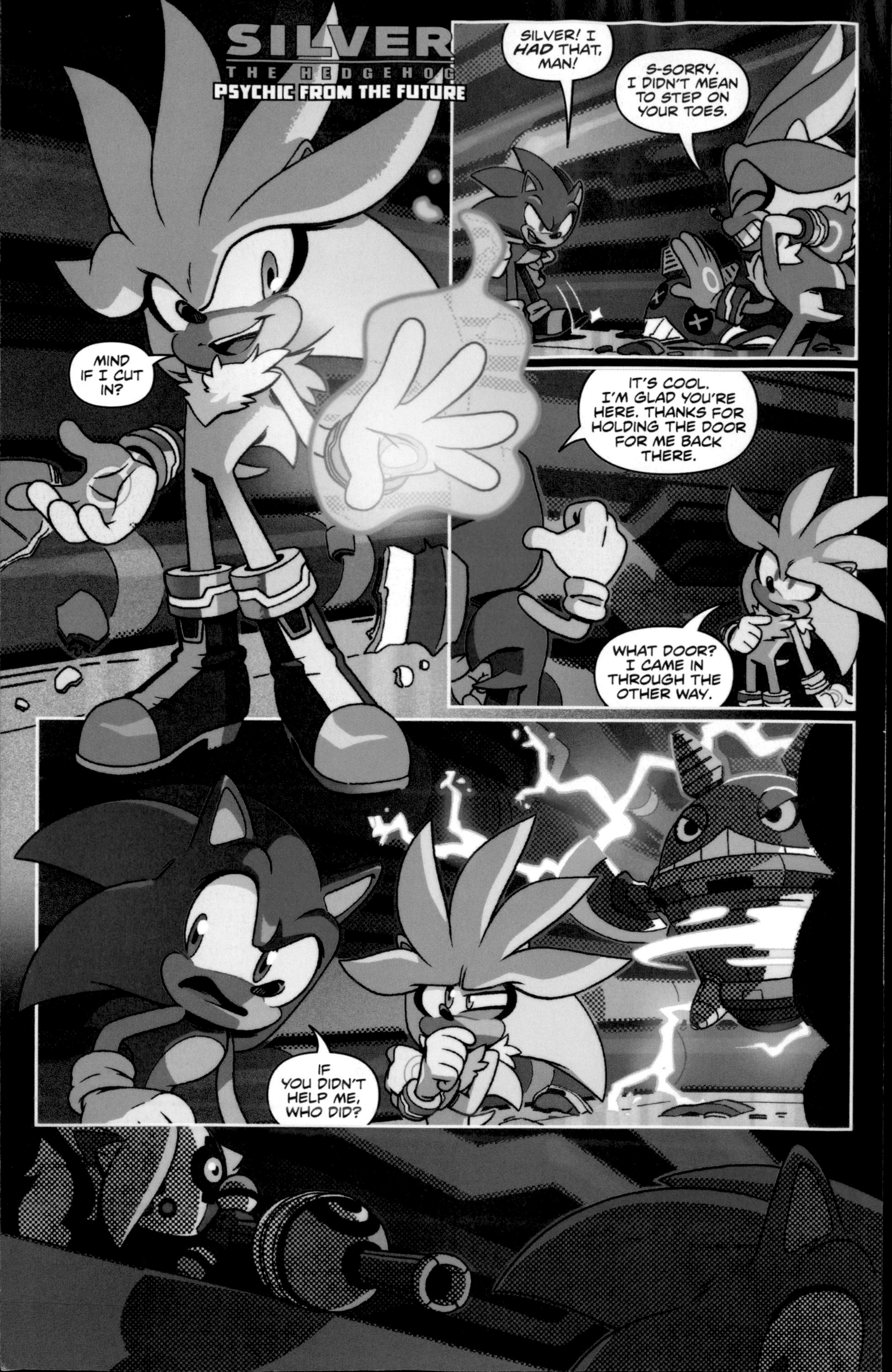
SILVER
THE HEDGEHOG
PSYCHIC FROM THE FUTURE
MIND IF I CUT IN?
SILVER! I HAD THAT, MAN!
S-SORRY. I DIDN'T MEAN TO STEP ON YOUR TOES.
IT'S COOL. I'M GLAD YOU'RE HERE. THANKS FOR HOLDING THE DOOR FOR ME BACK THERE.
WHAT DOOR? I CAME IN THROUGH THE OTHER WAY.
IF YOU DIDN'T HELP ME, WHO DID?

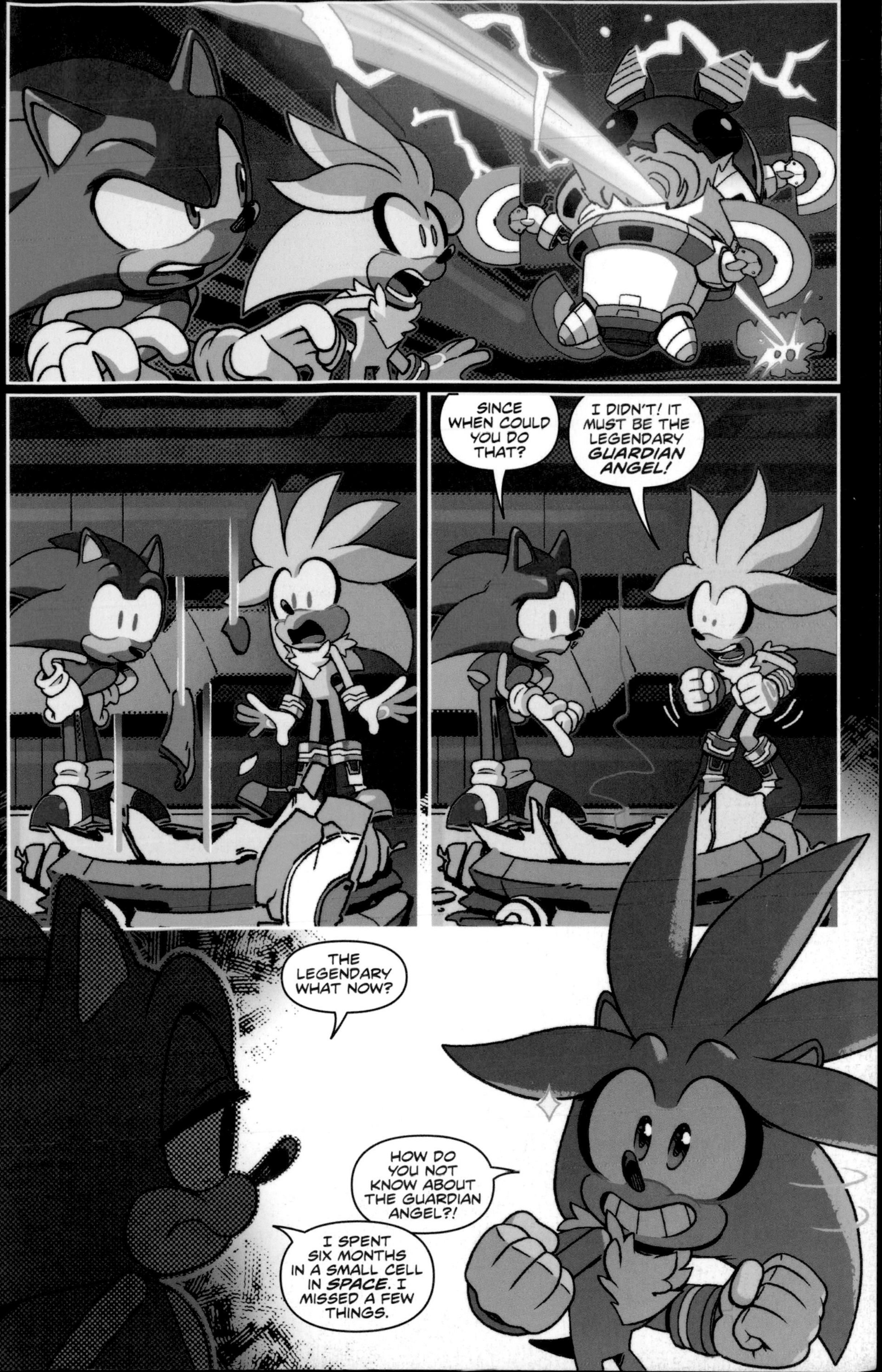
SINCE WHEN COULD YOU DO THAT?
I DIDN'T! IT MUST BE THE LEGENDARY GUARDIAN ANGEL!
THE LEGENDARY WHAT NOW?
HOW DO YOU NOT KNOW ABOUT THE GUARDIAN ANGEL?!
I SPENT SIX MONTHS IN A SMALL CELL IN SPACE. I MISSED A FEW THINGS.

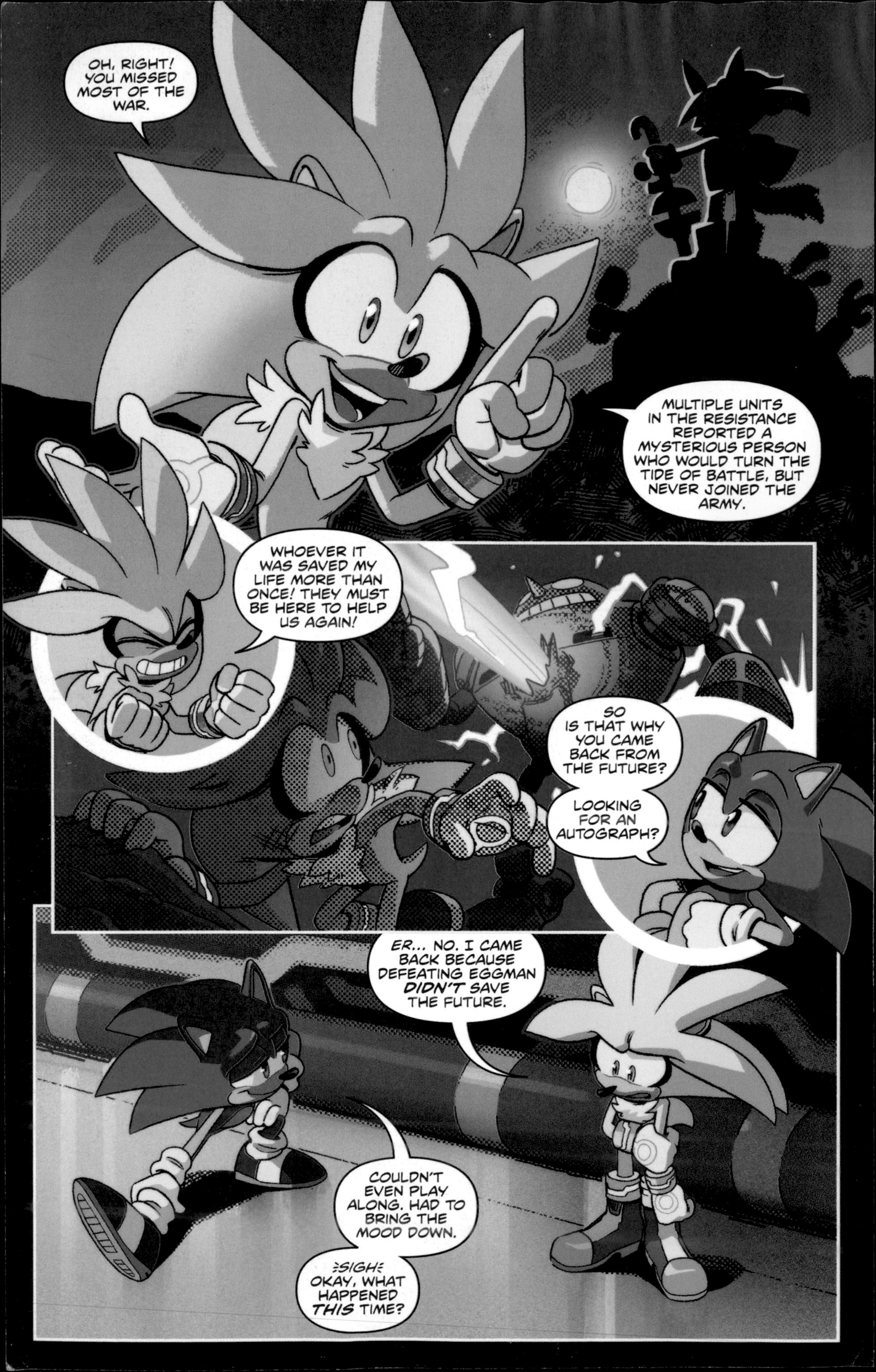
OH, RIGHT! YOU MISSED MOST OF THE WAR.
MULTIPLE UNITS IN THE RESISTANCE REPORTED A MYSTERIOUS PERSON WHO WOULD TURN THE TIDE OF BATTLE, BUT NEVER JOINED THE ARMY.
WHOEVER IT WAS SAVED MY LIFE MORE THAN ONCE! THEY MUST BE HERE TO HELP US AGAIN!
SO IS THAT WHY YOU CAME BACK FROM THE FUTURE?
LOOKING FOR AN AUTOGRAPH?
ER... NO. I CAME BACK BECAUSE DEFEATING EGGMAN DIDN'T SAVE THE FUTURE.
COULDN'T EVEN PLAY ALONG. HAD TO BRING THE MOOD DOWN.
SIGH OKAY, WHAT HAPPENED THIS TIME?

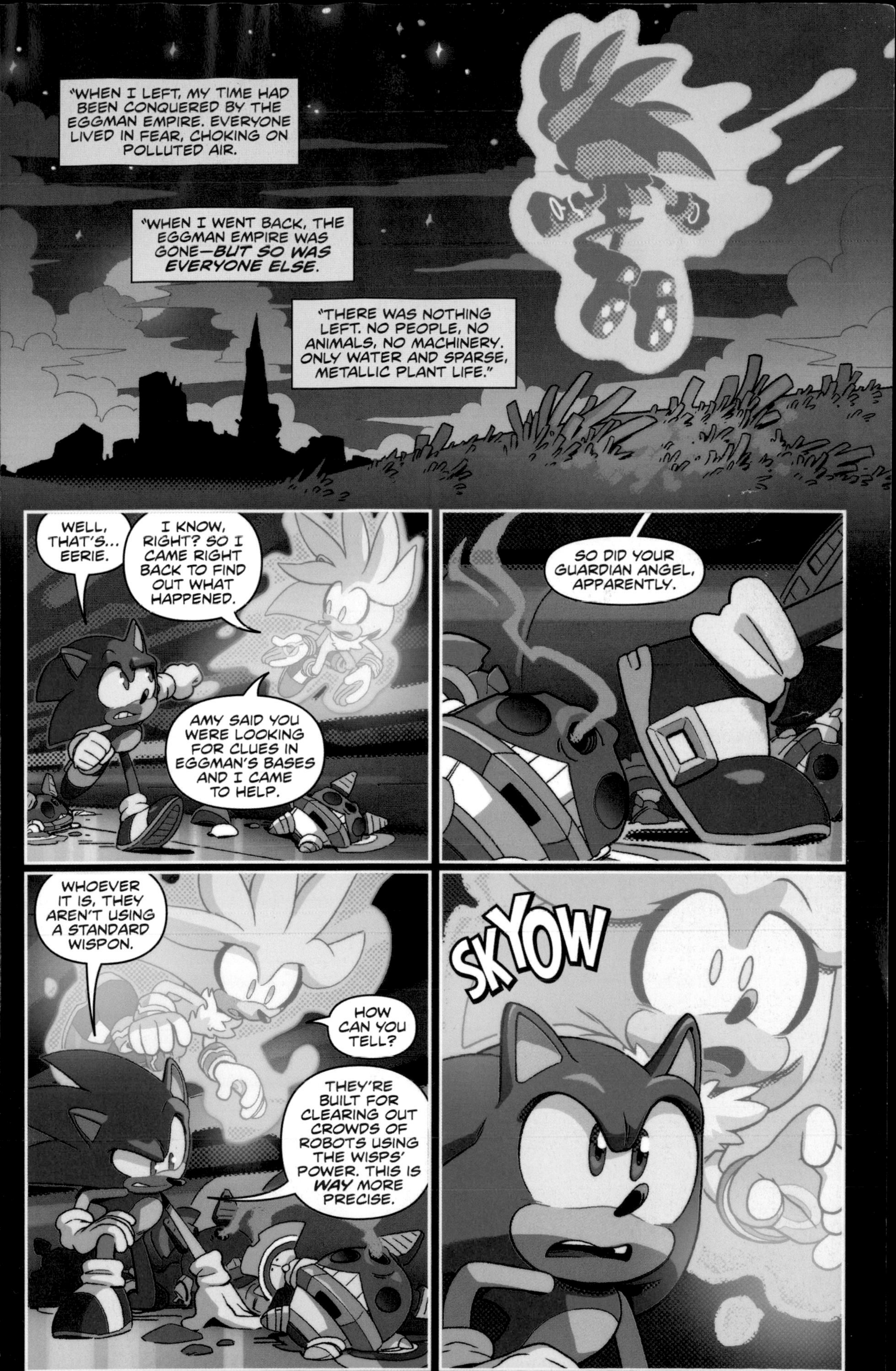

"WHEN I LEFT, MY TIME HAD BEEN CONQUERED BY THE EGGMAN EMPIRE. EVERYONE LIVED IN FEAR, CHOKING ON POLLUTED AIR.
"WHEN I WENT BACK, THE EGGMAN EMPIRE WAS GONE—*BUT SO WAS EVERYONE ELSE.*
"THERE WAS NOTHING LEFT. NO PEOPLE, NO ANIMALS, NO MACHINERY. ONLY WATER AND SPARSE, METALLIC PLANT LIFE."
WELL, THAT'S... EERIE.
I KNOW, RIGHT? SO I CAME RIGHT BACK TO FIND OUT WHAT HAPPENED.
AMY SAID YOU WERE LOOKING FOR CLUES IN EGGMAN'S BASES AND I CAME TO HELP.
SO DID YOUR GUARDIAN ANGEL, APPARENTLY.
WHOEVER IT IS, THEY AREN'T USING A STANDARD WISPON.
HOW CAN YOU TELL?
THEY'RE BUILT FOR CLEARING OUT CROWDS OF ROBOTS USING THE WISPS' POWER. THIS IS *WAY* MORE PRECISE.
SKYOW

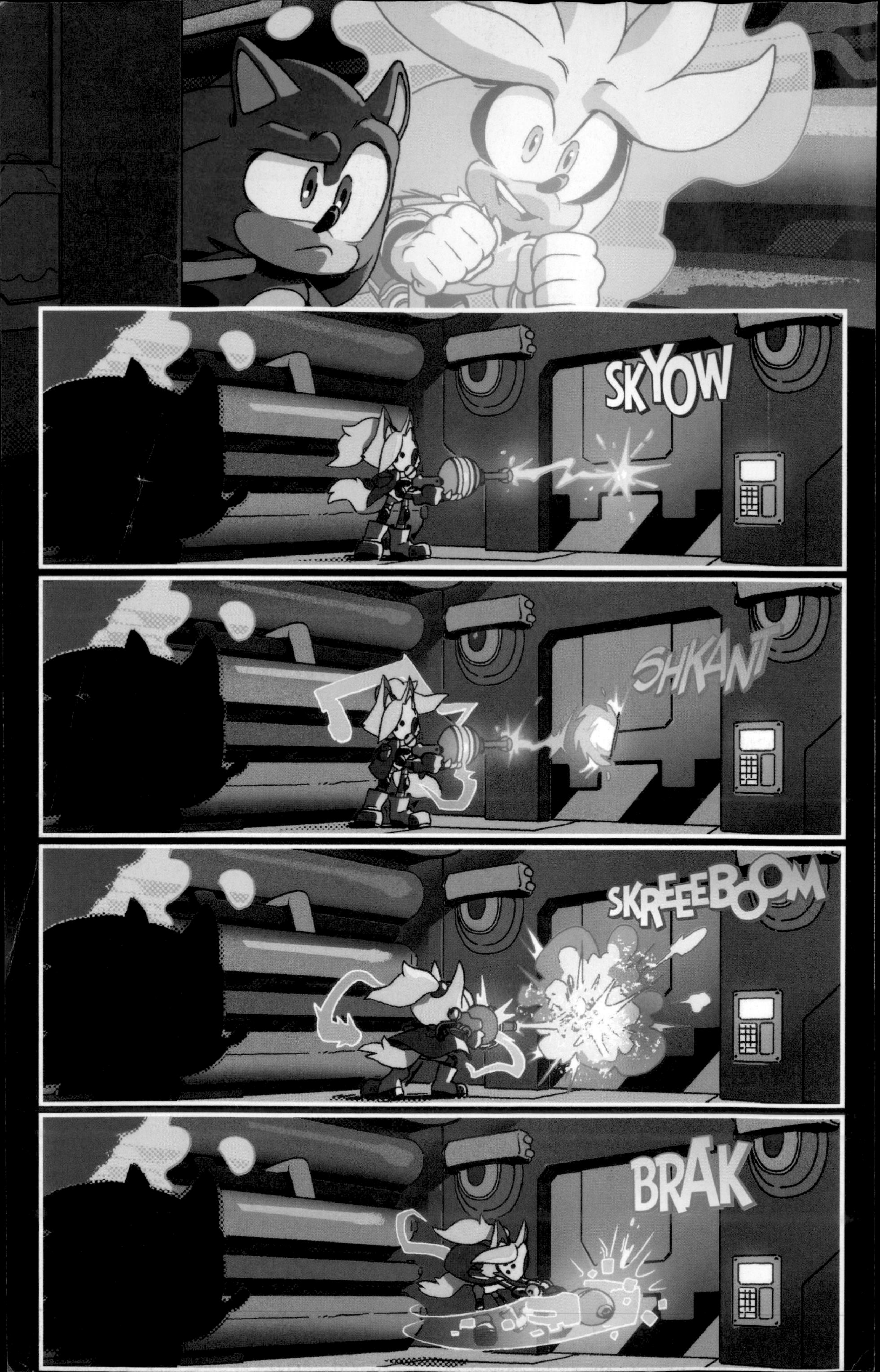
SKYOW
SHKANT
SKREEEBOOM
BRAK

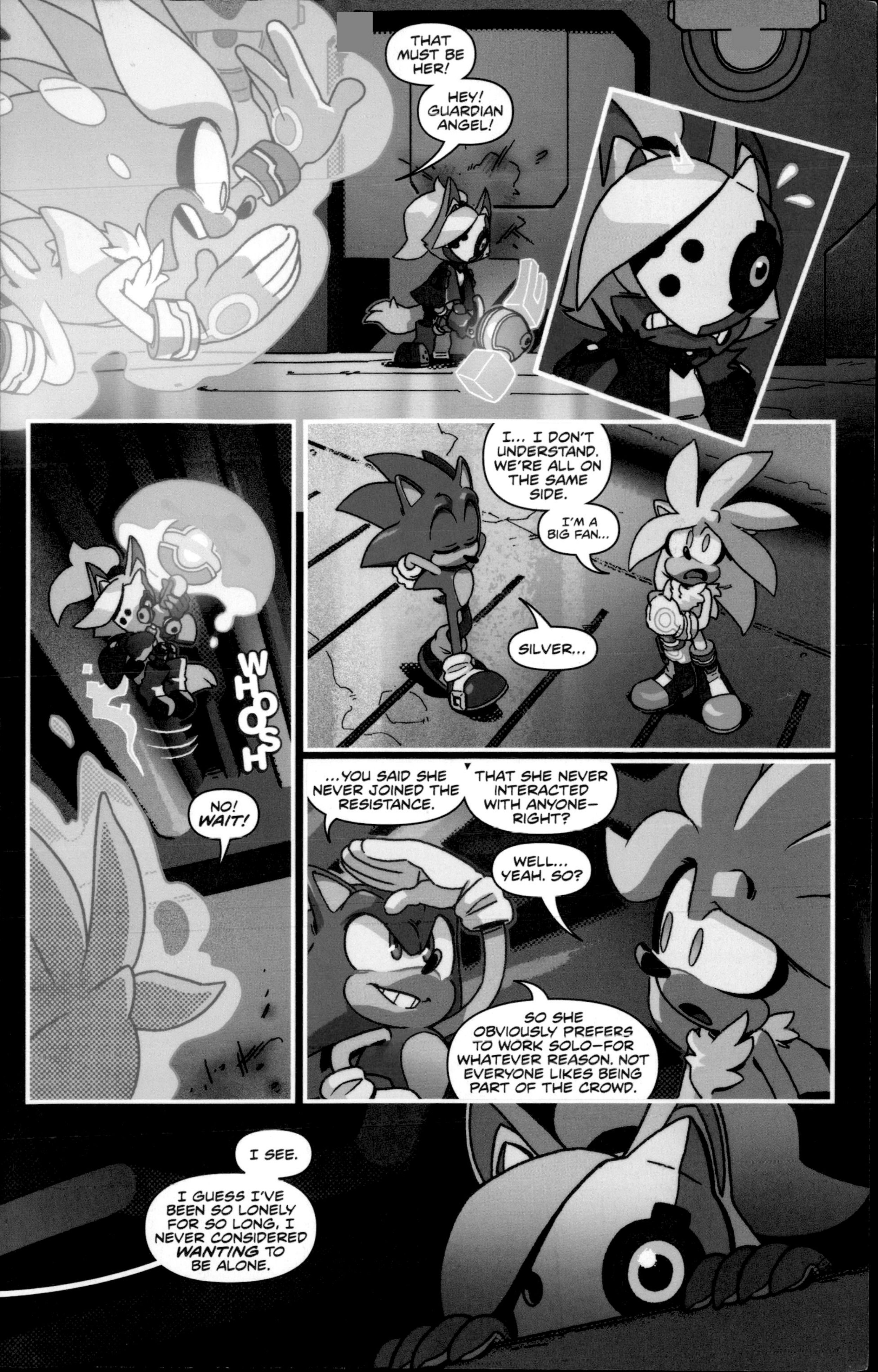

THAT MUST BE HER!
HEY! GUARDIAN ANGEL!
WHOOSH
NO! WAIT!
I... I DON'T UNDERSTAND. WE'RE ALL ON THE SAME SIDE.
I'M A BIG FAN...
SILVER...
...YOU SAID SHE NEVER JOINED THE RESISTANCE.
THAT SHE NEVER INTERACTED WITH ANYONE—RIGHT?
WELL... YEAH. SO?
SO SHE OBVIOUSLY PREFERS TO WORK SOLO—FOR WHATEVER REASON. NOT EVERYONE LIKES BEING PART OF THE CROWD.
I SEE.
I GUESS I'VE BEEN SO LONELY FOR SO LONG, I NEVER CONSIDERED WANTING TO BE ALONE.

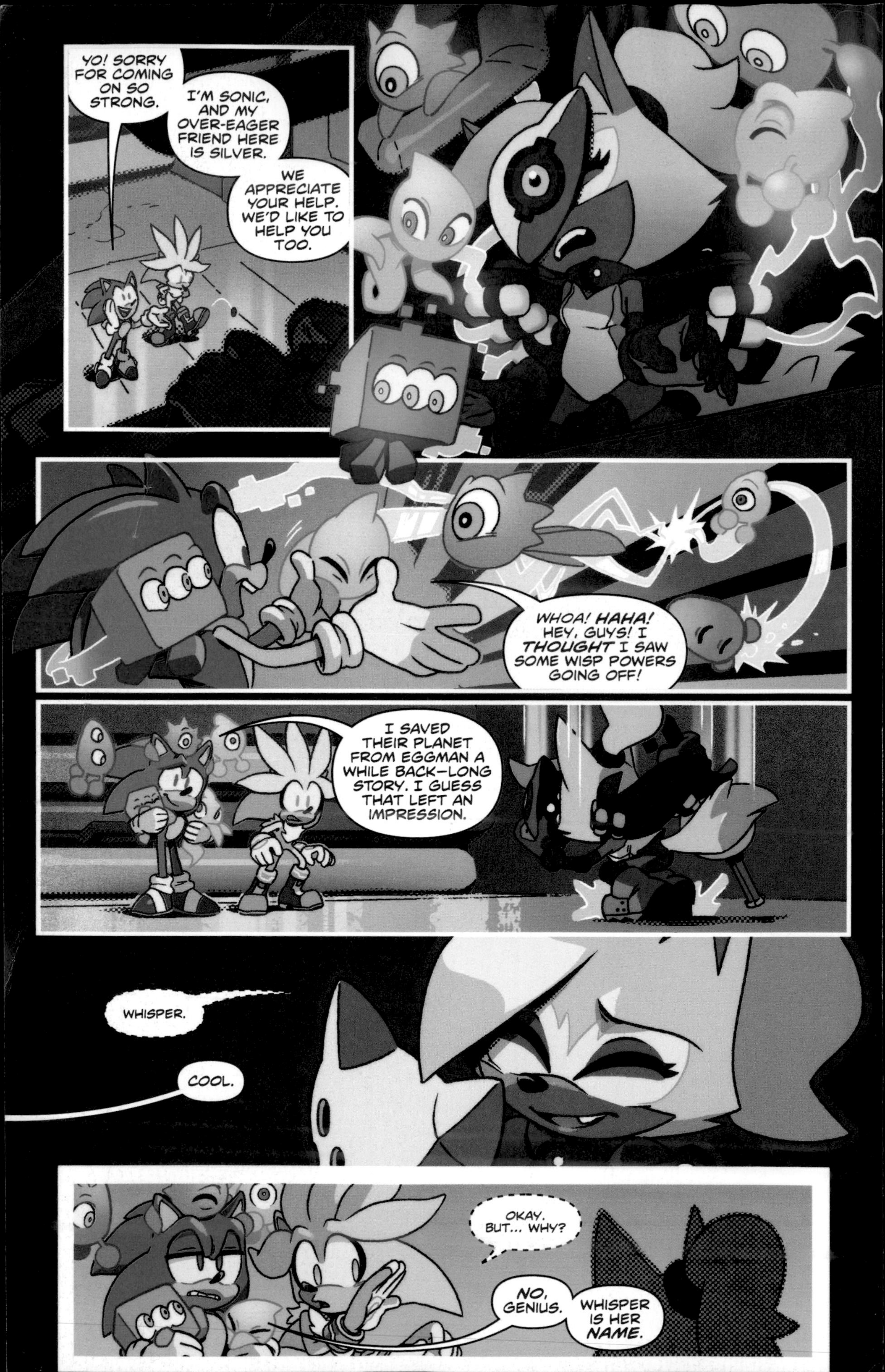
YO! SORRY FOR COMING ON SO STRONG.
I'M SONIC, AND MY OVER-EAGER FRIEND HERE IS SILVER.
WE APPRECIATE YOUR HELP. WE'D LIKE TO HELP YOU TOO.
WHOA! HAHA! HEY, GUYS! I THOUGHT I SAW SOME WISP POWERS GOING OFF!
I SAVED THEIR PLANET FROM EGGMAN A WHILE BACK—LONG STORY. I GUESS THAT LEFT AN IMPRESSION.
WHISPER.
COOL.
OKAY. BUT... WHY?
NO, GENIUS.
WHISPER IS HER NAME.

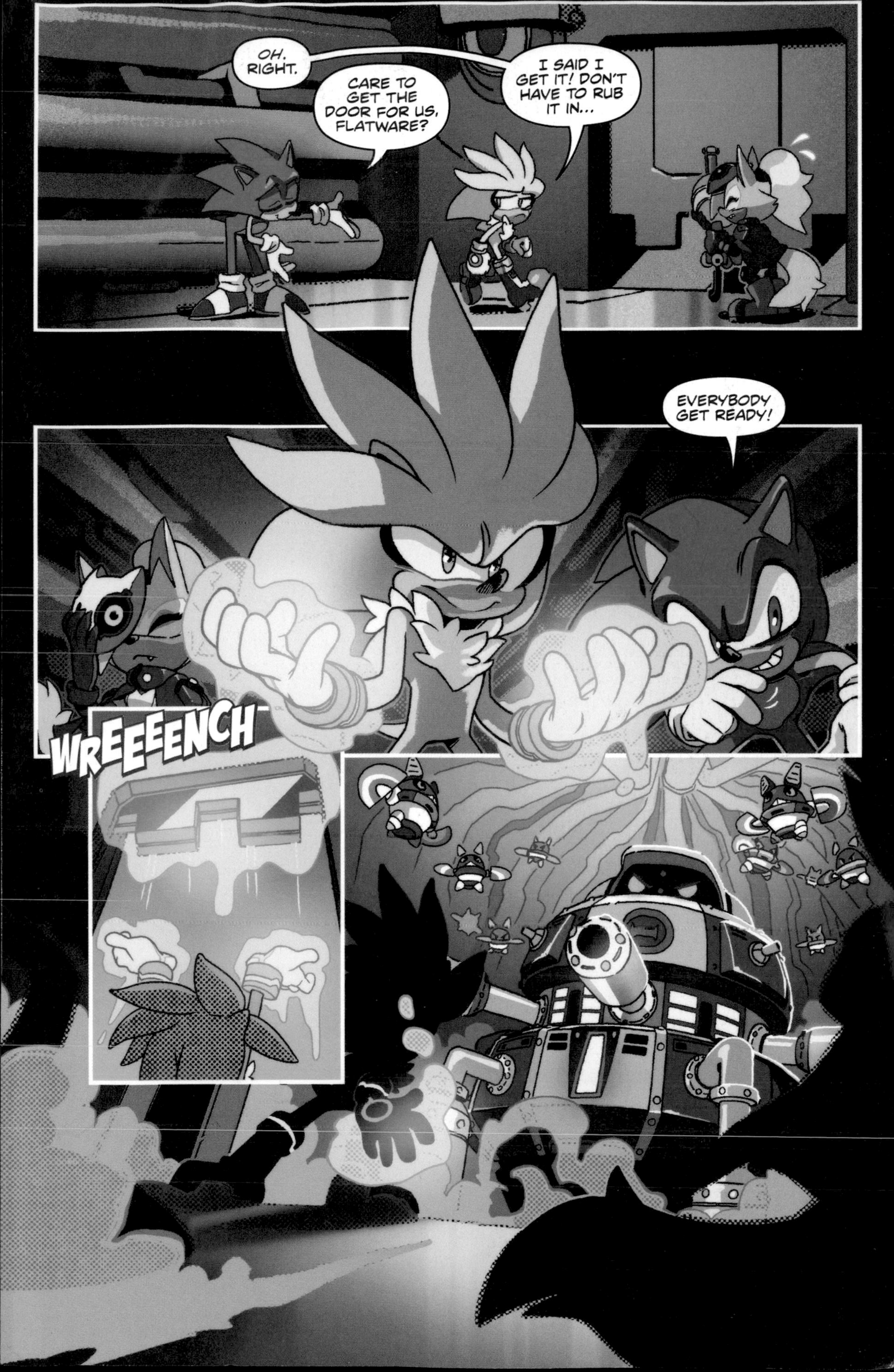
OH. RIGHT.
CARE TO GET THE DOOR FOR US, FLATWARE?
I SAID I GET IT! DON'T HAVE TO RUB IT IN...
EVERYBODY GET READY!
WREEEENCH

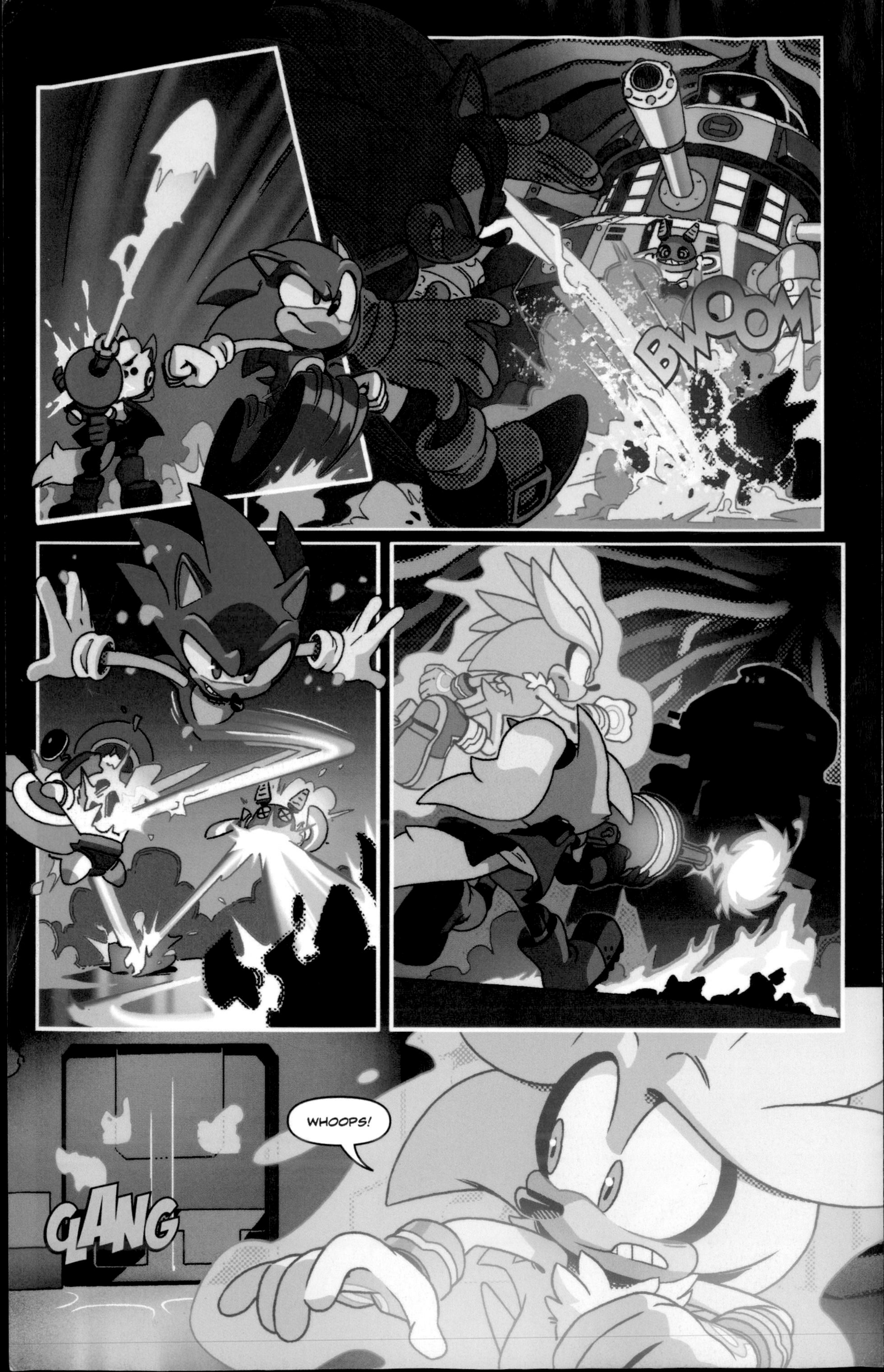
BWOOM
WHOOPS!
CLANG

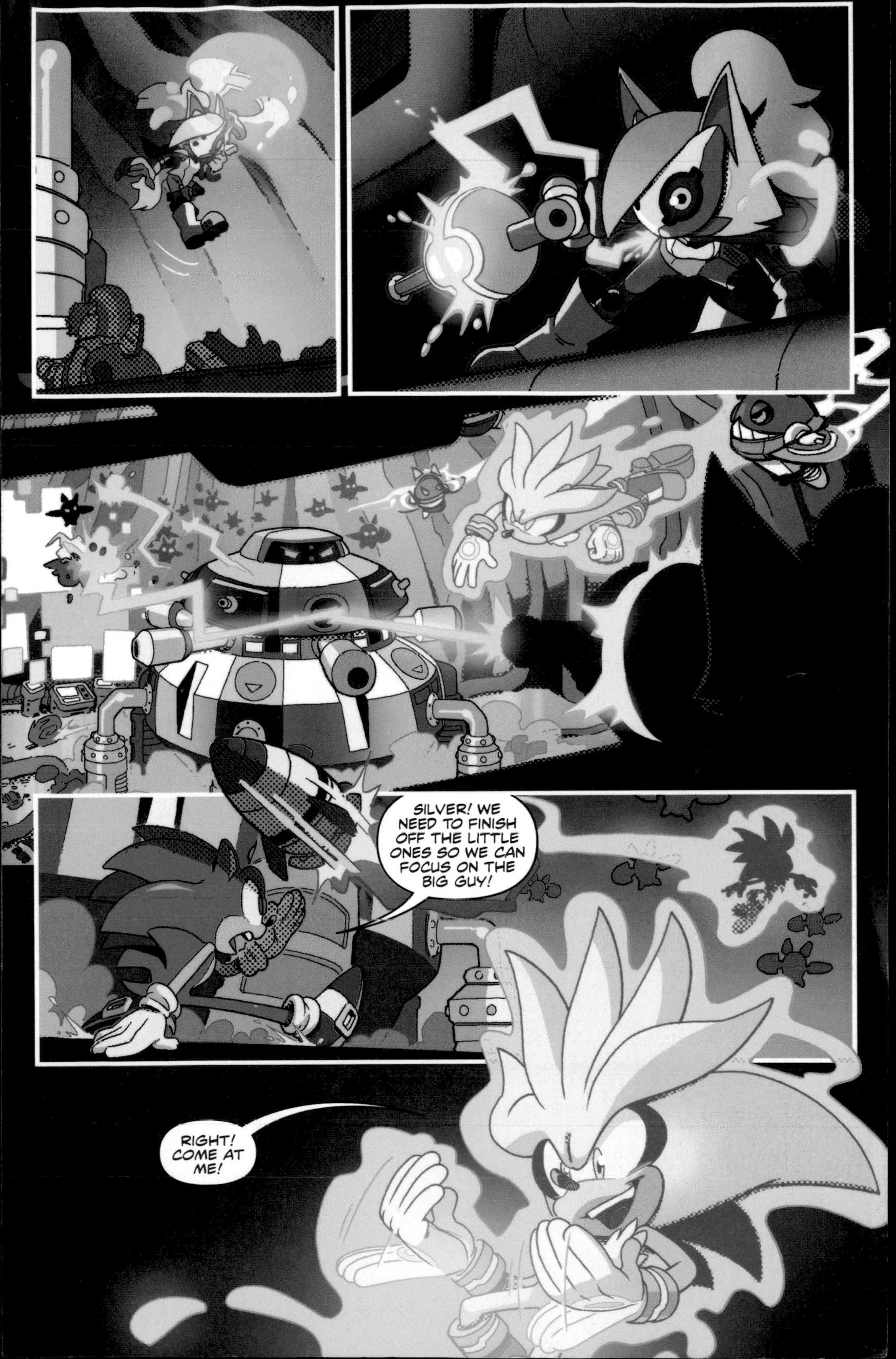
SILVER! WE NEED TO FINISH OFF THE LITTLE ONES SO WE CAN FOCUS ON THE BIG GUY!
RIGHT! COME AT ME!

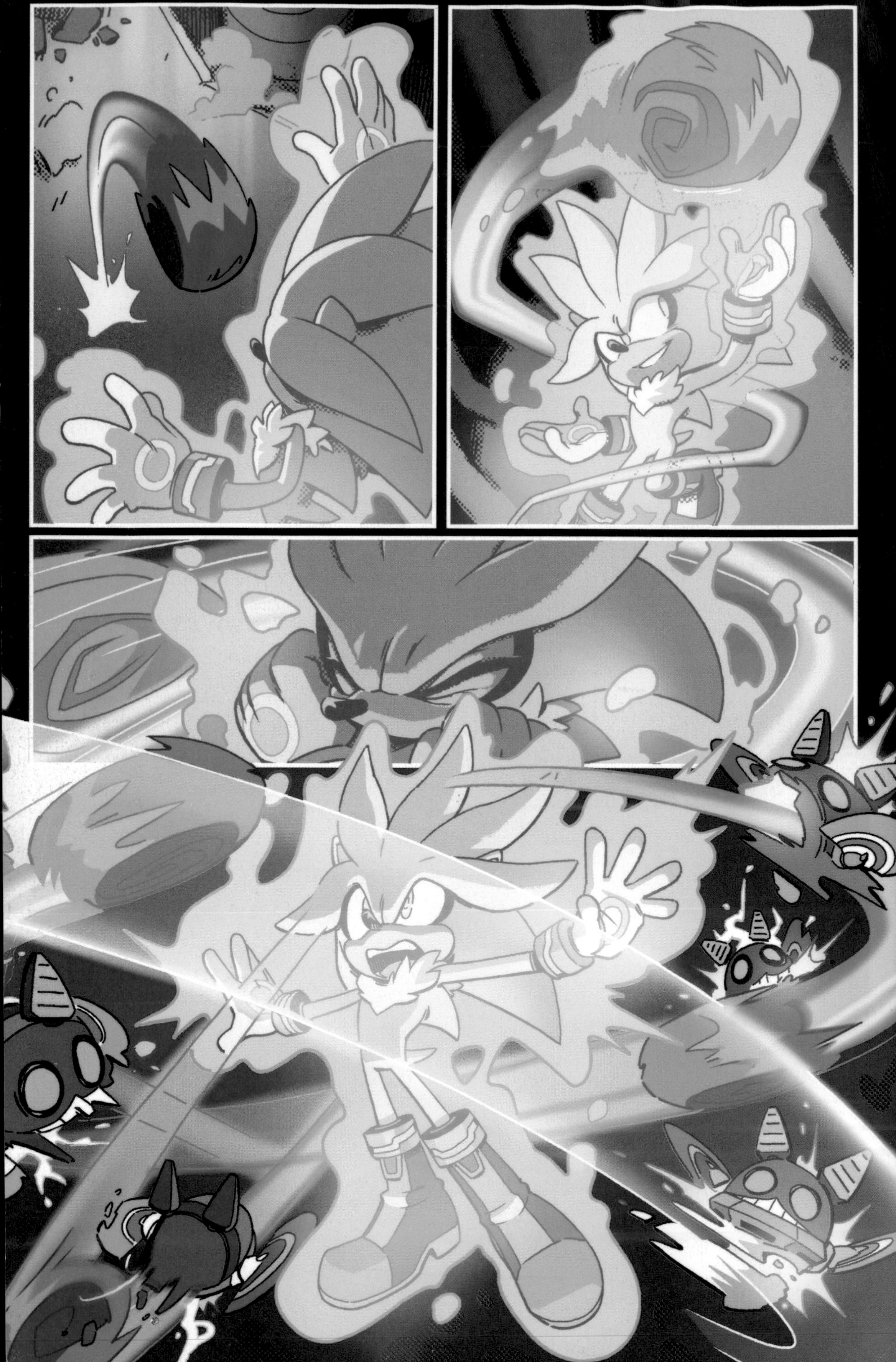

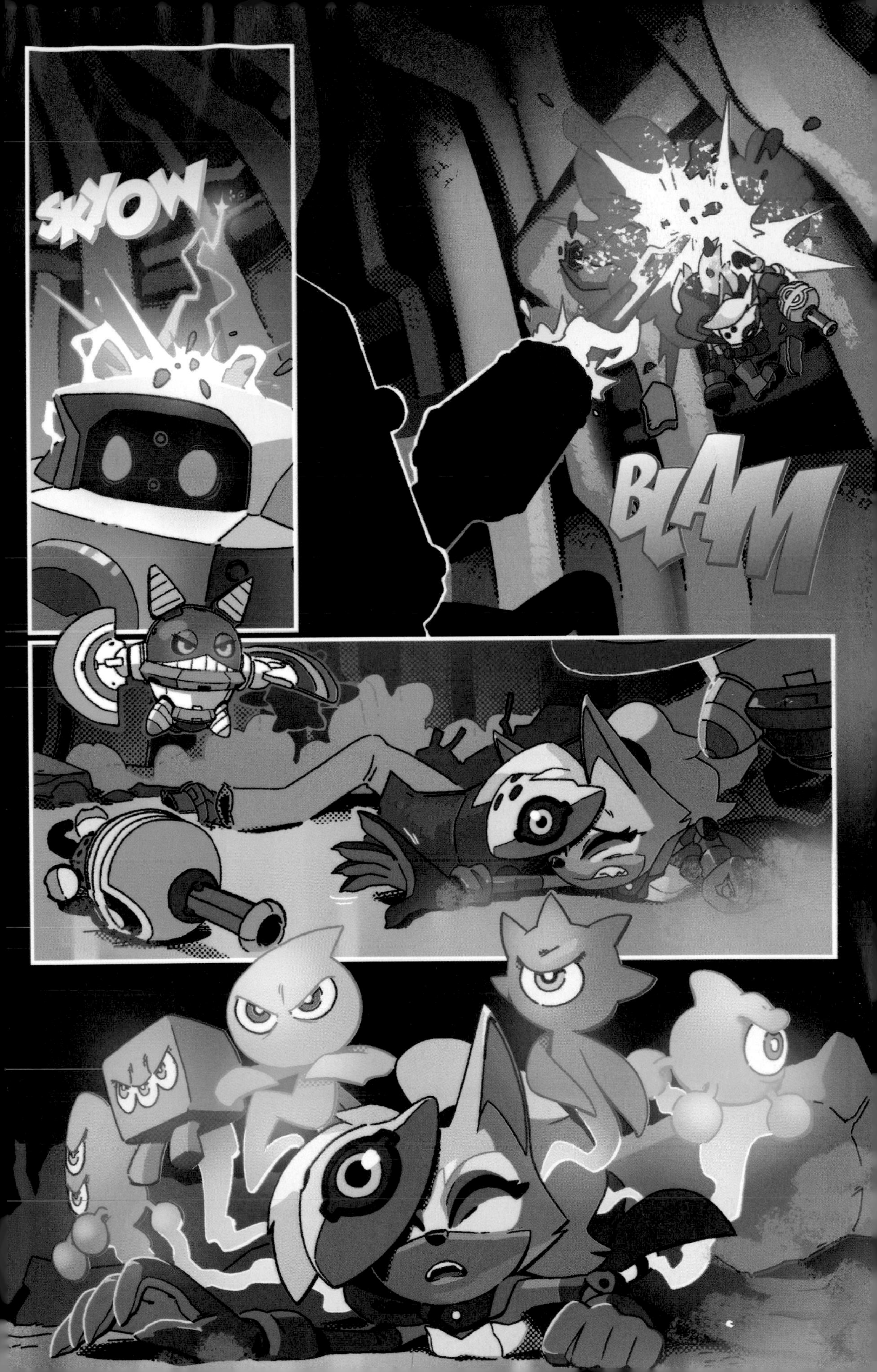
SKYOW
BLAM

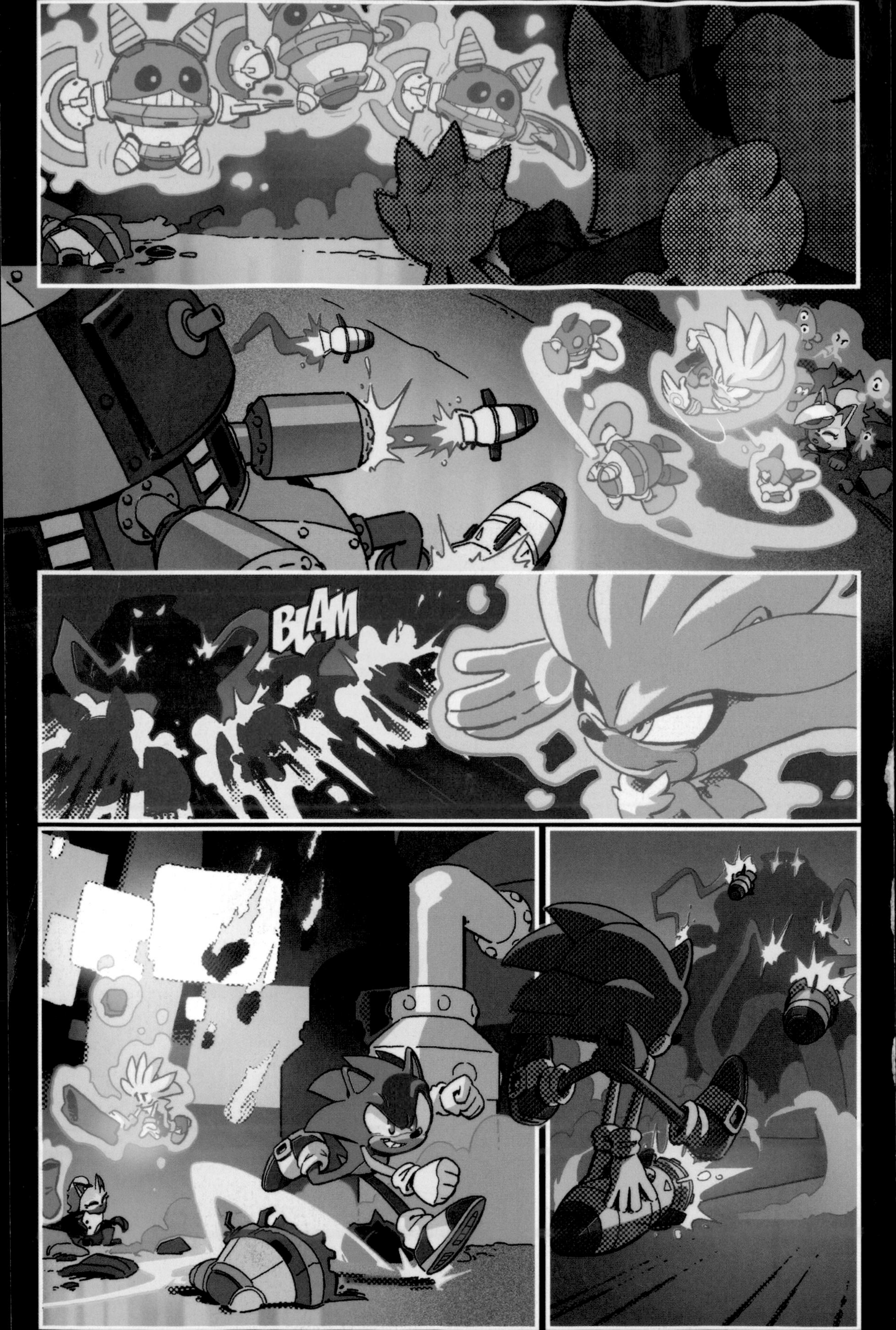
BLAM

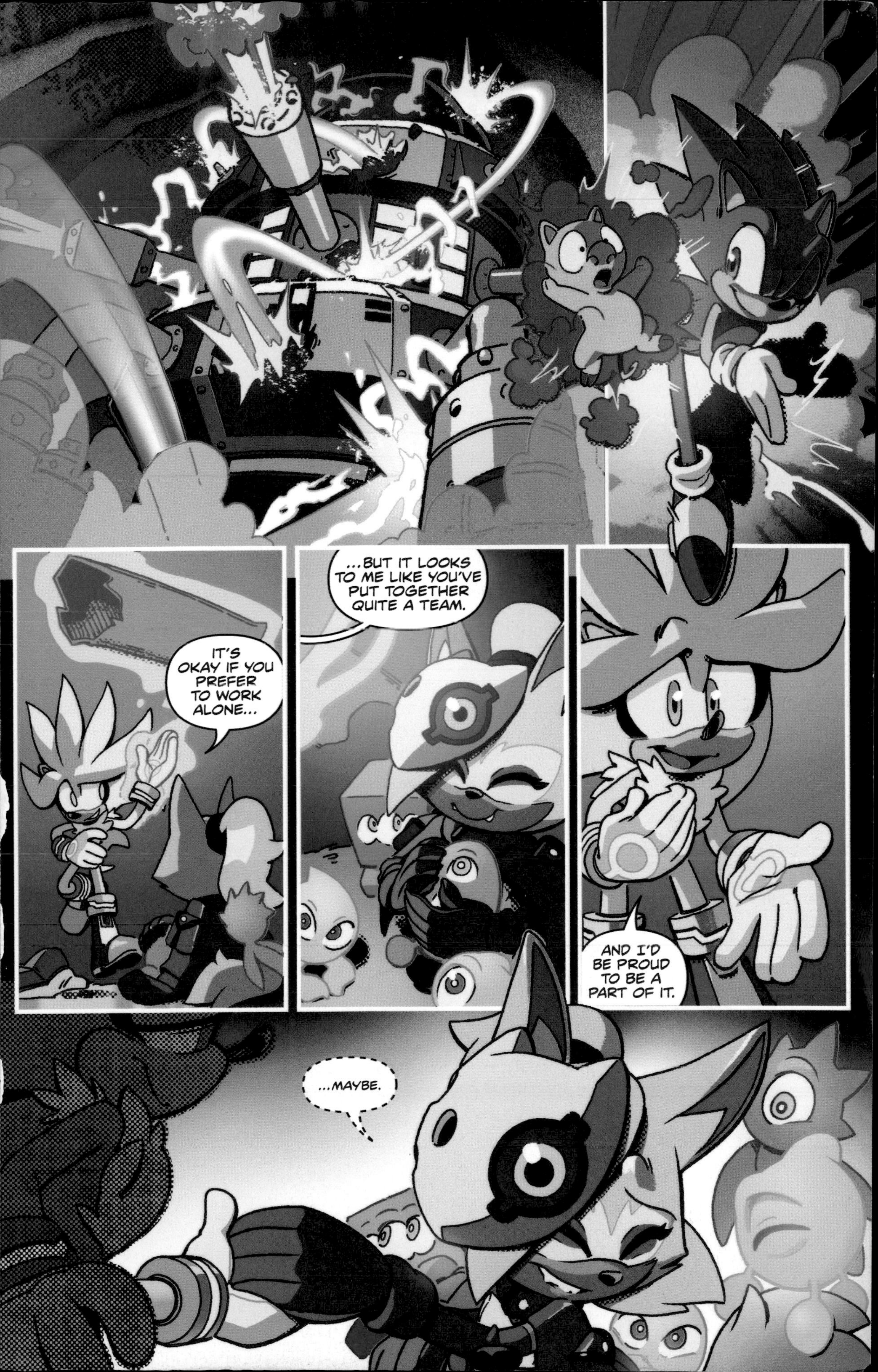
IT'S OKAY IF YOU PREFER TO WORK ALONE...
...BUT IT LOOKS TO ME LIKE YOU'VE PUT TOGETHER QUITE A TEAM.
AND I'D BE PROUD TO BE A PART OF IT.
...MAYBE.

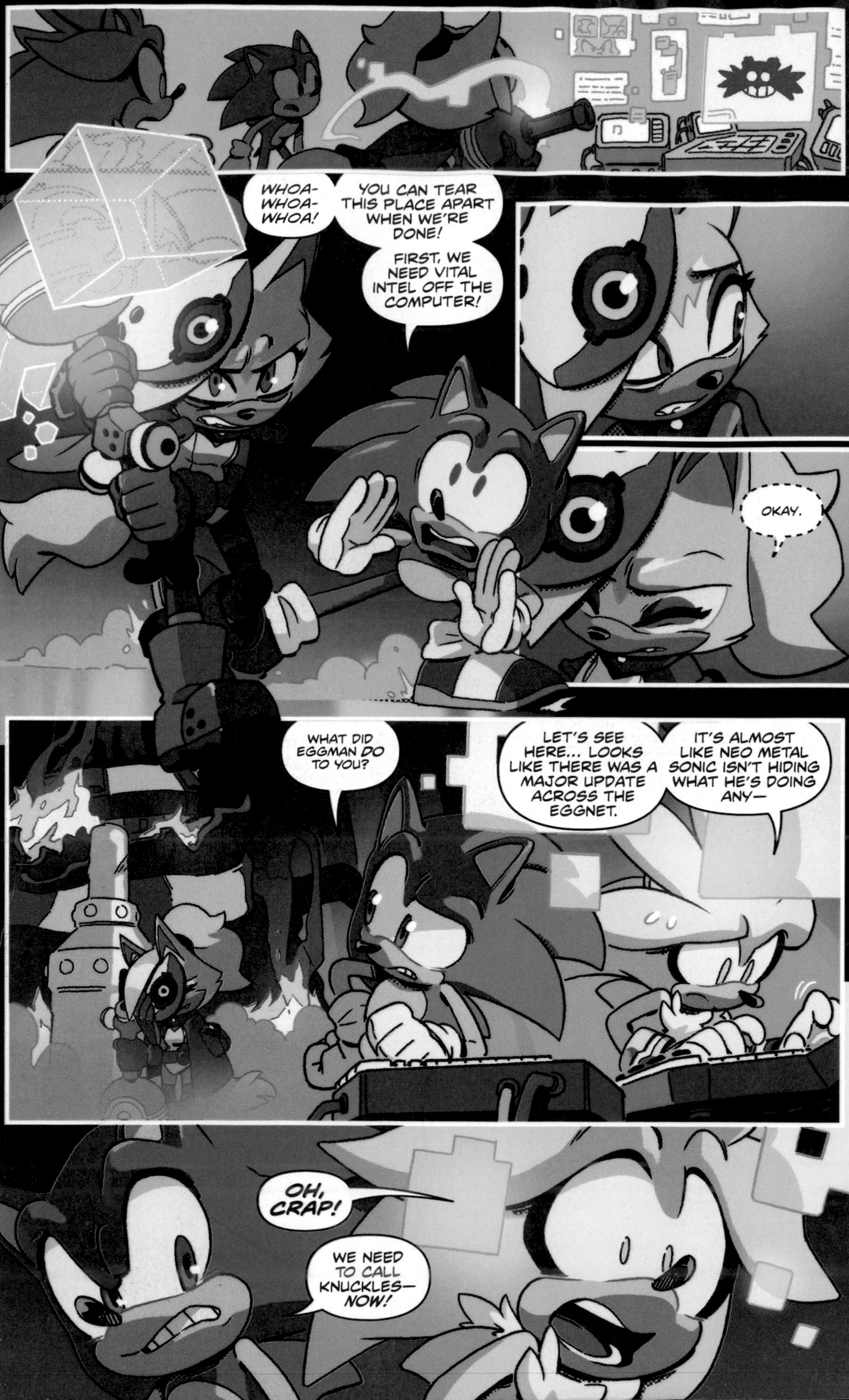

WHOA-WHOA-WHOA!
YOU CAN TEAR THIS PLACE APART WHEN WE'RE DONE!
FIRST, WE NEED VITAL INTEL OFF THE COMPUTER!
OKAY.
WHAT DID EGGMAN DO TO YOU?
LET'S SEE HERE... LOOKS LIKE THERE WAS A MAJOR UPDATE ACROSS THE EGGNET.
IT'S ALMOST LIKE NEO METAL SONIC ISN'T HIDING WHAT HE'S DOING ANY—
OH, CRAP!
WE NEED TO CALL KNUCKLES—NOW!

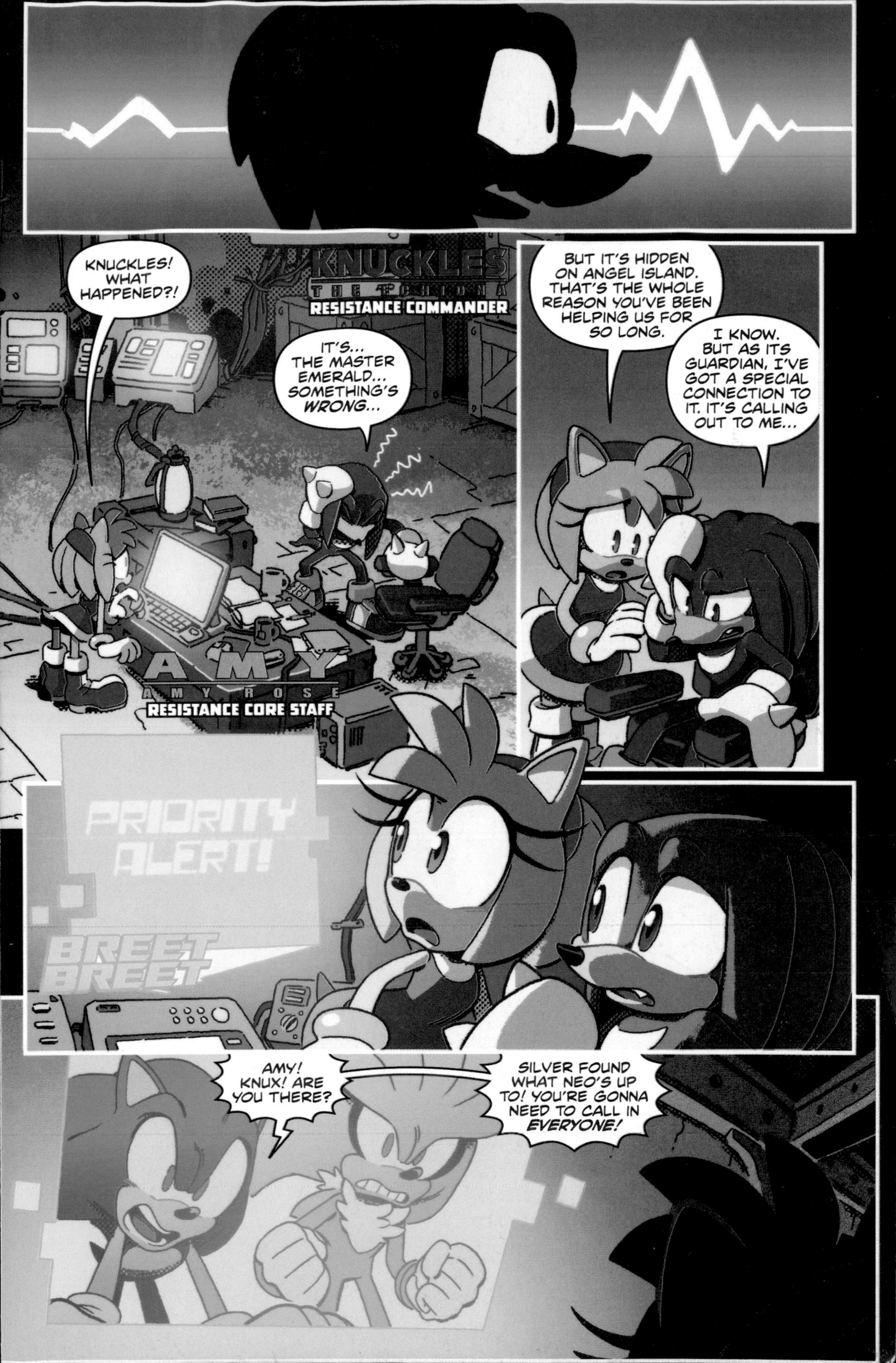
KNUCKLES! WHAT HAPPENED?!
KNUCKLES THE ECHIDNA
RESISTANCE COMMANDER
IT'S... THE MASTER EMERALD... SOMETHING'S WRONG...
AMY
AMY ROSE
RESISTANCE CORE STAFF
BUT IT'S HIDDEN ON ANGEL ISLAND. THAT'S THE WHOLE REASON YOU'VE BEEN HELPING US FOR SO LONG.
I KNOW. BUT AS ITS GUARDIAN, I'VE GOT A SPECIAL CONNECTION TO IT. IT'S CALLING OUT TO ME...
PRIORITY ALERT!
BREET BREET
AMY! KNUX! ARE YOU THERE?
SILVER FOUND WHAT NEO'S UP TO! YOU'RE GONNA NEED TO CALL IN EVERYONE!

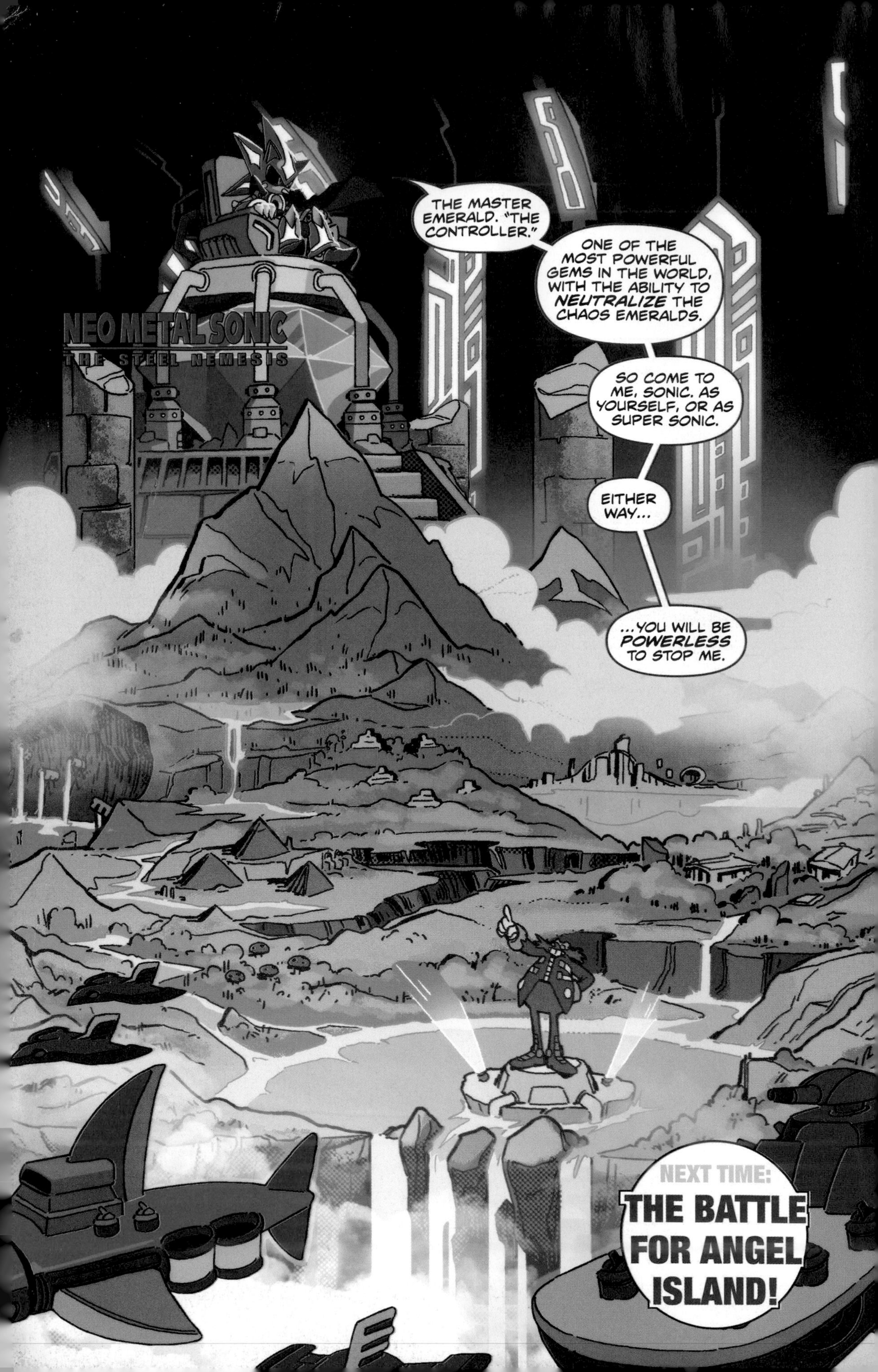
NEO METAL SONIC
THE STEEL NEMESIS
THE MASTER EMERALD. "THE CONTROLLER."
ONE OF THE MOST POWERFUL GEMS IN THE WORLD, WITH THE ABILITY TO NEUTRALIZE THE CHAOS EMERALDS.
SO COME TO ME, SONIC. AS YOURSELF, OR AS SUPER SONIC.
EITHER WAY...
...YOU WILL BE POWERLESS TO STOP ME.
NEXT TIME:
THE BATTLE FOR ANGEL ISLAND!

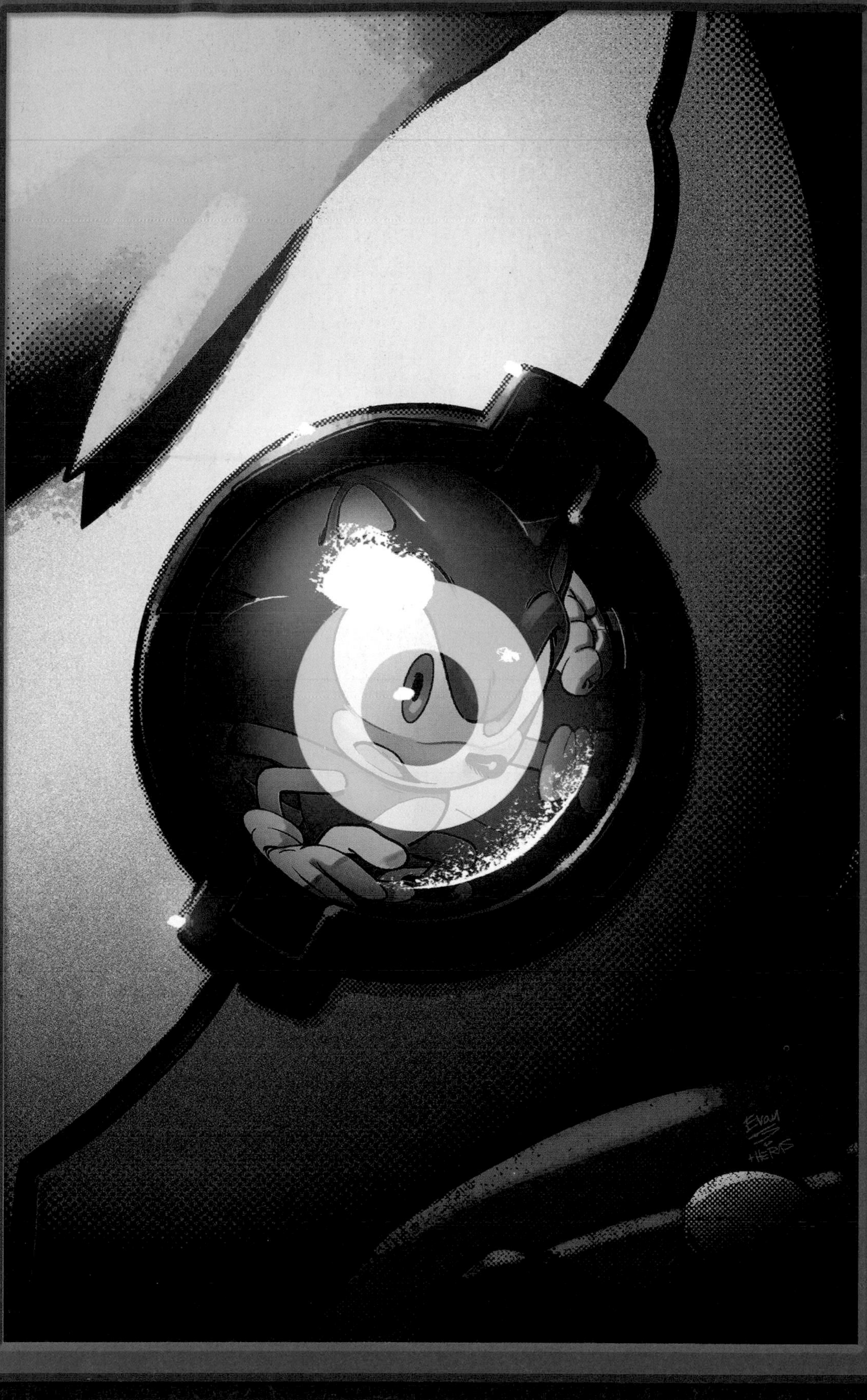

ART BY **EVAN STANLEY** COLORS BY **MATT HERMS**

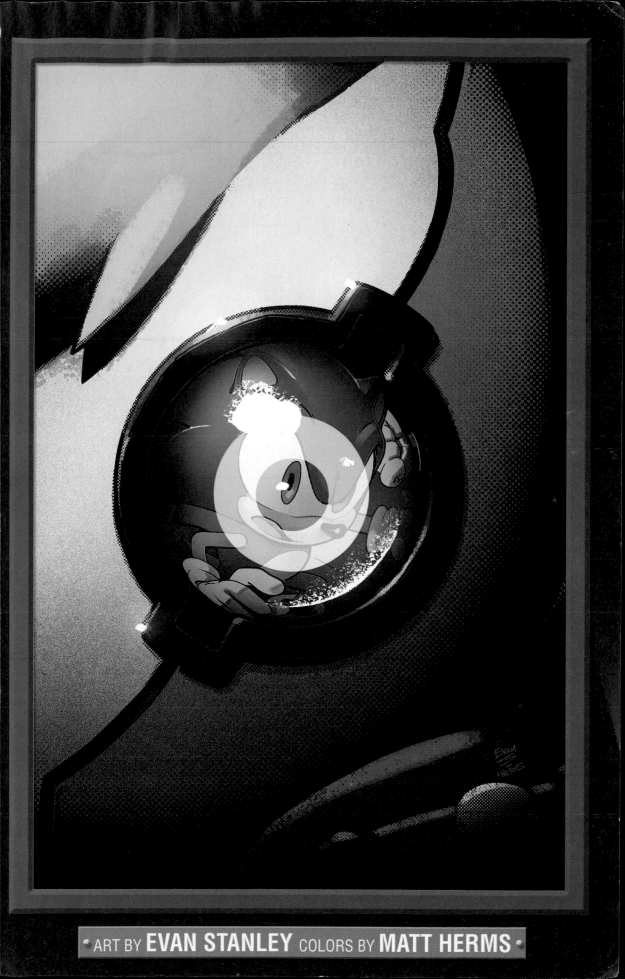

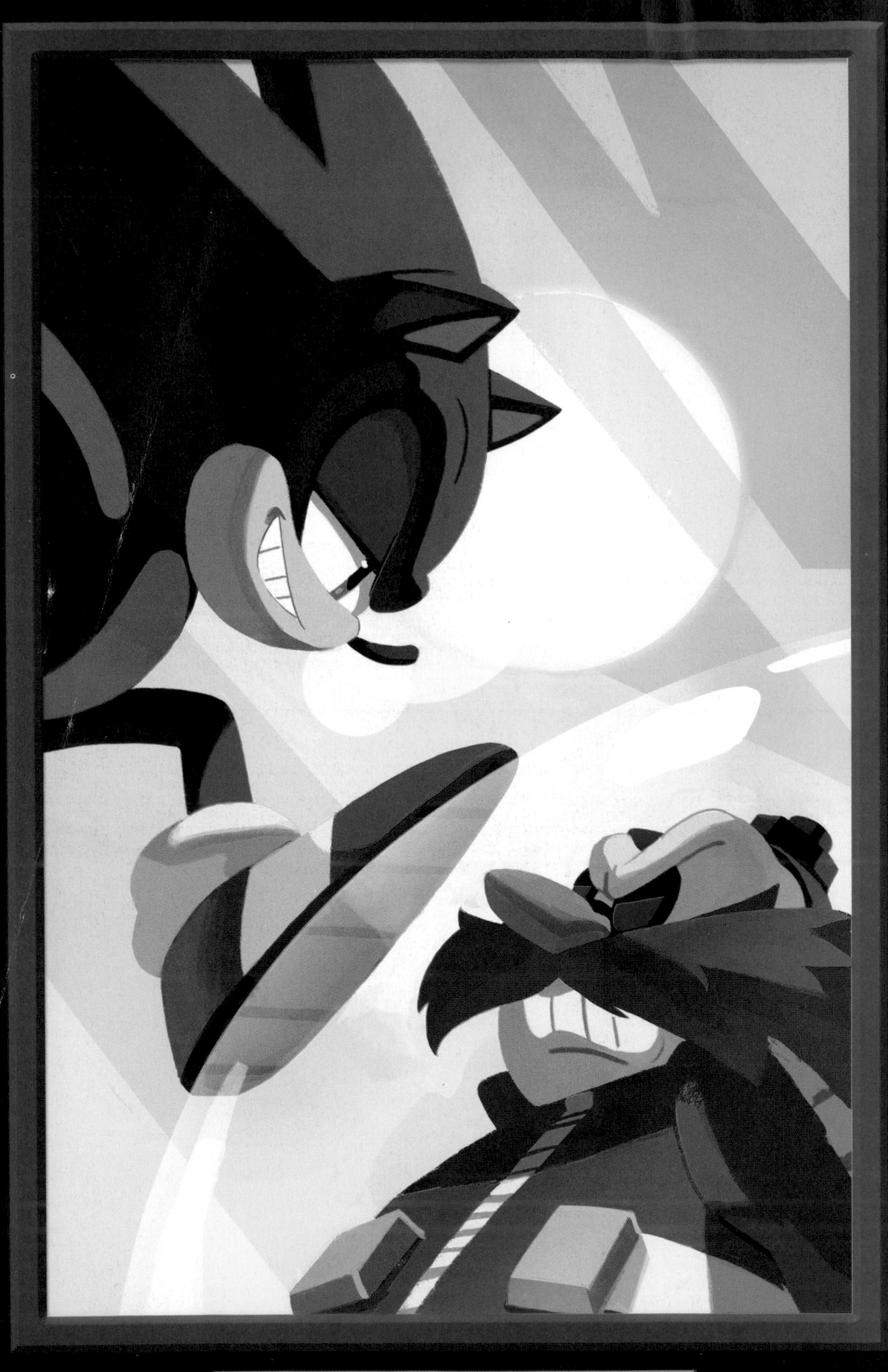

ART BY NATHALIE FOURDRAINE

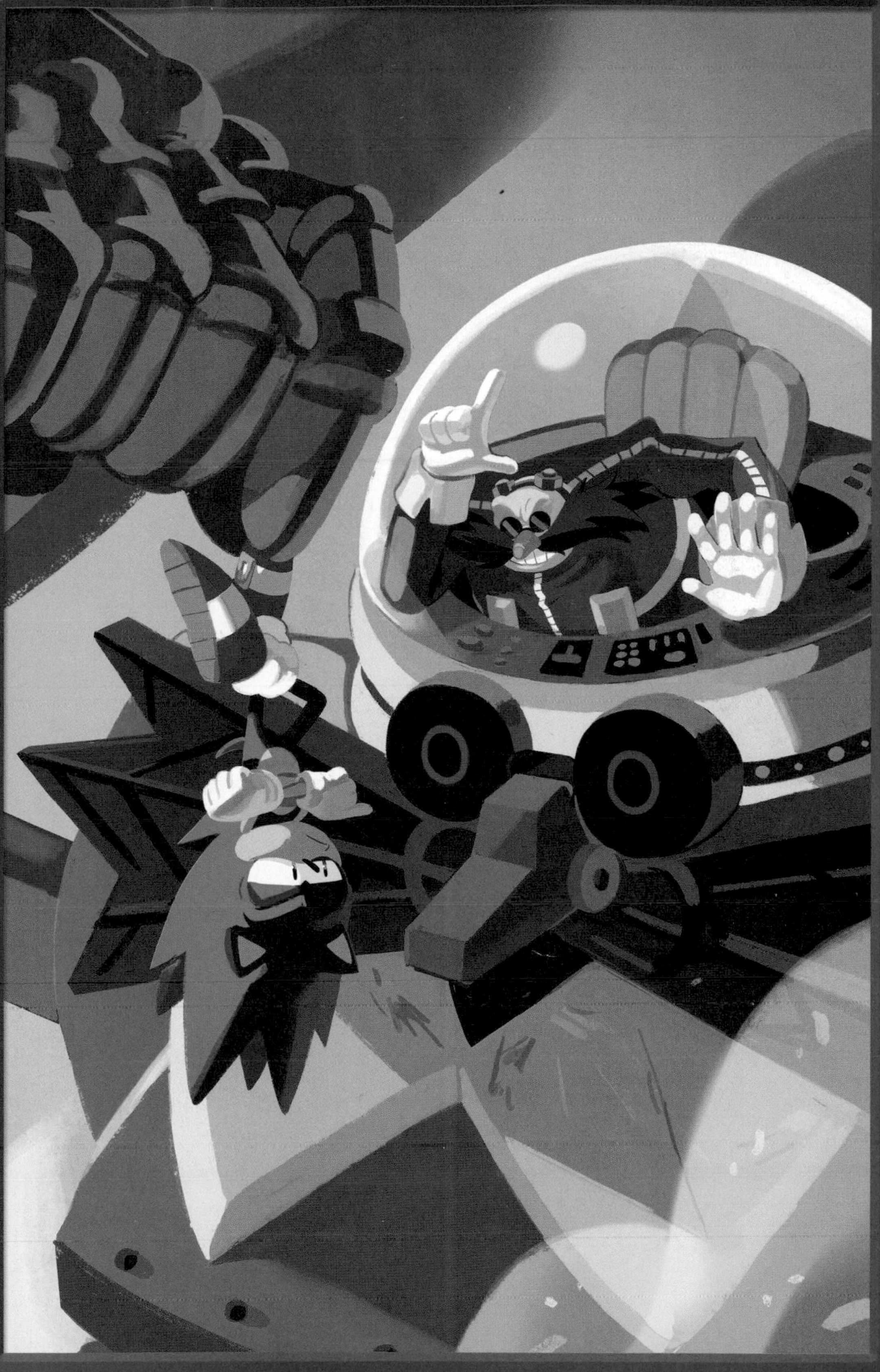

ART BY **NATHALIE FOURDRAINE**

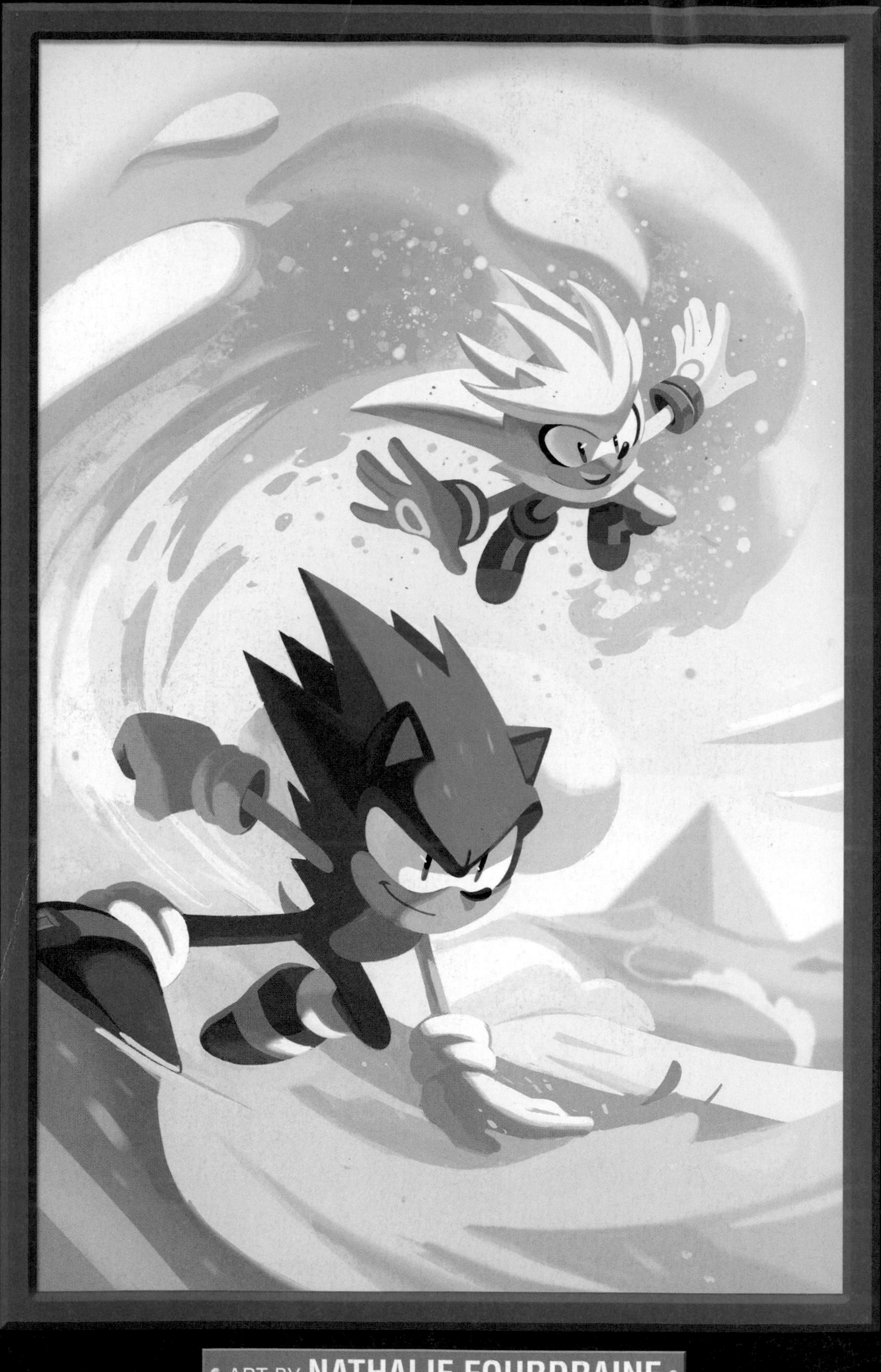

ART BY **NATHALIE FOURDRAINE**